D0340726

Ombria
in Shadow

Ombria in Shadow

PATRICIA A. MCKILLIP

Ace Books, New York

OMBRIA IN SHADOW

An Ace Book
Published by The Berkley Publishing Group,
a division of Penguin Putnam Inc.,
375 Hudson Street, New York, New York 10014.

Visit our website at
www.penguinputnam.com

Copyright © 2002 by Patricia A. McKillip.
Text design by Tiffany Kukec.

First edition: January 2002

Library of Congress Cataloging-in-Publication Data

McKillip, Patricia A.
Ombria in shadow / Patricia A. McKillip. — 1st ed.
p. cm.
ISBN 0-441-00895-X (alk. paper)
I. Title

PS3563.C38 O43 2002
813'.54 — dc21
2001046388

PRINTED IN THE UNITED STATES OF AMERICA

10   9   8   7   6   5   4   3   2   1

Ombria
in Shadow

ONE

Rose and Thorn

While the ruler of the ancient city of Ombria lay dying, his mistress, frozen out of the room by the black stare of Domina Pearl, drifted like a bird on a wave until she bumped through Kyel Greve's unguarded door to his bed, where he was playing with his puppets.

They looked at one another, the tavern keeper's daughter and the child-heir of Ombria, both pale, both red-eyed. Kyel lifted the falcon puppet on his hand. Its feathers were of silk, its eyes of dyed zirconium.

"Take down your hair," the falcon said.

Lydea lifted her hands; pearls, pins, gold nets scattered to the floor. Her hair, the color of autumn leaves, swept nearly to her knees. The boy gazed at it a while, unblinking, until Lydea thought he must have fallen asleep upright in his vast bed. But he shook himself finally. He had his

1

father's black-lashed sapphire eyes, and his black hair. His skin was white as wax, except for his nose, which was red. He wiped it on his sleeve.

"May I sit?" Lydea asked gravely. Tall and graceful, head always slightly bowed under the weight of a perilous love, she had come, barely more than a child herself, into the palace of the Prince of Ombria at his wife's death. In five years, Royce Greve had taught her presence and manners in that difficult place, but he could not stop her from biting her nails. She would have now, but Kyel tossed her a puppet.

"You must make it ask."

She wriggled her poor, torn fingers into its porcelain head: a goose head, appropriately, she thought.

"May I sit?" the goose asked, and the falcon answered, "Sit."

"Where are your guards?"

He shrugged slightly; the falcon said, "They were summoned away."

Her eyes widened. "By whom?"

"I don't know."

"And Jacinth? Where is she?"

"Domina told her to leave."

"To leave the palace?"

Both boy and falcon nodded. "She said I'm too old now for a nurse."

"Who said? Jacinth?"

"No. Domina."

A word Lydea had not said for five years jumped into her mouth; she pinched her lips with the goose's beak. Kyel's eyes looked suddenly bleak.

"My father is dying and Jacinth is gone. Will you stay with me?"

"For a bit." She remembered, made the goose speak. "For a bit, my lord," it said in the coarser accents of her childhood. "For a bite of time, my young duck."

"I'm a falcon, not a duck."

" 'Twas your grandfather a falcon. Peregrine Greve. Not you. You are a sweet duckling." She stroked his hair, trying to burrow through her sorrow to some thought. Sense eluded her; she felt heavy, resigned, boneless, barely able to lift the goose. "I will not leave you alone here," she promised, knowing herself good for that at least, even if she lost her life with him on that puppet-strewn bed. What to do, what to do . . . When Royce Greve breathed his last, his great-aunt Domina would make herself regent for Kyel until he came of age. If she let him live that long . . .

The goose descended, beak first, into the embroidered coverlet. Lydea gazed at it, her smoky eyes wide. Or had it been Ducon Greve, wanting to leave Kyel unprotected at Royce's death, who had sent the guards away? Could a bastard of the House rule Ombria? she wondered. If he were hard enough. A flea-bitten dog could rule Ombria, if it were ruthless enough.

The falcon nipped at the goose. "Talk." The falcon was tossed away then, replaced by the King of Rats, whose eyes were garnet, whose crown was gold. "Talk to me."

"Shall I tell you a story?" the goose asked.

"Tell me the story of the fan." Kyel rolled away from her, pulled the fan off an ebony table beside the bed. It was a delicate thing of slender ivory sticks and a double layer of folded rice paper. One side was a painting, the other an intricately cut silhouette, a shadow world behind a painted world that could be seen when the fan was held up to the light. It had belonged to Kyel's mother.

Lydea opened the fan slowly, revealed the colored side. "This is Ombria, my lord," the goose said. "The oldest city in the world."

"The most beautiful city in the world."

"The most powerful city in the world."

"The richest city in the world."

"This is the world of Ombria." The goose tapped a tiny jade-green palace overlooking the sea. "This is the palace of the rulers of Ombria. These are the great, busy ports of Ombria. These are the ships of Ombria . . ." The goose took the fan gently in its beak, angled it in front of the lamp. Light streamed through the fan. "This is the shadow of Ombria."

A city rose behind Ombria, a wondrous confection of shadow that towered even over the palace. Shadow ships sailed the waters; minute shadow people walked the painted streets. The future ruler of Ombria, lips parted, surveyed his domain.

"Tell me about the shadow city. Will I rule there, too?"

The goose's voice became dreamy, entwined in the tale. "The shadow city of Ombria is as old as Ombria. Some say it is a different city completely, existing side by side with Ombria in a time so close to us that there are places — streets, gates, old houses — where one time fades into the other, one city becomes the other. Others say both cities exist in one time, this moment, and you walk through both of them each day, just as, walking down a street, you pass through light and shadow and light . . . So, my lord, who can say if you will rule the shadow city? You rule and you do not rule: it is the same, for if you do rule the shadow city, you may never know it."

"Then how — Then how do they know it is there?"

The goose was silent. Above its painted head, Lydea's face with its autumn coloring and cloudy eyes was still, sculpted to a poised and timeless beauty by love and fear and grief. She was remembering the noisy, cluttered streets of her childhood: a blinding angle of light across an alley too black to see into, a house that was sometimes there and sometimes elsewhere. . . .

"Dea, Dea, how do they know?"

She blinked. Another voice had called her that: *Dea Dea*, a sigh of satiation, only at that time, only when they were most alone. There was not anything private in that house, not anything, nothing. . . .

She felt the heavy tears swell behind her eyes. The door opened abruptly. She turned, the goose turning with her, both faces staring, mute. But it was neither Domina Pearl nor her ensorcelled guard come to deal with the child. It was Camia Greve's bastard son, Ducon, who stood in the doorway, gazing back at rat and heir, mistress and goose, with as much expression, Lydea thought, as a halibut without a head.

He said to Lydea, "The prince is calling for you."

He did not resemble his mother, the prince's younger sister. She had died a decade after Ducon's birth without ever naming his father. Who he resembled still kept tongues busy. Even Lydea had tried to guess, but found no one at court with that stark white hair, those silvery eyes which gave nothing away but light, the thin, tight smile that challenged even Domina Pearl. Who he loved, what he did with his time, Lydea had only a vague idea. He treated his uncle's mistress with equal measures of courtesy and indifference; what he truly thought of her, she had no idea. He had odd interests in art and rambling; she guessed that from the watercolors she had seen of shabby doorways, broken piers, crumbling stairways, shadowed streets. He seemed to wander fearlessly through the darkest places in Ombria. Royce had been fond of his sister's bastard, and had treated him generously. But even after five years in the palace, Lydea hardly knew enough to be relieved or uneasy at his presence.

She put the puppet down and rose, looking anxiously at Kyel, torn between the unprotected child and the dying man's summons. Surely Ducon would not harm Kyel, she thought, but in that house who could assume that even fire and water would not conspire?

Kyel himself chose for her, speaking without fear, "My father wants you. Ducon will stay with me."

She made some attempt at her hair, noting, with a practical eye, that Ducon was unarmed. Ducon said briefly, "Leave it down. He will like it."

She dropped her hands, took a moment to give him what was left of her stunned thoughts. Kyel trusted him; she could only trust that. She said, desperate with fear, "Someone sent his guards away."

"I noticed."

"If Domina Pearl—if she has some plot—"

He was shaking his head; he picked his words with care in front of the boy. "Without Kyel there would be chaos. His rightful heirs are aged and frightened, and the

younger scions may decide to take what they will not inherit. She is better off regent for Kyel, than precipitating
a power struggle in the House of Greve that might heave
her out the door on her ancient backside."

She let her head drop an inch in resignation. "More
likely my fate, my lord Ducon: the back door and my backside. Domina Pearl will be on her feet when the House
falls down around her."

His light eyes remained on her face. "Do you have
some place—" He stopped, as Kyel stirred anxiously on
the bed.

"Lydea will not leave. I forbid it." He lifted the falcon
puppet; it stared fiercely at them both. "I will be Prince of
Ombria and I forbid."

"My lord," Lydea said gently, stirring her wits to answer them both, "will it please you to give me leave to visit
my father for a time? He was fond of me, and I have not—
I have not been home lately." Grief clawed at her voice.
She turned quickly, barely hearing Kyel's answer, remembering the young woman who, five years earlier, had entered the great palace by the sea giddy with love, spinning
dreams while the storm clouds gathered, too huge for her
to comprehend them. Silly dribbet of a girl. Bird nest for
a brain. Impossible she could have smiled so, been so blind
to her mother's horror. Her mother had died not long after
Lydea left. If she still had a father, he had not been inclined
to let her know.

The falcon gave her leave.

Then there was the waking dream: Royce Greve looking at her one last time, skin molded to the bones of his
face, his hand shaking, lifting to touch the long fall of her

hair. Something happened. She waited for his fingers to reach her, but they lay on the tapestry coverlet as if they had never moved. Around her, in the dead silence, the candles whispered his name, hers. Domina Pearl touched her.

Then she was walking to the west gate with the Black Pearl at her side to see that she did not linger a moment past her usefulness. The yard was deserted there. A stand of sunflowers hung their heavy heads like mourners; the sea drew slow, hollow breaths, loosed them as slowly. The palace stood listening, it seemed, to the tolling of the bells, with every window an eye, witness to her disgrace.

"You're best out of here," Domina commented. She was small, compact; she did not so much look old as emanate age, like a musty puff of air, or bone-creakings too slow to be heard. Her hair had been dyed black for as long as anyone had been around to remember; no one alive remembered a time without her. She wore it drawn back with pearls and tortoise-shell combs from a stiff face powdered dead-white. Her eyes were cold, barren moons. "There are those in this house who would strip you like carrion birds."

Lydea gazed back at her wearily. Domina Pearl had given her no time even to change her shoes, though the sapphire heels on them would shout to every moving shadow. "As will those in the streets of Ombria."

"Surely you expected no reward for loving."

"No. But, odd as it sounds, I didn't expect punishment."

Domina shrugged slightly. "It is not punishment. There is simply no place for you here, now. Go back to your father."

"I doubt my father will have much use for me."

"Then try the docks," Domina said without a flicker of expression. "Any tavern there will find a use for you."

"I'd rather die," Lydea said simply, and then, unbidden, her childhood tongue returned to her. "You raven-eyed hag, some bitter bird ate your heart out so long ago you don't even remember how to be human. I may be a fool-headed limpet with nothing left to cling to and about to be done to death for my shoes, but if I hear you've set your bleak eyes at harming Kyel Greve, I'll come shoeless out of my grave to put you in my place, you ugly foul mausoleum."

The Black Pearl opened the gate. She laughed suddenly, a little scuddering of dry leaves. "You won't live past midnight on the streets. Get out." The gate clanged shut with more force than necessary. "You are already dead."

Lydea, standing on the wrong side of the gate in the dark street, with her bright hair streaming down her shoulders and gifts from Royce on every finger, thought the old witch was probably right. She cast one final glance at the palace, saw the richly dressed courtiers clustered safely in the long halls, whispering about how Royce Greve had breathed his last, and that was the last any of them would see of his tavern-brew of a mistress, there one moment for five years and gone the next, as if she had, under Domina Pearl's arid glance, ceased to exist.

Lydea turned her back to them. "We'll see," she whispered, thinking of Kyel. "We'll see about that."

She braided her hair quickly, using rings here and there to secure it, then took off her shoes and tossed them into the sunflowers. Their great, strange faces, all eyes, trembled oddly; something rustled within them and was still. Lydea, with half the city to cross in the night, stared at them and realized that she even had sunflowers to fear; she could not trust that the Black Pearl had not planted her death among them. She took a step away from them, another. And then, tears of sorrow and terror sliding down her face, she ran from shadow to shadow into the dark.

She did not get far before the shadows began to reach out for her. She was pulled toward lit doorways, toward black alleys. Hands snatched at her hair, her bodice, her bare feet. She fled down a side street; someone caught her long braid, jerked her to her knees, wrapped the braid around her throat. She cried out, flailing at air. Stones echoed her cry, mocking, she thought, but she was free suddenly, for no reason. She stumbled up, reached the end of the street and ran into a body like a wall. A huge hand trapped her hands behind her back; a beard burrowed beneath her ear. A bird or a bat flew out of the shadows and the man was down, passed out drunk at her feet, she guessed, and moved again, frantically trying to remember the tangle of streets she had roamed so easily as a child. Voices plucked at her. *Where so fast, pretty one? Walk with us. What's your hurry? Stars, she wears, shining in her hair. Show us your stars, just show us, and we'll leave you be. That's a dead alley, nothing there, come back out here into the light. Stop her, catch her, she's stolen a treasure and hid it in her hair....*

She tore a ring out of her hair, threw it behind her, and half her ragged following stopped to scrabble in the street. She threw another ring; an urchin caught it, swallowed it, grinning. She threw another, and another, until her hair hung loose down her torn, dirty gown. Laughter came too close, retreated; signposts pointed in too many directions. Someone threw a bottle at her; it shattered under her feet. She cried out, running on thorns now, on broken splinters of fire. Tavern signs rocked overhead: the Iron Maiden, the Walking Oak, the Moon and Owl. Which was her father's? Was he there still? What was the name? Fingers clamped around her wrist, loosened abruptly, as if she burned. In that instant, she saw a face watching her that did not threaten; it seemed uncannily calm in the dusty streak of lamplight, as if the young woman standing there were a ghost. In that moment, Lydea remembered: Rose and Thorn, on Sheepshead Lane.

She gasped, "Sheepshead Lane—which way?"

The ghost pointed, and disappeared, was gone, was nothing. A sharp, bewildered sob broke out of Lydea. *Where can you go from here?* she pleaded silently at the empty shadows. *How do you find nowhere?* Voices gabbled at her; stray hounds had joined the pursuers, barking wildly. She ran again, on burning embers, on the razor's edge. She was stopped and caught and free again, for no discernible reason but that everyone must be blind, staggering drunk. Turning into Sheepshead Lane, she saw the painted rose hanging beneath the moon.

She flung herself through the doorway, fell on her knees in front of a short, bald, brawny man who was sweeping up beer-sodden straw on the floor. He stared at her; she stared at him. He turned his head, spat on the straw.

"Back, are you?"

She pulled herself away from the door so that he could bar it. The voices and barking faded into curses, laughter, the yelp of kicked dogs. She leaned against a bench, her eyes closed, listening to the brisk, angry strokes of the broom.

She spoke finally. "You've no one to sweep."

"I have myself."

"I remember how."

"It's not a broom handle you've held for five years."

She opened her eyes. He leaned the broom against the bar, folded his arms, his expression like another barred door. Sorrow caught fire in her throat; she swallowed the ember down, for he would have no pity. She asked, "Do you have someone to scrub tables?"

"My right hand."

"And to wash the glasses?"

"The street is full of taverns these days," he said, then grudged her another sentence. "I make do, with what I have."

"I'll do for nothing."

"So you have done, these five years."

Her mouth crooked. She looked at her torn hem, her bruised knees, the bloody straw where her feet rested. "You're right, there. I was that much a fool. I won't beg you—except, if you're going to throw me back out, I beg you wait till morning. It's fierce out there."

"I heard the mourning bells," he said. "But I didn't think you'd come here."

"No one there wanted me except the boy."

"The boy. Will they let him live?"

She shook her head wordlessly, her eyes burning. "I don't know," she whispered. "He is even more helpless."

He shifted straw with his foot, watching her. "I told you don't go."

"I know."

"So did she. She begged."

"I know."

"So now you're back."

"I'm not begging," she said carefully. "And you owe me nothing. But I will work."

"How, with those feet?"

"I'll work on my knees. In five years no one has had me but the Prince of Ombria, and I fought through half the city tonight to keep that true. There were other places that would have taken me in, but I'd rather wash the floor with my hair. And your windows. They could use it."

His jaw knotted; she saw a flick like a shutter opening in his eyes. He drew breath. "Then," he said softly, "you do that. You wash the floor with your hair. If you're still here by morning, for your mother's memory I will not throw you out."

She spread her hands. That morning they had been soft as feathers, jewelled, polished, perfumed. Now they were crisscrossed with blood and dirt, wearing only bruises for jewels. She said, "Where's the bucket?"

"I'll get that for you," said her father, and fetched her future from behind the bar.

TWO

The Enchanted Heart

M ag was seven when she discovered that she was human. Until then she had only been what Faey called
"my waxling." That Faey could make a child out of wax
to help her with this and that was scarcely in question.
Mag knew nothing of life before Faey made her, and when
Faey gave her memory, memory and her quick, curious
eyes that went everywhere in the ancient city of Ombria,
became her greatest assets.

Faey lived, for those who knew how to find her, within
Ombria's past. Parts of the city's past lay within time's
reach, beneath the streets in great old limestone tunnels:
the hovels and mansions and sunken river that Ombria
shrugged off like a forgotten skin, and buried beneath itself
through the centuries. Other parts were less accessible.
Everyone knew of past, like they knew the smells of wild

rose and shit and frying sausage, and the direction of the wind and the cry of gulls around the rotting docks. But though they relied on sausage and air, few paid attention to the city's past. That suited Faey, who lived along the borderline of past and present. Those who needed her followed the scent of her work and found her. Those who didn't considered her a vague seep out of someone's cistern, an imprecise shadow at the end of an alley, and walked their ceaseless, complex patterns above her head, never knowing how their lives echoed down the intricate passageways of time in the hollow beneath the city.

Mag, who did not consider herself human, moved easily in and out of the various places where Ombria crumbled into its past. By the time she was seven, she knew doors all over the city. There was the little worm-eaten gate in the sagging wall behind the stables in the yard of the Raven's Eye Inn. There was the shadow at the end of Glover's Alley, which Mag's sharp eyes noticed never changed position, morning or noon. There was the gaudy patch of sunflowers beside the west gate of the palace of the Prince of Ombria, that did nothing all day long but turn their golden-haired, thousand-eyed faces to follow the sun. The Prince of Ombria, whom Faey called the Reprobate, never bothered with what stood outside his iron gates on their graceful, gargantuan stalks and sometimes peered over his wall. If Faey wanted spare eyes, Mag knew how to grow them. The door to the undercity lay in the midst of the sunflowers: a hole between roots where what looked like some animal's den was the top of an ancient chimney. Steps leading down to the sea from the docks led farther than anyone guessed. Street drains, unused cellars, holes beneath steps, were doors that even the city urchins had discovered. Mag saw them sometimes, flitting through fingers of light from drains and broken windows and holes above their heads, exploring the secret streets, sitting on the walls of roofless houses, eating stolen apples or searching the rooms for treasure that lay just beyond their eyesight, in the moment just beyond their steps. They never eluded Faey's notice, and she never let them stay, as often as they planned to take up residence in the quiet, warm, secret place and fill a ruined city with a tattered population of waifs. They would get uneasy as the upper light began to fade, start glancing over their skinny shoulders and scratching for nonexistent fleas. Faey made the stones they threw into streams echo across vast distances; she made the old joists and chimneys whisper; she sent the icy breath of something snoring in a cellar curling around their ankles, so that they scrabbled with relief back up to the dangerous twilight of Ombria.

Mag had learned to move through the streets like a musician moves through music, tuning it note by note with every breath, every touch. A rough voice in the dark could render her invisible; at a touch, she was simply gone, up a pipe, down a barrel, down deeper than that, through a shadow or a door. Not being human, she never wondered at what humans did. She had seen them pilfer each other's watches, slit each other's throats, break each other's hearts. She had seen newborns tossed away with yesterday's rubbish. She had stepped over men snoring drunk on the cobbles; she had walked around women with bleeding faces, slumped in rich, torn gowns, weeping and cursing in tavern alleys. Since she was wax, none of this concerned her; they might have been dreams or ghosts she moved through, until they tried to pull her into their night-terrors. Then she melted as if flame had touched her, flowed away into a safer dream.

The day Mag turned human, Faey had sent her on an errand up into light. Mag carried a silk handkerchief loosely in one hand, like the ladies she saw taking fastidious steps through the streets. Now and then, like them, she touched the silk to her nostrils. Tucked within the silk, nestled against her palm, was Faey's spell: a tiny heart that looked of gold but was of many things. Faey had spent forever making it. Mag, watching and helping, had come as close as ever in her brief life to running like a street urchin up to the bumbling, crazed streets above. Even Faey looked affected, her pale skin glistening, her voice shaking with exhaustion. She barely had the strength to send Mag out. "Take this to the palace," she whispered. "Someone will be at the west gate." Mag, who had a vague, unwaxlike longing for light, chose to walk the upper streets to the Reprobate's house.

Dressed in a lacy gown she had torn to fit her, in fine black gloves some lady had dropped in the past, her feet bare, the silk to her nose, she turned her face to the sun like the sunflowers. She paid no attention to the women who flung her startled glances, or to the boys who minced, giggling, in her shadow. They were no more than smoke, the leftover dreams of the sunken, deserted city. So she thought, until Gram Reed, who pastured a cow in a bit of green behind the Raven's Eye Inn, led the cow into the street, looking one way at an oncoming beer cart while

Lady Barrow, looking the other way at a carriage and pair, led her old blind spaniel into the cow.

The spaniel yelped; the cow swung its head at the noise. Somehow teeth and great spongy nostrils collided. The cow bellowed; the spaniel lunged hysterically. Lady Barrow sat down on the cobbles, showing darned woolen hose under an avalanche of lace. Gram Reed, appalled, stooped to help her. The cow, jerking away from yellow, snapping teeth, pulled out of his hold and ran mooing into Amalee's Lady's Lace for Discreet and Public Occasions. An assortment of bird noises arose from within the shop: parrot screeches, peacock screams, the twitterings of finches. The cow bellowed again. There was a sound like the flat side of a door smacking a haunch of beef. The cow lumbered back out, trailing yards of eyelet lace and a pair of beribboned drawers from one horn.

Gram Reed groaned. Lady Barrow fainted, her wig toppling into a puddle. Mag laughed. She had never laughed in her life: wax does not. She was so startled by the sound she made that she jammed the handkerchief against her mouth. Something caught on her breath; she swallowed. It was then, poised between horror and laughter, a lunatic place where, she had observed, humans balanced most of their lives, that she saw she was one of them.

She swallowed again, felt the heart in her throat dissolve. For one second she was a slender, wild-haired, barefoot child in a woman's torn ball gown, a pair of gloves five times the size of her hands, watching a cow wearing underwear loom over her. Then habit moved her; she was halfway up a drainpipe, and the cow had careened into the Black Rose tavern. Gram Reed, who was fanning Lady

Barrow's face with her wig, cursed bitterly and flung the wig back into the puddle. Ladies from the lace shop came to her aid then, and Gram plunged into the tavern after his cow. Mag slid down the drainpipe and sat under it, blinking.

Something besides being human was happening to her. Everything seemed to be whispering secrets: the cobblestones, the gurgling drain, her heartbeat, the thin walls of the city through which voices and dreams flowed like blood or light. She wanted to touch everything, feel the pocky texture of granite, the silken slide of water, the tangle of human and horse hair in Lady Barrow's wig. She wanted to touch the blue-white pouch beneath Lady Barrow's closed eye, feel the quick life humming in it. She could hear everything, it seemed: Gram Reed and the tavern keeper arguing, a pigeon nosing under a feather for a flea, murmurings of love through the wall behind her, a footstep in a silent room, a drop of water rolling down the pipe, Amalee's indignant recountings, amid a chorus of shaking wattles and sharp glottals, of the cow coming through the door, and the more gleeful recountings of the street urchins in the next alley.

"... And then Faey's girl shinnied up the drainpipe, she moved so fast, like a spider jumping, here one, with the cow coming at her, and there the next, and the cow flying ribbons into the tavern, and old Beakernose Bailey didn't even take his nose out of his glass, he just reached out like he saw what he was expecting since the day he was born, and pinched the bloomers off the cow's horn and stuffed them up his sleeve ..."

Faey's girl. The street was suddenly far too noisy. Was

she truly visible for comment? If not Faey's making, then whose? She rolled onto her knees suddenly, feeling sick, and crawled a little way into the alley. There she slid into the window of a tiny room in a cellar that no one remembered was there. The room went down and down, a great bank of earth, for its floor had collapsed decades before. Dizzily, hearing stones and ghosts murmuring around her, she made her way along the silent river, where the reflections of invisible lamps along the bank patterned the dark water. Stepping across a bridge, she stepped across time. The lamps became real, lit her path to Faey's house beside the water. The door opened. The housekeeper, in archaic clothes and barely visible, greeted her. The only sound Mag heard in the rich, quiet house was Faey's snoring. Mag stumbled upstairs to her own bed and slept.

Faey, who missed little, watched her reel out of her room later and follow an erratic butterfly path to the water closet. She watched her come out again. Mag, feeling slow, blurred and jangling with a great city's noises, didn't see Faey's lifted hand or feel the blow. She skittered under it, came up sitting against the wall, staring like a rag doll, wide-eyed and stuffed. Faey, with all the work to do over again, and without the aid of her stricken waxling, said, mingling pity and exasperation, "It will only last three days."

But certain effects lasted years.

Mag never told Faey that she knew she was other than made. Human being what it was—raging, messy, cruel, drunken and stupid—she decided to remain wax. If, she reasoned, she did not say the word, no one would ever know. Saying "human" would make her so. Someone else might have made her body, but Faey had the making of her mind, and Mag had no desire to change the turn it had taken. Faey, who was efficient after a fashion, decided to expand Mag's usefulness, to give her an understanding of what she saw in Ombria. So she sent Mag to grateful clients in the upper world to be educated. Mag learned to read in the back room of an elegant brothel, following words across a page above a jewelled and scented finger. She learned languages from a retired smuggler, who spoke three well, seven well enough to live on, and whose parrot supplied her with a tantalizing vocabulary which the smuggler could be persuaded, with old sherry, to translate. She created eerie fires and stinks and subterranean bubblings in the book-strewn rooms of a brewer who, in the evenings, put on a long robe and a solemn expression, and spoke of the transmutation of the physical and spiritual world. Mag, whose idea of the spiritual world was what spoke out of Faey's fires, paid scant heed to the foggy, beer-steeped philosophy. Nor did she notice, for years, the cow-eyed glances of the brewer's young son. But she loved the colored fires and salts, the essences, the apparatus, the occasional explosions. She picked up math from helping a baker with his recipes, and the baker's wife with their accounts. The history of Ombria, the intricate and precarious structure of its ruling family, as well as the spider web of the streets, she learned by breathing, it seemed, or by listening to resonances in the air. Odd facts found her and clung; expertly, she wove the world around her, for ignorance was dangerous, and the heart she had eaten had become her defense.

Seven years passed before she met the woman to whom she should have given that heart. Faey had taken the second making herself to the palace, for her small assistant was still stupefied with impressions. Seven years later, a second request had come from within the gate. For what, Faey would not say, but Mag, watching her read the note the tongueless man had brought, saw Faey's mouth tighten.

"That woman." She turned, began rattling among jars, boxes, dried bats, moth-riddled sacks. "Old she-spider. She must have died a century ago; it's a wonder her bones don't clatter when she moves."

"What does she want?" Mag asked, putting a name to the description.

"Never you mind what she wants, just don't swallow it this time. Come here and hold this."

Mag rose from the gilt chair she sat on. Candle-like at fourteen, she was tall and lean and pale as wax but for her hair, which was a long, untidy straw-gold mass, and her odd, slanting eyes, the color of coffee with too much cream in it. She still wore whatever she found in the old chests and cupboards in the tumbledown mansions. That day it was black silk, jet beads, white lace, a sedate and scholarly look at odds with her unruly hair. Faey, who had been born in Ombria before it had a past, had sunk gradually underground along with it. No longer remembering her own face, she changed faces as often as she changed her clothes. Mag had gotten used to waking up to a stranger using Faey's rich, husky, imperious voice. Now, she had yellow-grey hair and violet eyes; she was dressed in what looked like an alchemist's robe with bits of mirror sewn all over it. She gave Mag a skein of silk on a spool to hold, and walked one end of the thread across the room. It had been a ballroom once. Ornate sconces and pastel colors still clung to the walls, despite spells that should have scorched the paint. Faey plucked prisms like fruit off the chandeliers when she needed them; she had worn all the faces in the paintings. The mirrors, overused, were shadowy with images. Mag, who had guessed from the length of the thread what Faey was making, felt a peculiar tightening in her throat, as if the gold heart were still caught there. She wondered who was about to die.

She said, hiding an edginess behind the sweet, equivocal voice she had acquired from the brothel, "Can't she do her own spells?"

"Domina Pearl? Some, she can do. But not this one. This one is old, and it casts no shadow of the maker and it leaves no trace." She sniffed, part at dust, part at Domina. "Her meanness outruns her talents. She's mostly imagination. But up there, that mostly works."

Standing at the far wall, she measured a shorter length, severed the silk with precision, her teeth snapping like shears. Mag watched her out of still eyes. This was what humans did to each other: took one another's lives and then pretended they had not. Faey was honest in her own way; she was too powerful to need to lie. But Mag, feeling the gold heart again in her throat, sensed that dealing death to humans would make her irrevocably human.

"Hold steady," Faey said.

"I am."

She measured another short length and bit it off. Holding the three ends between her teeth, she braided the two shorter lengths down the long strand Mag held. Mag, watching shadows quiver at the edge of the room, heard Faey's murmuring with occult clarity. The spell seemed to tremble down the strand into her ear. Faey took the thread ends from her mouth and pinched them. Three drops of blood fell on the floor. She took the light from a candle behind her onto her fingers, applied the tiny flame to the braid. It worked its way down, while she caught falling ash and blood in her palm. Mag stood quite still, expressionless, a thing carved of wax. A bird fluttered above the flame, a carrion crow of smoke, watching, waiting. Mag stared it down: it was dream, a wish of Domina Pearl's, nothing. The flame reached the end of the braid, began its long, slow journey down the single strand, leaving an unbroken gossamer strand of ash in its wake.

"Hold steady," Faey whispered. "Steady."

"Yes," Mag said, thinking: I am wax, I am a making, I am nothing. Slowly the flame came toward her; a drop of sweat rolled down her face like wax. Words followed the flame down the ash; she wanted to tilt her head, shake them out of her ear. The flame reached her finally; Faey's voice, ragged and toneless, came from the other end of the room.

"Blow it out."

She ducked her head, sucked it in between her lips.

Either Faey did not notice, or it did not matter. She began looping the thread of ash in her hand, while Mag toyed with the taste in her mouth, and wondered whose life it was. Faey set the coil of ashes into an ivory box, and sent Mag with it to the palace.

The sunflowers drooped beside the gate; their eyes had been picked out by birds. Mag stood among them in a chill autumn wind, alone in the streets of Ombria, her quick eyes missing not even the slink of black cat in the dark. She saw the shadow that came out of the palace before it saw her. A small woman moved into the torchlight between the gates. She wore black, close-fitting silk like a shroud, and a fantastic hair style: a tall, severe hillock above her brow in which she could have hidden an arsenal of dainty weapons. Mag smelled the age wafting from her, not even living ravages, but the dusty scent of old bones. She stood as intent as a cat among the sunflowers, her breathing hidden beneath the murmuring leaves. The woman sensed her finally; she stared into the withering stalks with a long, unblinking gaze. She lifted a finger, crooked it.

"Come here."

Mag moved into the light. The woman's eyes seemed to see more of Mag than anyone had ever seen in her life.

"You are Faey's making."

Mag said nothing, not willing to give this old raven even the sound of her voice. Domina Pearl smiled, a thin smile like a wrinkle in old leather.

"Who made you really, I wonder? Did she find you in some doorway? Or do you have a more complex history? Is she too stupid to know you know you are human? You are curious. You like knowing things, seeing secrets. I will tell you this: if I find you watching me again I will unmake you so well, past and future, that not even Faey will remember you existed. Give me the box."

That night, the Prince of Ombria, who had suffered odd, sudden ailments all his life, grew very ill. Mag sat long past morning beside the chimney that rose into the roots of the sunflowers, listening to snatches of gossip echoing down the stones, as carriages of physicians and far-flung family rattled through the gate. She fell asleep listening, her head against the chimney stones. In her dreams, she heard the voices drift down from above, telling her that the prince's life had been mysteriously spared; he would not die that night. The last thing she saw, in memory or warning, were two eyes as black and still as a toad's eyes watching her.

THREE

Cat and Mouse

W hen the prince finally took to his deathbed two years later, it was without Faey's help. Receiving word of his uncle's death, Ducon Greve picked the weeping Kyel up in his arms and disappeared, as far as anyone could tell. Exactly where they vanished on their way to bid farewell to the dead man, no one was able to explain to Domina Pearl, though everyone, she was assured, had been watching the two of them at all times.

"I was afraid of this," the Black Pearl said sharply. "The bastard will kill the boy. Find them."

Ducon, who had spent much of his life exploring the honeycomb of secret passages, hidden doorways, stairs behind stairs in the ancient, rambling palace, listened to this exchange as he walked along a narrow passage behind the corridor wall where the guards and courtiers were gathered. He held Kyel in one arm, and a candle in one hand. Kyel clung to his neck, silent, wide-eyed, watching the shadows plummet down the panelled walls ahead of them. There were unlit tapers Ducon had placed in sconces during other rambles; this time, knowing they would be sought, he did not leave a trail of light behind him. How well Domina Pearl knew the palace, he had no idea. If she found them alone, without witnesses, she might kill them both and lay Kyel's death on Ducon's own mute head.

"May we talk yet?" Kyel whispered. Ducon, still hearing the murmur of voices beyond the wall, put his finger to his lips. The boy was silent again; he was still too astonished by the secret paths within the house to remember to cry. It was his small pale face, his quiet, hopeless weeping when he had been told that his father was dead and that Lydea did not want to stay with him any longer, that had cut Ducon to the heart. Without thinking, he had the child in his arms; without thinking, he had taken Kyel as far as he could get from time and death, to quiet his grief.

He stopped at three hinged panels limned with carved roses. The panels opened under his touch. A few steps upward took them into a windowless chamber on a secret floor of rooms invisible from outside the palace. The rooms were full of moth-eaten tapestries, tiny, stiff, ornate chairs, paraphernalia from forgotten centuries. He set Kyel on his feet.

"We can talk now."

Kyel gazed around him, then up at Ducon, out of his father's dark blue eyes. He said, "Is this a secret place?"

"This is your place. All these secrets, this house, all of Ombria is yours."

"Not yours."

"No. Not mine, nor Domina Pearl's."

"But you," Kyel said, "know all these secret places."

Ducon smiled a little. "Your father knew a few of them."

"Is this where Lydea went?"

"No." His smile had vanished. He knelt, drawing Kyel close to him so that the child could not see his face. Lydea was a blown flame; Lydea was yesterday; Lydea, alone on the streets of Ombria, was already changing into something neither of them would recognize, if she survived to see them again. "Lydea went back to her father."

"Domina Pearl said she didn't want to stay with me."

"Domina Pearl was mistaken. Lydea loves you very much." He hesitated, not knowing how much bitterness the boy could understand that night. "She would have stayed for you."

"Domina made her go," Kyel whispered. He pushed his face hard against Ducon, burrowing away from what he saw. His voice rose suddenly, muffled in Ducon's shirt. "Domina made Jacinth go, and Lydea — will she make you go?"

"Maybe." Kyel lifted his head; his face was scarlet, tear-streaked. He drew breath to shout; Ducon pulled him close again, his face against Kyel's hot, wet cheek. "Shh. If they hear us, nothing will be secret."

"Tell her no!"

"You will tell her. Not now, but when you are older. Now, you must do whatever she wants, and when you want to tell her no, you must draw a picture of what you want to say no to. I'll show you a secret place to leave it.

Never tell her no to her face, until you are old enough to make her do what you want. I'll help you when I can. Promise — "

"Ducon, don't go."

"I won't, unless I must." He held Kyel's face between his hands, seeing his uncle again. A thumb of grief pushed against his throat. He swallowed, dropped his forehead against Kyel's. "Please," he whispered. "Play this game with me, of silence, secret drawings, secret places. Please. Promise."

Kyel slumped against him. The promise was a long time coming; when it came, it was little more than a breath of shaped air.

Ducon took him higher in the palace, showed him spider webs of passages, cunningly wrought doors opening into bedrooms, council chambers, ballrooms. The secrets there did not interest Ducon much; having learned to thread through them, he used them only to get to the place that intrigued him most, where he was slowly leading Kyel. Kyel, sometimes in his arms, sometimes holding his hand, went willingly, though his face was stiff and white with grief and shock. He seemed to hope that if they walked far enough, Ducon would lead him out of sorrow and fear and uncertainty, into a morning in which his father only slept and Domina Pearl did not exist. They went to the hidden, forgotten crown of the palace, so high that when they first heard the mice-like pattering on the roof, Kyel asked in astonishment,

"What is it?"

"Rain."

The rain came down and down and down, like the song

Ducon heard Lydea sing to Kyel one night, her voice lilting down, down, down as Kyel's eyelids slowly drooped. Kyel clung hard to Ducon's hand, for there were more noises around them than the rain. The old walls wept water; timbers were rotting, old mortar crumbling, newer plaster bleeding damp, swelling, as if the inner house were in pain. Roosting pigeons heard their steps, fluttered off exposed rafters into the dark. Ducon felt rain in his hair. Vast rooms loomed about his fluttering candle; the shadows moved and sighed. Fire pulled gold out of the dark: flaked gold trim around doors and long windows in rooms where the patterns of slow, complex dances had worn into the floor. Ducon had sketched that door, that window; he watched them now, as he stood at the elusive boundary between light and shadow, and wondered if the fiery star of light in a shard of glass was a reflection of his candle, or another light moving to meet him.

The palace, like the city, had been sinking into itself longer than memory, floors shrinking, chipped paint revealing underlayers, joists and beams shifting restlessly, night by night, century by century. Ducon, for reasons he scarcely understood, had made himself witness to the changing, in hundreds of sketches and watercolors he had made through the years. The Black Pearl occasionally rifled through them, left them disordered without caring that he saw. He wondered if she knew why he would paint the same door again and again in changing lights. Mingled among the doorways, gates, thresholds, stairs and alleys of Ombria, they deceived her eyes; she thought he wandered only in the streets to find all his ruined doorways. So he guessed, and hoped it was true, and that they would not find her waiting for them in the old palace's heart.

Kyel made a sound and stumbled; Ducon realized he must be walking half-asleep. He stooped, picked the child up. Kyel was trembling with cold, his eyes smudged with weariness, but he turned in Ducon's hold, gazing ahead toward whatever hope Ducon had walked so far to find for them. It was only another doorway: this one distinguished by painted irises twining up the carved wooden posts. One post was cracked, bent under the shifting weight of the ceiling, the paint long warped away. The other still bloomed irises in delicate greens and purples. Ducon stopped.

He stood there for a long time, at the threshold beneath the lintel, in the moment between worlds, watching the flat slab of dark not even the light of his candle could enter, while Kyel finally fell asleep against his shoulder.

Air trembled on the threshold, smelling of grass, slow rain, lavender. A light sparked, reflecting Ducon's candle; how near or far, he could not tell in the utter darkness. There were voices, whisperings. A bell began its slow dirge, faint and far away within the shadow, for someone who had died. Ducon felt the icy hand of sorrow and wonder glide over him. Shaken, unable to move, he heard a second bell, louder, on this side of the shadow, its great open mouth speaking the word that Royce Greve could not. Ducon closed his burning eyes and wondered if, in the shadow city, someone stood like him, in a secret place, listening to the mourning bell of a city within a tale.

Kyel woke when they left the rain behind, entered the maze of secret passages again.

"Are we there?" he asked. Ducon walked quickly, taking a shorter route, alert for footsteps, unexpected voices.

"Not yet."

Kyel drowsed again, woke when Ducon stopped beside a little door. He blew his candle out, set it in the sconce beside the door, and shifted the sconce. The door clicked, opened a crack.

He whispered, "This is Jacinth's room. Since you have no nurse now, it will remain empty. This is where you can leave drawings for me. The other side of this door is a mirror. Within the mirror's gilded frame, there are two red jewels. Push them both at once, and the door will open. Can you remember that?"

"Two red jewels," Kyel said obediently. His eyes were half-closed.

"It's a secret," Ducon reminded him. "Our secret." He pushed the small door open, stepped through. As the mirror clicked shut behind them, the tip of a rapier blade, quick as lightning and burning cold, snaked past Kyel to hover in the hollow of Ducon's throat.

Kyel moved abruptly; the blade cut. "No," the boy said, shocked out of sleep. Ducon, frozen, stared into the cold eyes of one of the household guards who had watched his eccentric roaming in and out of the palace for years without question. The guard's bleak, empty face was so expressionless it seemed entranced. He no longer recognized the man he might kill, Ducon realized; he would recognize only Domina Pearl.

Ducon saw her then, standing quietly beside the doorway between Kyel's bedchamber and the nurse's. More guards poured past her into the room, their swords drawn, their empty eyes intent on the Black Pearl's prey. Ducon could not tell if she had seen him come out of the wall; her eyes told him nothing either. It will not matter anymore, he thought in sudden surprise that his life ended there, at a step through a mirror.

But again, he was surprised.

"Take the prince to his bed," Domina Pearl said to the guards massed and prickling like a hedgehog around Ducon. "Summon his attendants. Leave the bastard to me."

The rapier loosed him. Ducon set Kyel down gently, feeling him tremble. The child drew breath to speak. Ducon shook his head slightly and Kyel swallowed words, his mouth pinched tight. His eyes clung to his cousin until guards falling into ranks around him hid him from view.

Domina Pearl closed the door behind them. She gazed at Ducon a moment without speaking. Her face, he thought wearily, resembled some barren landscape, a desert, a cliff, more than anything human. He matched her stare for stare, feeling the blood seep into his shirt from the rapier's cut.

The old jaws creaked open. "Ducon Greve. I don't need you in order to rule Ombria. I do not even need the boy. Any of his doddering, whey-faced relatives in line to inherit would do as well for me, likely with less trouble. I am older than the memory of anyone alive in this court. I have been called great-aunt to rulers and their heirs far longer than anyone would care to delve into. With a prince scarcely out of his cradle and his direct heirs glimpsing into their open graves, I can finally assume power. No one would dare argue rights with me to my face. Would you?"

The question seemed rhetorical, but he opened his mouth to offer a reckless answer anyway. A spider web of lines covered her face; her voice thinned. "Yes. I know you that well. So I will warn you once, now, that if you challenge me, or conspire against me, or interfere with me in any way, I will kill Kyel and lay the blame on your head. Do you understand me?"

"No," he whispered. "I don't understand you at all."

She showed him cracked yellow teeth, like some ancient, feral street cat. It was, he realized, her version of a smile. "Good. I have many eyes in this palace, many ears. If you betray me, I will know. I would prefer to keep the boy alive to maintain a semblance of continuity. An illusion of hope. The prince is dead, long live the prince. I may need that illusion to suit my purposes with other courts, other countries. But his life depends upon you, my lord Ducon. If you do nothing to harm me, I will do nothing to harm him."

She turned. In that brief moment he thought how easy it would be to crush those dry bird-bones at her neck between his fingers. She stopped, glanced back at him, and he felt hands as cool and smooth as the glass behind him slide around his throat and tighten. "A word, my lord Ducon," he heard through the sudden black wind roaring through his head, "of warning."

He woke some time later at the foot of the mirror, his throat as raw as if he had swallowed a rapier. He managed to find his feet and stumble into Jacinth's bed. There he took some comfort in her lingering scent of violets and the memory of her delicate hands before the long night opened its toad's eyes in his thoughts and watched.

FOUR

The Alchemist's Riddle

"So the old besom cleared the Reprobate out at last,"
Faey said. A bell in the palace had tolled its solitary
dirge all night long. At dawn, other bells in clock- and
watch-towers all over the city had joined it. The air seemed
to pulse with ponderous, invisible wings of iron. "Leaving
a child to rule and a senile great-uncle or herself as regent.
I don't need a crystal ball to tell me that she'll make herself
regent, and that the bastard will be her next prey."

"Not the child?" Mag asked. They were eating breakfast for once at breakfast time. Faey was dressed in deep
mourning. She had borrowed her wan, beautiful, grief-
stricken face and her clothes from a painting that hung
above her on the wall. Shadows served them, vague
sketches of color and movement dressed in a motley of
fashions, who often seemed not to see one another. Faey's

cook was a mountainous, efficient woman who kept the
kitchens dim and pretended not to notice who among her
staff was real and who was shade. "Ducon Greve won't
inherit; why would Domina Pearl fear him?"

"He won't inherit, but he may decide to take. She can
control the child for many years — forever if she begins
right. But Ducon is an unknown quantity."

He was indeed. For all her listening beneath the sunflowers, Mag had heard little about him. She broke a corner off a piece of toast and winced. She had sprained her
thumb in some altercation during the wild run the night
before. Remembering the argument at the sunflower gate,
she felt a sudden urge to dabble in politics. The palace,
which for years had seemed less accessible and far less
interesting than the streets of Ombria, was taking on in-
triguing hues of light and dark. People emerged to line
themselves on either side. The child and the old woman
faced one another. The outcast mistress, a mop in her
hands, took her stand beside Kyel. Where, Mag wondered,
would Ducon Greve stand? On his own? A divided man,
one foot in shadow and one in light? Or beside the child
prince? Surely not with the old besom, who might sweep
him from present into past as tidily as she had done his
uncle.

Faey, calmly eating kippers underneath her own de-
spairing face, flicked a glittering jet glance down the long
table. "You're not thinking, are you, my waxling? I didn't
make you to think."

"Occasionally," Mag admitted, "I have a thought."

"Well. Makings such as you are difficult and seldom
flawless. You keep away from Domina Pearl. She's busi-

ness for us, but she's ruthless. I don't want you anywhere in her thoughts."

"I thought you said she is mostly imagination."

"So she is," Faey said softly, "and so are you. She'd melt you down like a candle if you got in her way. Don't niggle arguments at me, just keep out of her shadow."

"Yes, Faey."

"I want you to go above. I need certain things. Don't be long; we'll have work by noon. Those who fear Domina Pearl's housekeeping will be scattering through the city looking for protective charms."

"How can you do for them," Mag asked curiously, "and at the same time do for her? You'll undo your own spells."

Faey shrugged. "It's business. Those who paid for protection won't be around to demand their money back if it fails." She tracked a stray fish bone with her tongue, removed it delicately from between her lips, and rose. "Come to me when you've finished; I'll give you a list of what I want from up there."

Mag, alone but for the ghosts, toyed with a crust and entertained a carefully chosen thought or two. Coffee flavored with mint and chocolate was poured into her cup. She raised it to her face like a flower and inhaled noisily, then took a fashionably mincing sip. If the Black Pearl sent to Faey for help in ridding the world of Ducon Greve, would that be the world's gain or its loss? Faey was rousing her powers and her waxling to deal in death again. Mag wanted to know for whose sake she might risk Faey's fury and mistrust by thwarting her spells. To Faey, business was business. She bore no one ill will, even those she harmed, and she assumed her waxling thought as she did.

But her waxling felt, as strongly as wax feels flame on the wick, that Domina Pearl was another matter entirely.

Her bones and her shadow and her dank eyes boded nothing but ill for Ombria. Her ways had eaten the heart out of its better days; she was busily turning the city into a parched, crippled, bitter husk. Faey seemed indifferent to the Black Pearl's workings in the city or the palace, as if, living beneath and in the past, she could not be touched by the mausoleum's schemings. But Domina Pearl had above all a power for hatred of which Faey seemed oblivious. The Black Pearl had thrown the prince's mistress out to be murdered in the streets, for no other crime than an upside-down innocence. She would at least contemplate the death of a child. She would kill again in secret, with or without Faey's help. Mag, who was fascinated by secrets, studied the coffee trembling under her breath. How much power did the old besom wield? Where had she gotten it? Who was she? Was she even of Ombria, or had she been born in some distant country so long ago that nothing was left of it now but its name and its dubious achievement, the indestructible Pearl?

The woman in the painting suddenly found her mouth and spoke. "Mag!"

She started guiltily. "Yes, Faey."

"You are thinking, my waxling."

She made a swift decision, and finished her coffee on the way up. "I'm coming," she said, both to Faey and to the young woman on Sheepshead Lane, whose sapphire-heeled shoes Mag had tossed down the chimney beneath the sunflowers.

She took them with her when she went above into day.

She bought a lamb's heart at the butcher's. She waited at a familiar doorway in a back alley for goats' eyes and candles made of goat fat. At a small shop with dusty windows and an ancient apothecary sign, she picked up powdered bone and extractions from strange, fleshy plants that had been diverted from Domina Pearl's pirate ships. For the cook, she bought violets. At the brewer's, she traded silver for quicksilver, and a crock of Faey's favorite ale. The brewer's son had trouble counting change and kept dropping coins until his amiably chatting father went to load a few kegs for a merchant. Then, as Mag worried the crock into her basket, trying not to squash goats' eyes and violets, the young man reached across the counter and seized her hand. She gazed at him in wonder. He had thick, moist fingers, and she needed her hand to shift the eyes.

"Mag," he said huskily. His heavy, earnest face was sheened with sweat and the bluish shadow of his first beard. "How can you not see how we belong to one another? We've grown up together, like night and day. You are moon to my sun, you are silver to my aspiring gold — You would complete me —"

"Wait," she pleaded. "The crock is on the violets."

"Marry me. Together we would become the marvel we seek, the transmutation of time into eternity —"

She snorted inelegantly, and felt something peculiar flowing through her bones, an unaccustomed panic, a desperate urgency she barely knew words for. He thought he recognized her as human. "You are mistaken," she said coldly. "And from what I've seen of both alchemy and marriage, all the marvels lie in the expectation."

"Mag!" He was clinging to her basket now, while she settled the crock.

"Besides, I belong to Faey."

"But she doesn't own—"

"She does. I am her waxling."

"But—"

"Wax transmutes to smoke and air, not gold."

"But I love you!"

She only stared at him, perplexed. He tossed his hands into the air with a groan, and she escaped.

Shadows in the street told her time was passing, but she stole a little of Faey's, taking shortcuts through an abandoned shop and what looked like the walled end of an alley to get to Sheepshead Lane. There she found the Rose and Thorn, where she had last seen the harried, bleeding woman who had fled across the night locked safely away behind its door. The limping tavern-wench serving beer and boiled mutton did not notice Mag. Her eyes were swollen with grief and weariness; her bright hair was bundled away into a cap. The man behind the bar, burly and bald as a bed knob, watched her narrowly. She worked patiently, without complaint, though her jaw tightened now and then in pain. Mag dropped one sapphire shoe into the empty bucket in a corner behind the bar and slipped away before they saw her.

She descended, not through the nearest hole as was her childhood habit, but more sedately down a marble staircase that began life in the upper world as an innocent stairway from a cellar door. Below, Faey complained about her tardiness, but was too busy to press for explanations. A gentleman from the palace had sent a request, with gold, for a method of detecting poison. Mag sighed. It would be a smelly afternoon.

By evening, there was more work. Two days later, Mag stood on the bank of the river outside Faey's house, blinking tiredly at the slow dark water. Lamps along the banks, iron-wrought fantasies of palaces and carriages and wind-blown galleons that Faey lit when she happened to remember, tossed flowers of fire on the water. Houses on the river crumbled in the damp, revealing pale, elegant rooms, massive hearths, delicate paints. Their roofs sometimes rose to support the streets above. Rooms still sealed emitted frail lights; shadows moved like dreams across silk curtains. The undercity wandered into caves, bridged side streams, flowed toward a distance with no horizon, its streets breaking over chasms in which, far below, other lights patterned the dark water.

Mag could smell the spells in the ruffled ivory taffeta she wore. She could smell them on her skin. The spells lay in small, expensive boxes, ready to be called for. *Swallow this and nothing you eat or drink will harm you. Unwind this and stretch it across your doorway; no one will be able to pass over it. Place this beside you at night: it will cry out if it senses danger.* Domina Pearl would find them, these trinkets of sorcery, and send her own request to Faey: a spell to undo all spells.

As Faey said, no one would be alive to complain. Mag swallowed a yawn and contemplated a finger of sunlight falling a long way from a chink in a drainage ditch onto the water. She would find a chink to meddle with that spell, she decided. The Black Pearl should not have her own way so easily. Above her, cobblestones rattled continuously under carriages trailing black ribbons from their doors, making their way to the great, solemn funeral that would finally put an end to the tolling of the bells.

"Mag!" Faey called within the house or within Mag's mind; she was too tired to tell which.

"Coming," she answered, but lingered a moment longer, her eyes narrowed, searching the shadowy riverbank for the place where some woman might have come, years earlier, to bear a nut-eyed child in the dark and leave her there, wailing in the forgotten city, until the city's sorceress stumbled out of bed, prodded her ancient face into some recognizable shape, and went to see what was disturbing her sleep.

"Mag! My waxling! I need you now, not tomorrow."

Or, Mag wondered dispassionately, was I just found abandoned in some gutter above, and traded, along with a bucket of salamanders and some mandrake root, for a few coins to the sorceress who lives underground?

She moved at last. "I'm coming."

"I want you to go out again," Faey told her, and gave her a list. "When you come back, you may rest. I can do these last myself." Then she sniffed. She was not ordinarily sensitive, but her spells had been potent. Her own eyelids hung like crescent moons with weariness, but she moved busily, gathering this and that. "Change your clothes and get aired, my waxling. A lady should aspire to smell of roses, not sulphur."

Rose, thought Mag.

An hour or two later, errands finished and the sorceress satisfied, Mag sat down among the idlers in the Rose and Thorn. Like them, she wore black. The entire city seemed to be dressed in funereal shades, not only for the dead prince, but in vigorous, reckless mourning for the hope being buried with him. Mag, in brocade so old that its interweave of silver thread had tarnished, was scarcely visible behind the long black veils she had pinned to her hat. Those who caught a glimpse of her slender waist and the graceful fingers exposed beyond the lace of her finger-less gloves, came up against the ghostly swaths of black and turned uneasily back to their cups. The tavern maid, her eyes glazed by sorrow and the incessant clamor of the bells, limped over to Mag. Even she seemed startled out of her grief by the apparition.

"What would you —" She saw the sapphire heel flash from beneath the veil and her voice died.

"I brought your other shoe," Mag said softly. The woman's attention riveted itself on the opal mounted on gold between two pearls on Mag's forefinger. She closed her eyes suddenly as if they stung. Mag added, "And this belongs to you. I took it from a sailor. The others were lost."

The woman's eyes rose from the ring to the lacy dark obscuring the face within. "It was you," she whispered. "Helping me that night. That's how I made it through the streets alive. But how? Why did you help me?"

Mag, who hadn't stopped to think about it, shrugged lightly and then discovered answers. "I like meddling," she said simply. "And I dislike Domina Pearl. I was hiding in the sunflowers at the west gate when she threw you out of the palace."

The woman seemed to be trying to guess at the strength, the agility hidden beneath brocade and lace. "But how?" she repeated. Mag worked a jet pin idly out of her hat, touched the long, barbed shaft to the tip of her finger. The woman's mouth opened, but nothing came out; she watched wordlessly as Mag replaced the pin.

"Lydea!" the tavern keeper barked from behind the bar. "Take the lady's order and get this beer before it loses head."

Lydea shifted position from one bandaged foot to the other, but did not turn. She asked abruptly, "Where can I find you later? He's counting off hours for my transgressions. Right now I doubt that I could live long enough to satisfy him."

"Who is he?"

"My father."

Mag examined him curiously. "I never had one."

"They're a mixed blessing. But I owe him for taking me in that night. And I owe you a great deal, it seems. Where do you live?"

I live underground, Mag said silently, *with a sorceress named Faey*. The facts had never surprised her before. But Lydea's weary, harrowed eyes trying to see her clearly within the shadows disconcerted Mad oddly. People knew her only vaguely as belonging to Faey. She had never been asked to explain herself in human terms. She said weakly, "It's not an easy place to find."

"Oh."

"You could help me now, though."

"How?" Lydea asked promptly.

"You must have known Ducon Greve while you were at the palace. Is he worth saving?"

"Worth—" Lydea echoed bewilderedly. "Worth saving how? From what?"

"From death."

Lydea stared at her. At the next table, her father rattled a tray irritably; heavy glass and pewter careening together could not produce his daughter's attention. Lydea found her voice finally. "Is he in danger?"

"Faey—the woman I live with—thinks he will be." Lydea was still perplexed. Mag sighed noiselessly, scarcely disturbing lace, and put it more clearly. "Faey thinks that Domina Pearl will ask her to make something that will unmake Ducon."

"Unmake?"

"Something subtle. A spell no one would suspect."

Lydea's brows leaped up; so did her voice. "To kill him?"

"It would be something Faey is quite capable of doing."

Lydea groped for the back of a chair, but she did not sit. Her eyes, stunned and horrified, seemed to expect nothing predictably human beneath the veil. "She would do that?"

"It's business," Mag said fairly. "But I think that Faey must care a little about Ombria, because she doesn't approve at all of the Black Pearl."

"And you." Lydea's voice was disappearing, burrowing high up into her throat. "What do you do?"

"I help her."

Lydea backed a step at that, then stood still again, gazing in complete confusion at the veiled contradiction under her nose. "You help her kill?"

"No," Mag said very softly, her eyes on a knothole between Lydea's clogs, as though Faey might be under the floorboards listening. "She rarely does that, and when she does, I find ways to meddle without her knowledge." She paused, remembering the taste of blood and fire when she had first given breath back to one of Faey's undoings. "That's why I asked you about Ducon Greve. If he is worth saving, or if Ombria would be better off without him. It's not easy, changing Faey's spells. And I don't know what she would do to me if she caught me. What do you think? Should I bother?"

Lydea stared at her, dumbfounded. Then her gaze grew inward, searching memory, and Mag glimpsed beneath her careworn, grieving face, the fine-boned beauty who had been a prince's mistress scant days before. Lydea said slowly, "I never knew him well. He kept his life and his thoughts private, from me at least. Kyel trusted him. Which may be to Ducon's advantage now, or may not be. I couldn't say. He has no love for Domina Pearl, but then who does? I know he wanders through the city. He would show Royce his drawings of odd things that caught his eye in the streets. Doorways, crooked alleys, barred cellar windows. I didn't understand them. Royce would tell him to be more careful, but he'd go out alone, unarmed, come back whenever he chose. He had no place in the world, he said once, therefore he could go everywhere."

Like me, Mag thought, startled by the recognition. She asked, "What does he look like?"

"Like no one I've ever seen. He's striking, with his silvery eyes and hair as white as fish bone, though he's not much older than I am. He looks capable of taking care of himself in Ombria at night."

"Like me," Mag murmured, curious now. Behind the bar, the tavern keeper upended an entire tray of mugs into a wash basin; Lydea started at the clatter. Still she lingered, caught by another memory. "He mentioned a tavern once. What was it? The King of Flounders. The name made Kyel laugh."

"I'll look there for him," Mag said. She slid the ring off her finger and dropped it into an empty cup. The shoe she slipped from beneath her veil into Lydea's apron pocket so quickly that only a single jewel flared before it vanished. She would have risen then, but Lydea had shifted closer to her, perplexed again, uneasy at what she might have loosed into Ducon's life.

"Please," she begged. "Let me see your face. You chose to save me; now you have put Ducon in your balance. You're someone dealing with life and death, and I need to put a face to that, or I'll see you as you are, all in black with your face invisible, in my nightmares."

Mag, mute at the unexpected image of herself as someone's bad dream, pulled the pin out of her hat. The tavern had all but emptied for the [cf4]funeral; those left had forgotten their interest in her. The veils parted easily at the back. She sat blinking at the sudden light, gazing back at Lydea while she straightened the pins in the improbable golden stork's nest of her hair.

Lydea, astonished again, touched a tendril of the wild hair. She breathed, "You're so young. Was it you I saw in the lamplight that night? Who told me where to find the Rose and Thorn?"

Mag nodded. "You seemed a little lost, then."

"I was very lost, then. What is your name?"

"Mag."

"Just Mag?"

"It's what the sorceress named me." She tucked her hair back into her enormous hat, adjusted the veils and rose. Lydea watched her, brows puckered worriedly, but at what, Mag was uncertain.

"If I wanted to find you, ask you about Ducon—"

"Don't look for me," Mag advised. "I'll come to you, whatever happens to him."

"Maybe," Lydea said somberly, "but if you keep passing the Black Pearl's name around in broad daylight, I'll be waiting here until I've paid off the entire city's transgressions. You be careful of that woman."

Once warned, no fool, Mag thought. Twice warned, once a fool. And so on. She stepped outside the tavern and stopped, oddly disoriented, as if the sky had turned grass-green, or the sun had taken to changing phases, like the moon. Then she realized that the city's noises had become familiar once again.

The bells of Ombria were silent.

FIVE

The King of Flounders

Ducon Greve stood in front of the mausoleum of the House of Greve. The bald dome and the squat pillars holding it up enclosed the lichen-stained central cube, whose ponderous doors were open to accept yet another ruler of Ombria. The white marble had darkened, weathered through centuries. The mausoleum sat on a broad green knoll overlooking, between neat rows of cypress, a swath of glittering sea. The iron fence beyond the trees held back a black tide of mourners from the city. Courtiers from the palace, nobles, and relatives of the family were scattered in a crescent moon before the face of the mausoleum. All were silent, motionless, spellbound, it seemed, by the constant, jarring clamor of bells.

The child-heir of Ombria stood beside the Black Pearl. Both were surrounded by an escort of guards. Ducon was

never far from Kyel, though the guards were so thick a-
round the boy that he could barely be seen. As if, Ducon
thought, Domina Pearl feared some bloody rebellion to be
instigated by red-eyed great-aunts and their elderly con-
sorts. He had chosen a place within a cluster of minor
cousins and relatives whose names dangled like spiders
along the edges of the family tree. He could see Kyel most
clearly among them. The boy looked for him once, his eyes
widening suddenly at all the strangers around him, his face
flushing as if he were close to tears. Ducon shifted a little
and Kyel found him. Ducon smiled; the panic receded from
Kyel's eyes. Domina Pearl moved between them.

Then Kyel's father was carried into the candlelit dark
within the mausoleum. The courtiers came back out; the
dead prince did not. After what seemed a long time, during
which nothing moved but the wind, and the long banners
flowing and coiling like black flame, and the distant, froth-
ing sea, Ducon realized that the bells had finally stopped
tolling.

"The prince is dead," someone said softly behind him.
"Long live the prince."

Trumpets flashed then, a shout of gold before they
spoke. Ducon turned. Camas Erl, who had in earlier years
been his tutor, was watching Domina Pearl, a mordant
light in his yellow eyes. Long, sonorous cadences from the
trumpets moved the groups of mourners down the hill toward the line of carriages. Camas, a tall, lean man with a
dry voice and chestnut hair lightly threaded with silver,
had been at the palace since Ducan was five. He had been
unfailingly even-tempered and kind to the fatherless boy,
and he seemed to know everything worth knowing, from

the names of moths to the history of Ombria and the House
of Greve, even, Ducon discovered eventually, how to make
paints.

"Be careful," Ducon advised him. "She is culling her
court. None of us is safe."

"I am," Camas said. "She has asked me to stay and
tutor the prince, as Royce Greve wished."

"You'll stay?"

"Oddly enough, for such an indolent court, the palace
has an extraordinary library. I would hate to leave it. I am
still working on my history of Ombria." He paused then,
studying Ducon. "I trust," he said slowly, "that you are not
contemplating anything stupid?"

"Not at the moment. The Black Pearl and I have
reached a compromise of sorts. I won't fight her, and she
won't kill me."

"I see," Camas said aridly. Domina Pearl passed them
then, and he said nothing more. The Black Pearl walked
beside Kyel, one hand on his shoulder. Ducon watched his
stiff back, his small, clenched fists. He would not cry and
he would not look at her. Once he turned to give an in-
credulous glance back at the mausoleum. Ducon saw his
face clearly then, bewildered, colorless. The boy stumbled
a little; Domina's fingers tightened on his shoulder. He
stared ahead, trudging wearily down the hill. He would
return to the palace to rehearse for his coronation the next
morning.

Ducon's own hands had closed. He watched the child
blindly, shaken by ideas, impulses he did not dare put into
words, even in the privacy of his own head. Camas's long

hand on his shoulder, a light, familiar touch, conveyed both sympathy and warning.

"You must give her no excuse," the tutor murmured.

"I know."

"The boy needs you."

He drew breath, his hands opening. "I know."

"Promise me something." Camas waited, until Ducon met his eyes. His voice was very soft. "If you decide to act, tell me first. Before you make a move, or say a word to anyone else. That way, if anything does happen to you, I'll know why. I have known you nearly all your life. It would be hard for me to have you disappear and not to know why."

Ducon shook his head a little, touched. "I don't have a coherent idea in my head," he assured Camas. "Except to take the paper and charcoal out of the carriage and join the rest of Ombria for my uncle's wake." He paused briefly, remembering, his mouth tight. "He was good to me. And to my mother. I'll miss him." Another figure formed in memory, with impossibly long, autumn-leaf hair, and perpetually chewed fingers. She might have died as well, so quickly and utterly had she vanished into the night of Ombria. "Poor Kyel," he whispered.

"Pity us all."

"Come with me?"

"I haven't your fondness for the stinking back streets and churning taverns," the tutor said mildly. "I prefer to spend the afternoon in the library, contemplating history and your uncle's place in it. But at Domina Pearl's command, I will spend it gutting the traditional coronation ceremony and filleting it into something more suitable for a five-year old. Be careful."

"I will," Ducon promised absently, and went to join the crowd beyond the fence, which was dispersing through the streets of Ombria in search of a suitable place to mourn.

Some of the younger nobles and courtiers shared his taste for the unseemly side of Ombria. They had no idea why Ducon would stop to sketch a window whose small, thick, cracked panes of glass made the world beyond it undefined, elusive. They would criticize his drawings, follow him into taverns and drink with him, until they recognized what they wanted at the bottom of a bottle or in a face. Then they would let him drift away to find other windows, other doors and passageways that seemed haunting in their ambiguity, as if they led both out and in at once, and to the same place.

This time, a small group of nobles clung to his side all afternoon, made uneasy by death, he thought, and irritatingly noisy. They would not let him wander off pursuing shadows. They pulled him ruthlessly into taverns and inns, where they bought him fine wine or ale, depending on the place, and stood around him, laughing and drinking, while he picked out faces in the blur of black shoulders and veils, and sketched them. Every face that emerged on his paper seemed not so much in mourning for one ineffectual ruler as in fear of the next. He wondered, at one point, if he were simply shadowing every expression he drew with his own thoughts.

He didn't notice the painted flounder dancing improbably on the crest of a wave, its gold crown sliding rakishly toward eyes protruding like carbuncles, one above the other on its flat body. He had seen the tavern sign many times. This time, near that nebulous edge of day between light and night, all the inns and taverns were blurring into one, and he had no idea where he was in Ombria. He floated on the will and fumes of the young nobles, some the sons of dissipated courtiers, others cousins of confusing degree, who rarely appeared at court except for coronations and funerals. He had spent some time in one inn, he remembered vaguely, trying to chart their relation to him, at their insistence. It occurred to him then that their true interest lay in Kyel, and the likelihood that the young prince might not survive his bleak-eyed regent to rule Ombria himself. Where, they might wonder, did that put them along the line of power? A dangerous and compelling question, but not, in the end, what they asked him.

He recognized the tavern when he walked in: the painted plaster above the mantelpiece depicted a line of flounders swimming sedately behind one another, blowing bubbles in strands of graduated pearls. There was the familiar crush of black, ribbons streaming from hats and sleeves, a funeral dirge sung in too many parts, and as tongues loosened recklessly toward the end of the long day, the unexpected barb of politics.

It was a laugh into the dragon's maw, he heard someone say of the rousing dirge, because that's what Royce Greve's death had brought Ombria up against: the twin-headed dragon of a child-ruler and Domina Pearl.

"Not that Royce Greve had much of Ombria at heart, not like his father did, but at least he kept the Black Pearl pretending to be honest while she ran her pirate ring and dabbled in sorcery. Now she won't have to pretend." The speaker held up his glass. Ducon recognized him, despite his patched black: he had owned a fleet of ships and been extremely wealthy until Domina Pearl turned her eye toward him. "To her," he offered. "The Black Pearl and her sea scum that closed the ports of Ombria."

Ducon sank into a chair at the only empty table. "There," he commented, "is a dead man."

Wine appeared before him magically, as it had done all afternoon. He drank half of it before he noticed that none of the courtiers' sons or cousins were drinking with him. They were not even talking. They ringed the table, gazing down at him, their eyes narrowed, speculative, their faces no longer bland and foolish with drink, but hungry, he thought, and wondering how he might do stuffed and served on a platter.

A third or fourth cousin pulled a chair back abruptly, dropped into it. Ducon tried to remember his name. The cousins all looked alike by then, dark-haired, dark-eyed, vaguely resembling the dead prince. Protective coloring, he guessed.

And then the seated cousin said very softly, "You could rule, Ducon. You could be regent instead of Domina Pearl."

His head cleared very quickly. He glanced past them at the crush, shifting paper, raising charcoal, as if he were seeking inspiration. Everyone near their table was talking at once, passionately and obliviously. Nobody appeared to be listening to anyone, except perhaps the slender woman clad in outdated black brocade and an enormous hat like a mushroom shot through with jewelled pins, whose veil totally obscured her face. She leaned against the wall near him, languidly fanning the air with a hand enclosed in black lace. In front of her, two men with red faces and black rosettes on their sleeves were speaking to one another, loudly and earnestly, about two entirely different subjects. She seemed to be brushing their words away from her like gnats.

Ducon said, sketching her absently, dark graceful lines with little more than an upraised hand to render them human, "You don't know Domina Pearl. She is a crafty old spider and she has woven her web through Ombria longer than anyone can remember."

"She can't live forever."

He raised a brow, working on a hatpin. "I think she died a century ago. She found some way to outwit death and make her bones do her bidding."

A hand came down over his wrist, stilling the charcoal. "Ducon." The cousin leaned closer, his fingers tight, his bloodshot eyes burning blue and cold, somehow at the same time. "How long will she let Kyel Greve live? Who inherits after him? Some doddering, snail-eyed great-uncle of Kyel's, who would fall to pieces if Domina Pearl crossed her eyes at him. What good is that for Ombria? You may be of dubious pedigree, but you have brains, you know Ombria, and you know Domina Pearl's ways. Strip her of her power. We'll help you. You find a way; you tell us how, and we will do whatever you say."

Ducon took the charcoal with his free hand, sketched the shadowy suggestion of a face beneath the veil. "She'd kill me," he said briefly. "Or she would kill Kyel, if I threaten her."

"Then," the cousin said, his voice a breath of air, an evanescent bubble, "Kyel would be out of your way."

Ducon's charcoal stopped. He gazed back at the fierce blue eyes, his own eyes the color of the pewter wine cup and as opaque. He finished the wine in the cup abruptly and stood up.

"This is no place to talk. She grows ears everywhere, like mushrooms." He tucked the lady under his arm. "Come with me."

He led them away from the crowded streets to the sea.

On the end of a weedy pier, where they could see the waves through rotting wood glide and curl beneath them, he let them speak again. The warehouses facing the water were empty; so was the harbor except for a few fishing boats and a black-sailed pirate ship heaving to port at one of Domina Pearl's guarded docks. They gathered around him, a dozen or so frustrated young nobles, who looked to him, for reasons he could not fathom, to save them all from Domina Pearl.

He asked succinctly, "Why me? I'm a bastard of the House of Greve, without a father anywhere on the horizon. Why not one of you? Or do you just want to use me to get rid of Domina Pearl, and then declare me illegitimate?"

He saw genuine surprise in their eyes. "We all know you're a bastard," someone answered earnestly. "But none of us are any closer to inherit. What we want, we must take. There's us. There's our fathers, none of them powerful enough to fight her. And there's the legitimate line, all of them with one foot in their graves and looking over their shoulders to see that Domina Pearl doesn't shove them in alive. Who else could challenge her except you?"

"How? With a paintbrush? She will kill me if she thinks I am plotting against her. I don't know what she might do to Kyel."

"Kyel is hers now," the ruthless-eyed cousin said pithily. "She'll have a decade at least before he grows his first beard. By then, there will be nothing left of him but Domina Pearl's will. Kyel is lost. You cannot let him matter."

Ducon was silent, wordless at the idea, though they assumed he was merely taking the measure of them while his eyes shifted from face to face around the circle. He said carefully, "Leaving Kyel aside, there is the matter of the Black Pearl. She has mysterious origins and powers that no one understands; she is unscrupulous, unpredictable, and she has turned Ombria into this." He reached down, pulled a flourishing thistle out from between the planks. He tossed it down a hole in the pier to the waves. "You want me to fight that?"

"Yes."

"With what?"

They were silent then, but not dissuaded; one shrugged after a moment. "You have mysterious origins, too, and you're the only one living under the palace roof with her who isn't too terrified of her to think. You find a way to rid Ombria of her, and we'll help you. We'll back you against our fathers, and the House of Greve. You will become Prince of Ombria; we'll pledge you that. And then you can weed these piers to your heart's content. Ombria was a great, thriving, beautiful city once. Not in our memories, but that's what all our fathers say. We want that city back."

The black ship drew closer; Ducon thought of them

all, visible and vulnerable to a peering glass eye. "Is any one of you sober?" he demanded. "You have no idea how devious she is. You may not even live long enough to find your way to your beds tonight."

He recognized the hand that reached out to grip his shoulder, the stark, burning vision in the eyes holding his. "Take Ombria away from the Black Pearl. Give us back our city. You would do it if you were the true heir of the House of Greve. You would do it or die trying. Find a way, Ducon Greve."

"Kyel—"

The hand tightened. "Let him go," the cousin said softly. "Just let him go. Do what you must to save Ombria. She must have no hold on you, through the boy. No power over you because of him. You act for yourself and Ombria, not for him. She's got her hand on his heart and she'll take root there. Fear him. He could be the death of you."

He stepped back out of the fervid hold, and glanced at the ship. "That could be the death of us all."

"You'll give us an answer now." There was both threat and plea in the demand.

He looked down, watched the last of the fading sun gild the water through the ragged holes in the pier and slowly fade, leaving them in shadow. "Go home," he told them. "Forget everything that you've said to me. When I need you, I'll find you. I have drawn all your faces."

He left them edgy, unsatisfied, he knew, but there was nothing anyone could do then, and they were facing Ombria's night. He followed them off the pier. An odd drift of black stopped him briefly, a windblown shadow he glimpsed through a hole as the pier passed over the shore. But it was gone before he saw it clearly, and, glancing over the side of the pier, he saw no footprints in the sand.

SIX

Dancing Shoes

Lydea, hearing the bells of Ombria stop tolling, burst into tears.

She was carrying a tray of ale and mutton for a table full of mourners who hadn't managed to find their way out of the tavern to the funeral. They were making elaborate, lugubrious speeches to one another about the dead prince when her tray crashed down on the table among them and she wept suddenly, wildly, inconsolably. She wept for Royce's touch and his smile, for Kyel's soft hair under her hand and his eyes when she told him stories; she wept for her lost love, for her dead mother, for her father who could not seem to remember one tender word, for her throbbing, bleeding feet. She pulled the cap off her head and wiped her face with it; the stunned mourners watched her hair tumble to her knees. She wept for the child-prince of Ombria, lonely and in danger, for Ombria itself, for the Black Pearl's cruelty, for the shoes she would never wear again, for her lost innocence. She did not see the ale she had spilled in the mutton, or the aghast and speculative faces around the table. She felt someone's hand on her arm, pulling her. She stumbled on her poor, minced feet as far as the bar, and then sank behind it into the shadowy corner where her father piled dirty aprons and towels, and she cried for her lost years, all the years she had left behind her in the palace when Domina Pearl cast her out and slammed the iron gate.

She felt her heart empty finally, a limp nothing with no more glittering, hard-edged diamonds cutting their way out, no enormous pearls that ached through her throat before they spilled out of her. She leaned back against the scarred wood, letting a grain of sand fall, now and then, out of her swollen, gritty eyes. The tavern was unusually silent, but she had not emptied the place out entirely. She heard her father exchanging morose complaints with someone between swallows and thumps of pewter.

"I don't know what to do with her," he said. "She's neither fish nor fowl. She's not what she was, neither here nor there."

There was a hiccup; a burly voice that belonged to the butcher across the street suggested roundly, "Marry her. That'll put her in her place."

"Marry her to who? To what? She's lived for five years as the prince's mistress, and now she's back here washing beer mugs. There she was a tavern-wench dressed like a princess; here she's a princess dressed like a tavern-wench. Once she knew her job here. Now she can barely keep an order in her head. She serves beef instead of beer, and takes away half-full mugs from under the drinkers' noses. Look at this place. Echoing, on the afternoon of the Prince of Ombria's wake."

"Marry her," the butcher said with annoying persistence.

"To who?"

"Anyone. It doesn't matter. The coffin-maker over on Plank Street just lost his wife. And him with five, the smallest barely cutting teeth."

"Who? That scrawny little bantam with a nose like a pug? He has five?"

"And no wife."

Lydea picked up a soiled apron, wiped her eyes with it wearily. She remembered the coffin-maker, who barely came up to her chin, and whose upturned nostrils were uncannily expressive: they followed her like eyes, and leered when she looked at him. The butcher's notion was ludicrous, but her father had a point. She was floundering in the tavern just as she would have been floundering at the palace, if she had been permitted to stay.

She slipped her clogs off to ease her feet, and remembered what she was sitting on. She groped through the pile of aprons and towels until she felt the sapphire-crusted heels where she had hidden them.

"You could marry," the butcher told her father. "Someone who could work with you, take care of the place."

"I'm no good company," her father said shortly. "I should know. I've had to live with myself these past years, after they both left me."

The butcher swallowed beer audibly. "That's a lot to lose at once."

"Neither of them gave me a choice. One walked out the door into a fine carriage, the other out of life into — Well, it wasn't fine at all. Nothing like what's being buried today in that marble house overlooking the sea."

Lydea's face pulled against itself. The men, hearing a sound like torn cloth from behind the bar, went silent. She quieted, fighting sorrow; they spoke again, cautiously, their voices lower.

"I never thought I'd see her again. I thought she'd do anything to keep from coming back here."

"She should have married."

"She should have thought. She should have managed more cleverly and got something for herself. But no; she did all for love and wound up with nothing."

She turned a shoe in a stray beam of light from high, grimy panes, watched it spark and flare in the jewels.

I have something, she thought. I have dancing shoes.

She burrowed beneath her until she found the other one. Then she crawled out from behind the bar, her feet bare, her hair hanging limply, her eyes, she knew, a terrifying red in a face like a stiff white mask.

Even the butcher in his blood-streaked apron looked uneasy at the sight of her. Then their lowered eyes found the shoes in her hand, the sapphires catching light and casting quivering rays of blue everywhere, as if a star had fallen into the tavern.

Her father spoke finally. "Is that — What — "

"Sapphires," Lydea said. "The prince gave them to me. I doubt that I'll be dancing in them ever again, so I'll sell them. They'll pay for my keep while I look for other work. That way you won't be burdened by me."

His face, hard and furrowed like a walnut shell since she had returned, slackened suddenly as if she had hurt him. Then the shell formed again.

"You weren't wearing them the night you came back," he commented gruffly. "How did they walk their way across the city?"

"I threw them away at the palace gate," she answered steadily, "so I could run better. Someone found them and brought them back to me."

"Who?" her father demanded. "Who in this city can afford to be so honest?"

"And why?" the butcher asked bewilderedly.

She remembered the young, composed face hiding secrets the way her hair hid its barbed, jewelled weapons. "I don't know why," she answered slowly. "To make me trust her, maybe."

The butcher extended a filthy finger to the fine cloth covering the shoes, dyed the color of the stones. "What's that?"

"Silk."

"Did you really dance in them?" her father asked, looking torn between wonder and suspicion, as if, like her life, he could not quite bring himself to believe in them.

"Once." She set them on the table in front of him. "So, you see, I'm not entirely helpless. I'll be out of your way as soon as I can sell them."

"You could marry, with those," the butcher suggested, still staring at them, his round eyes as blue as the stones.

"Find yourself a husband instead of a prince, give your father some grandchildren."

"I'll never marry," Lydea said shortly. "Anyway, why would I want someone who'd marry me for my shoes? I'm no good here in the tavern anymore, but there must be something I can do to take care of myself."

Her father picked up a shoe, turned it to watch the light. "You used to know what you were doing in here." Then he looked at her, absently scratching the frown between his brows with the tip of a silk toe. "This is no life for you, once you've danced in these."

"Maybe not. But I was also thrown out into the streets for wearing them. They could have been the death of me. This place saved me. It was my only hope."

He loosed a short, harsh breath at the idea. But the frown was only skin deep now; it had left his eyes. "Why did you stay, if they treated you like that?"

She had to swallow hard before she could speak. "Royce was good to me. But he was all I had. Nothing else, no one, no true place. You said it. I was a tavern-wench dressed like a princess. That's how they all saw me. Except for the prince. And his son. They saw someone they loved."

They were both gazing at her now, with the same expression they had worn for her shoes.

"They wouldn't let you stay even for the boy's sake?" her father asked.

"He didn't want me to go." Her throat ached again. "But she even sent his nurse away. She was busy cleaning house, the night the prince died."

"She?" the butcher prompted.

"Domina Pearl."

The name cast a pall over them; they seemed to see past the death of the prince to what Ombria truly mourned. "Domina Pearl," the butcher echoed glumly. "She rules us now." He drank deeply, then wondered: "What's she made of? I heard she's been alive for centuries. That dust comes out of her when she sneezes."

"She's good for another century," Lydea said, "if no one challenges her. And she'll have no more mercy for this city than she did for me."

"What about the bastard?" her father asked. "Ducon. Will he fight her?"

"I don't know. Mostly he just draws."

They were silent again, bleakly contemplating the star-shot air in front of them. Her father placed the shoe he held precisely beside the other on the table. He said to the shoes, "You never gave me a chance to be angry with you before you left."

"I know."

"So I've had to wait all this time." He pushed the shoes an inch toward her. "Find other work if you want. But don't go. It'll come back to me, how to live with someone besides myself."

She felt the tears sting her eyes again. "For a while, then," she said stiffly, to keep her voice from shaking.

"You're not going to cry again, are you?" he asked warily.

"Well, not this minute."

A group in solemn black splintered away from the crowded streets, opened the door abruptly and staggered in. "Where is the keeper of this tavern?" a young man demanded. "We are in mourning and we need spirits."

Lydea rolled the shoes into her apron as her father rose. She went back behind the bar to hide them again. Kneeling in the laundry, she watched blue fires leap from jewel to jewel and thought with wonder: Where was the young woman who had danced in them somewhere on the other side of the chasm of memory and death? Her hair had been scalloped and scrolled into a rich, coppery crown festooned with strands of sapphire. She had worn pale blue silk to match her eyes; lace the darker blue of her jewels spiralled around the skirt. The prince dancing with her had eyes of the same dark blue. No matter who distracted him, those eyes always returned to her face. Their smiles reflected one another, all evening. No one else smiled at her like that, with eyes and mind. The courtiers stretched their lips and considered that a smile. Their eyes saw the tavern-wench. Or worse: they calculated methodically, as if they were listing household expenses, what about her had captivated Royce. Only he had seen beyond that, into her mind and heart. He and Kyel.

She remembered the vast bed where she had last seen Kyel, talked to him, touched him. She felt his soft cheek against her fingers, and pushed her empty hand against her mouth. "I wish . . ." she whispered, scarcely knowing for what. "I wish . . ."

But Kyel had vanished along with that beautiful young woman in sapphire heels who had danced with a prince. She was as dead as Royce was, she knew. That's what the courtiers would think, having seen her abandoned in Ombria at midnight. Murdered, or locked in some dingy room above a tavern on the water where the Black Pearl's ships docked. Either way, dead to their world.

They would never recognize me now, she thought dispassionately. Not even the ones who took me apart with their eyes and put me back together. I don't exist beyond the palace walls.

"Lydea," her father said, with less bark in his voice than usual. She could hear the place beginning to fill again, now that the funeral was over. She pushed the heels back among the soiled linens. And then she sat frozen, staring at them, her mind seeing something in the wrinkled aprons and stained towels that she could not yet put to words.

She forced herself to rise, find her tavern clogs and step into them, ignoring the splinters of pain in her feet. She pushed her hair back into her cap, and what was forming in her mind became a little clearer, something seen by first dawn light, rather than in the black hour after moonset.

She pieced the idea together, winding endless circles among the tables, setting down ale and bread and cold beef, picking up empty mugs. She never met eyes, and so no one looked directly at her; she kept her hair hidden, her voice toneless. She never smiled, which was easy. Her scratched, chewed hands, blistered lately by broom and scrub brush, were all that most ever noticed of her. Even the ones with straying hands who got the smack of her tray against their heads never really looked at her.

Certainly she had scarcely noticed the shadows that came and went in the palace, carrying trays, changing linen, dusting, polishing, picking up broken pieces of this or that, making fires, taking soiled garments away to be cleaned, and bringing them back. Kyel's nurse, Jacinth, had supervised much of that for him. But Domina Pearl had sent her away. He would have other attendants now, chosen by the Black Pearl to give orders to the faceless company, numerous and quiet as mice, that flitted through the halls of the palace.

No one, she thought, cold with wonder at the idea, *would recognize me among them. Not even Domina Pearl.*

But what exactly could she do that would bring her most consistently into Kyel's presence? She tried to remember her previous life, while responding to the details and demands of the present. The crowd, trying to drink its way past the uncertainty and peril of the changing rule, kept her working long past midnight. With some regard for her poor feet, her father put her behind the bar to wash mugs for a while. She gave that idea scant thought: stuck in the palace kitchens, she would never see the child-prince. She wouldn't dare wear the starched aprons and caps of those who carried trays here and there, even if she could talk her way into such a position. One hard-eyed glance from Domina Pearl, and she would find herself among the crabs at the bottom of the harbor. She had to attract no attention, no interest from anyone.

Laundry?

She could not remember, she had never noticed, who took the bed linens, the towels, her clothes. A haughty attendant pointed to something soiled, and it vanished. Someone like that, she thought, as the sweat from the steaming water rolled down from her hairline into the suds. Someone without a name, without a face, only a pair of hands to carry with and a pair of feet to move her.

But carry what? What would move her in and out of Kyel's life with no one, not even Domina Pearl, thinking twice about her?

The tavern finally quieted. Her father took the broom in hand before she could reach for it. She sank gratefully back down in the laundry pile, too tired to wonder what she was doing there. A shoe heel nudged her hip. She pulled it out and remembered the sunflowers shivering after she had flung the shoes into them.

I must have hit Mag, she thought surprisedly, and found her answer there, glittering in her hand.

Mag.

SEVEN

Sleight of Hand

Mag stood beneath the palace of the rulers of Ombria. She had taken a turn underground past the sunflowers and the great, crumbled hearth with the chimney beneath them. Water from rain and drainage had eaten away at the face of the mansion containing the chimney. It stood very near what turned out to be the palace's cellars. Mag had wandered through them curiously, a taper in one hand, for what seemed hours. The outer rooms were ancient, ornate, as if they might have once existed above the earth as part of the early palace, and had gradually sunk to resume life in the maze of cellar rooms. Spiralling stone arches framed doorways; gargoyles depended from kitchen pipes, mouths open to issue rainwater, but only managing, at best, a suspended spider. Others, froglike chins in hand, contemplated centuries of boredom atop an archway, guarding the room within from nothing.

There were no ghosts. Mag, moving as quietly as one toward the busier inner cellars, wondered if Faey's peculiar existence, half-alive, half-past, had wakened the memories in the ghosts who lived with her. She heard voices now and then, abrupt, echoing distortions of sound that might have lost coherent shape passing between now and then. For a long time, she found no way up.

She began to smell things besides stone and standing water. Tapers lit here and there showed her enormous urns, barrels, little pools of carelessly decanted liquid. One unlit room smelled of vinegar, another of leather, another of lamp oil. She passed into a vast holding place for ancient carriages. They were lined against the walls, ranked by age and ornateness. On impulse, she climbed into one, sat regally on moth-eaten velvet, one hand out the window, lightly stroking the gaudy bauble of gold on wheels that might have carried a princess to her coronation.

She hardly looked the part. She wore black again, borrowed from a servant's chest she had found in Faey's attic. She might pass, she hoped, for a housekeeper or some such, if anyone glimpsed her through a closing door, or disappearing down a staircase. She had not come on any errand of Faey's. It was the middle of the night, and Faey, trailing smells and colors of spells like rotting silk, had tumbled so deeply into sleep that her face, slipping free from its own spell, bulged oddly here and there like a sack of potatoes. Her snores, reverberating through the undercity, had followed Mag for an astonishing distance. Had she

known where Mag was going, she would have taken her
waxling promptly in hand for repairs.

Mag had come to explore the palace, to find its disused
passageways, its hiding places, the secrets known to harried servants and mice that everyone else had forgotten.
She wanted to know the palace as she knew the streets of
Ombria. She wanted to be able to disappear into it, to
disguise herself so well that she might appear, to the most
acute eye, of no more interest than a noon shadow or a fire
iron.

She wanted to spy on Domina Pearl.

What she told herself was that she needed to know
more about Ducon Greve, so that if Faey was requested
to become his undoing, Mag would know if she should
bother meddling to protect him. The bits and pieces of
plotting she had heard in the King of Flounders and under
the old pier made meddling seem moot: the conspirators
had made it quite clear that a dead Kyel would be far more
convenient to Ducon. Mag had never seen the child, but
she had an idea that killing the rightful heir of Ombria and
usurping his crown might be the last nail hammered into
the coffin of the city's fading hope. She did not want to
help Faey kill, if it came to that; neither did she want Ombria to die. On the other hand of this many-handed di-
lemma, if a crown were at stake, Ducon might actually be
inspired to find a way to stop Domina Pearl. In that case,
Mag should find a way to help him before Faey killed him.

So she told herself. But while Ducon Greve was her
excuse, Domina Pearl was her quarry, and she moved as
if every subsequent step might bring her under the Black
Pearl's eye.

Did the she-spider sleep? Mag wondered. Or was she too old to need to dream? Who would likely be awake? Guards, bootblacks, pages, perhaps some in the kitchens preparing for tomorrow's coronation feast. Perhaps others decorating a ballroom, though Mag doubted that anyone would feel like dancing at the Black Pearl's ascent to power.

Her taper was burning low. She slipped out of the carriage and went to find the bottles: the great racks and casks of wine that a prince might demand with his dinner, causing the household to find the quickest way down to them.

She found the wine cellar, and the nearest stairs. She went up, listening at every step. At the top of the narrow stairs, she heard voices. She blew out her taper, then leaped adroitly into the corner behind the door as it swung suddenly open. It swung back, revealing a round woman in black, weighted and clinking with dozens of keys swinging on ribbons at her side. She muttered to herself as she descended into her small pool of light. Mag followed the door as it fanned on its hinges, and found herself among long racks of sweetmeats and confections so beautifully crafted they might have been worn as easily as eaten. A small boy lying beside the glowing coals in the vast hearth looked at her, yawned, and closed his eyes again.

She found another door, interrupted a man in black, surrounded by hanging cheeses and haunches of meat, polishing his eyepiece.

He put it on, but she gave him no chance to see her. When he came out a moment later to look for her, she was under a table, the last place he would expect to find her.

He disappeared back into the pantry. She tried another door.

The kitchen, like the cellar, was a warren of rooms, but she found her way beyond it finally into a vast room where more yawning servants were laying cloths as broad as sails onto tables. She kept to the shadows, moving quickly and purposefully to the opposite door. They only glanced her way as the door closed behind her. The palace, it seemed, was as restless as the streets at night, and possibly as hazardous. The armed guards she found standing on both sides of the hall beyond the door looked, with their blank, cold, mindless eyes, as if they did not recognize her as human. She felt their eyes on her back all the way down the endless hall. The Black Pearl's many eyes, she realized suddenly, and disappeared down a narrow marble stairway to get away from them.

At the bottom of the stairs, she saw a man appear out of a wall.

She flattened herself against the stairwell, became a shadow clinging to the flickering web of shadows just beyond the spray of tapers in their sconces around the corner. He did not notice her peering eyes behind the flames. He glanced swiftly up and down the hallway. The doors and walls were of polished oak, plainly adorned; the sconces, few and far between, were equally simple. Servants' quarters, perhaps, quiet and sparsely lit, a safe place, Mag thought curiously, to emerge from a wall in the middle of the night. But for what?

Burglary or an assignation suggested themselves promptly. The man was dressed in black like everyone else that day; nothing immediately indicated his place along the social strata. He carried some papers in one hand, which seemed inappropriate for a lover or a thief. The one on top, covered in a chaos of thick black lines, looked like a child's drawing. In the other hand he carried a candle, which he raised to his lips to extinguish. Mag saw his face then, suddenly and dramatically, glowing with light, young despite his white hair. The flame in his pale eyes and the planes of shadow shifted across his face as the candle moved, giving him a masked, enigmatic look. He blew out the flame. As he put the candle back in the empty sconce from which, she noted, he might have taken it, she saw his face through a different shadow: her black veil. She had watched him in the King of Flounders, and he had watched her, his questing charcoal trying to search out her face beneath the mourning veil.

Ducon Greve.

She followed him at a distance down the dim lower corridors, which remained silent and unguarded. Beside a great marble urn placed in the narrow hall for no apparent reason except that no one wanted it anywhere else, he vanished again. She saw the small door open in the wall on the other side of the urn, but she couldn't tell how it opened. It had closed by the time she reached it. Nothing she did to the urn had any effect on the door. She heard a murmuring within the wall, and put her ear against it. Somewhere within the secret walls a woman laughed lightly. Mag's mouth crooked. He might be there until dawn.

She retraced her steps to the marble stairway and spent some time trying to turn sconces, pry open grooved slats of oak, and feel, along the center molding on the wall, the lines where that door cut through it. She was so occupied that she did not notice the man at the top of the stairs until he spoke.

"You, down there. Come with me."

She froze for a breath. Then she forced herself to move, bob her body into some kind of stiff curtsey before she was able to see past the sudden flare of fear behind her eyes. But it was not one of Domina Pearl's guards challenging her. It was a plump, hastily dressed man with a black bag in one hand and a small, laden tray in the other. As she stared at him, he motioned impatiently with the tray. Something sloshed out of a glass and he cursed.

"Come and carry this for me."

She nodded wordlessly and went up to take the tray.

She followed him into the upper halls, which were heavily guarded and well lit. The walls and ceilings turned into subtle, ornate sculptures of whipped cream and meringue, white birds flying overhead, white roses opening as they passed. The heavy double doors grew gardens on them also, in dark, glossy wood. Sobbing, rhythmic and hopeless, came from behind one door: a high-pitched child's voice. The man with the bag stopped in front of it and knocked. It opened abruptly to a scene of domestic chaos: two servants trying gently to remove the satin sheets from an enormous bed upon which a small boy, his nightshirt soiled with what looked like supper, wept inconsolably. The servant who opened the door, holding a clean nightshirt, looked harried.

So did Domina Pearl, whose brow had cracked like fine porcelain beneath its glaze. She said to the physician, while she tried to coax the prince off the sheets, "He had a nightmare about his father. I think he is fretting about the ceremony tomorrow."

"This will make him sleep," the physician answered. He gestured to Mag, who was frozen again on the threshold. "Come, girl, gather your wits."

She did, as she trailed after the servant with the nightshirt. The physician and the Black Pearl bent over Kyel. The sheets, freed finally, floated gracefully down into a heap in a corner. Kyel took a sip from the glass and promptly spat it out. The physician put the glass back onto the tray, which the servant carrying the clean nightshirt discovered in her other hand.

Kyel demanded shrilly of Domina Pearl, "Where is Ducon? What did you do to him? Did you send him away like you sent Jacinth and Lydea?"

"Find him!" the Black Pearl snapped at the servants. "Leave those. Go and search for Ducon Greve."

"Let me try something else," the physician said worriedly, opening his bag. "You, girl! Move the prince into the next room. Where is the girl? Did she — Ah, well." He gathered the noisily weeping child up and headed into the adjoining chamber. "Mind like an empty casket," Mag, shrouded in stained satin, heard him mutter.

The Black Pearl answered acidly, "Let us hope there is something more in yours."

The prince did not quiet, and Mag, blind and motionless beneath the sheets, did not dare move until Ducon Greve finally entered. She wondered how the servants had managed to get his attention. Guards followed him in, apparently; she heard Domina Pearl order them,

"Two guards watching the prince at this door, and two

outside in the hall. Leave the doors open at all times. Stay with him, my lord Ducon, until morning."

He murmured something; the young prince was finally quiet. Mag held her breath and listened. But even with her acute ears, which noticed a crumb of dirt dislodged from the streets when she prowled below, she did not hear the sound of the Black Pearl's steps when she left.

The servants came for the laundry at dawn. The sheets, which had crept inch by inch under the bed when the rooms had finally darkened, emerged in the arms of a rather oddly-dressed servant, who might have borrowed her grandmother's uniform and most certainly never combed her hair. But no one spoke, for the prince still slept and the handsome bastard, dressed and sleepless, cast them a glance out of his silvery eyes to quiet them. The sheets followed the servants out and vanished for days, until someone found them in a kitchen cupboard stuffed into a silver soup tureen.

EIGHT

Masquerade

The coronation ceremony, though mercifully brief by ordinary standards of time in Ombria, seemed endless to Ducon Greve. In view of the young prince's age and bereavement, Camas Erl had cut short much ritual fanfare, including the traditional parade of the newly crowned ruler through his city. Given the cynical and desperate mood of the city, Ducon thought it a prudent decision. As he stood in the great hall watching the nobles file slowly toward Kyel to put their trust in him and pledge their fidelity, he heard the words, repeated again and again, tossed like false coin into the shadow cast by the Black Pearl. No one trusted in anything but a savage and uncertain future, and the only fidelity pledged with any degree of truth sprang out of terror. The numb, weary expression on the child's face changed only once, when Ducon knelt before him.

Then, a spark of recognition, hope, had struggled into Kyel's eyes. He seemed to listen carefully to Ducon's pledge, as if he believed the promise within the ritual words, and would hold Ducon to it. The spider binding Kyel carefully day by day into her threads stood beside the throne, paying no attention to words, Ducon guessed, but to every expression and intonation behind them, and putting to memory every face that pledged her anything but fear.

The tense coronation was followed by a feast and a truly lugubrious ball. Everyone ate and danced dutifully to uphold the illusion of continuity and hope; no one, however inclined, flung a plate of pastries on the floor and demanded to know what, exactly, they were celebrating. Ducon hovered where Kyel could see him, at a table near the throne. Camas Erl, his long chestnut hair rumpled as though he had tried to pull it out of its tie while he pared the ceremony down to its core, drifted up to him.

"It was still too long," Camas murmured flatly, an eye on his new pupil. Kyel sat on a throne covered with flowers and cloth-of-gold, his feet dangling, a makeshift crown hastily sized to fit sitting precariously on his head, his eyes still swollen from the previous night's tempest. The Black Pearl kept her place beside him. There was a bright, ominous glitter in the child's eyes. "I amputated speeches by ministers and city officials; I threw out the entire ritual surrounding the regent's coronation. Except that one sentence. I looked as far back as I could go into Ombria's history; this was about as barbaric as anything early rulers sat through. And look at him. You can almost smell the lightning."

Ducon took a sip of wine. "It was an impossible task," he said softly, "given the circumstances. He is simply inconsolable."

"Go to him."

He shrugged slightly. "She won't be pleased."

The tutor turned a fretful eye at him. "Would you rather see him in hysterics?"

"Maybe," Ducon said recklessly. "No one else here can afford to be honest."

But he set his cup down and went to Kyel's side. He sensed the Black Pearl bristle at his company, her hair and back growing stiffer, even her shadow elongating. He bent, his hand on Kyel's shoulder, his face close to the boy's. "Be patient. It will be over very soon."

Neither Domina nor the prince spoke. The Black Pearl, her face arranging itself in what she thought was a smile, warned with her eyes: *He is mine now, in this public place. He must look to me.* Kyel's eyes warned him of what no one else dared: an incipient, passionate attack of truth, impelled by too much loss, too much change, and accompanied by a battery of furious tears.

Ducon's hand tightened on Kyel's shoulder; he breathed quickly, "Draw it for me. You promised."

Kyel swallowed, his face rigid as he stared at the listless dancers. Domina Pearl gestured imprudently at a passing tray of sweetmeats. The prince, presented with them, gave her an astonished, contemptuous glance but refrained from kicking them all over the floor.

Ducon rejoined the desultory company. He made polite conversation, danced with a couple of his great-aunts, returned them to his melancholy uncles, and eluded trouble in the form of the young conspirators, who, fierce and anxious, stalked him from group to group but never managed to speak to him alone.

He had rescued himself for the third time, leaving the conspirators abruptly as a group of young women adroitly plucked them away from one another to dance. Ducon joined what looked like a harmless cluster of aging courtiers, the brilliance of their dress and medals of rank drawing attention, so they must hope, from the expressions in their eyes.

They were of the oldest and wealthiest of the families connected to the court of Ombria; most had been councillors and ministers of the dead prince. They had reason to be bitter, Ducon knew. Domina Pearl, reducing Kyel to a puppet-prince, would make puppets of them all. But they chatted idly as Ducon joined them of what was farthest from their minds: hunting lodges, favorite dogs, farms their tenants worked in the country around Ombria. A tray of wine and pastries, following Ducon, passed among them.

One, Greye Kestevan, asked, brushing a speck of cream from his mustache, "Do you still paint, my lord Ducon?"

"I have little enough to do," Ducon answered mildly. "It passes the time."

"Still haunting taverns and odd corners of Ombria?"

"Still."

The man, his hair as white as Ducon's around a perfect bald circle, his dark eyes bland within their hooded pouches, glanced at his companions and replaced his empty glass with another. His hand closed lightly above Ducon's elbow as a young woman with a sweet and determined smile stopped to cajole a dance.

"No, leave him to us a moment; we've scarcely seen him since the — Since. So. My lord Ducon. You must see and hear things in odd corners of Ombria that the rest of us miss."

Ducon shrugged; the hand did not loose him. "I wander everywhere. As I said, it — "

"Passes the time," another man, Marin Sozon, interrupted genially. He had little enough to be pleasant about. The crazed human face of the manticore rampant across his tunic seemed to display his true feelings. He had been one of the dead prince's ministers, and occasionally Royce's sharpest critic. The Black Pearl had already stripped him of all power. Ducon, feeling her eyes on his back, paid careful attention to a quail egg stuffed with roe. "Perhaps now, though," Sozon continued, "with the prince fatherless, you might spend more time with him?"

"I spent half the night with him," Ducon said. "He was having nightmares."

"Domina Pearl summoned you?"

"No. Kyel did. The prince," he amended, "I should say now." He gave them a thin smile. "It is still hard to believe that my uncle is dead and my very small cousin rules Ombria."

"It is indeed," a third, Hilil Gamelyn said with a glance over his wine toward the prince on his throne and the regent standing beside him, a ring of gold and onyx and diamonds circling the base of her domed hair. The dome looked higher than ever; Ducon wondered what she was hiding in it. Gamelyn added casually, startling him, "Since it is not true."

"No," Ducon said equably after a moment, aware of the hand still closed above his elbow. "But for the sake of the occasion it is polite to pretend." He finished his own wine, turned abruptly to leave the glass on a tray, freeing himself. "And safer," he breathed. For an instant their masks dissolved; he saw the questions, the urgent, dangerous calculations in their eyes as they looked at him. He stepped away; they turned to one another, voices bland again, expressions hidden. But they had given him too much, he understood. They had no idea where his loyalty lay, and if it ended where ambition began.

He went within the walls the next morning to gather whatever comments on the ceremony Kyel might have left for him behind the mirror. There were several drawings, as confused and poignant as dreams. Ducon did not linger there to study them. He had no idea what the mirror was reflecting at that moment. If it was Domina Pearl's eyes, turning at a mouse-rustle of paper behind the mirror, she might remember where she had found him the night he had spirited Kyel away. He took a turning in the rambling, secret corridors that brought him to a hidden door behind a fan of giant fern leaves in a small conservatory. The walls there were inlaid with stained glass depicting a graceful bower of ivy and flowing vines blossoming frozen sprays of white and lavender flowers amid perfect clusters of grapes. The conservatory was rarely occupied, though the living plants were scrupulously tended. Ducon crossed a marble floor patterned with more flowers, rolling Kyel's drawings absently into a scroll, and passed through the open doors into the very company of men whose grasp he had eluded the evening before.

They might have been waiting for him, though they looked as surprised as he. But they wasted no time; they took him lightly in hand and drew him back into the empty conservatory to a circle of marble benches within a ring of potted palms.

"My lord Ducon," Marin Sozon said, his pale blue eyes no longer genial but very cold. "The House of Greve will not survive Kyel's rule. Domina Pearl will destroy him, the family, and Ombria. It will be years, if ever, before Kyel produces an heir, and his consort will be chosen by his regent. The House of Greve is dead. I warned your uncle repeatedly about her; he did nothing. What will you do?"

Ducon sat down. The half-dozen courtiers closed around him, their aging faces grim. They had watched Domina Pearl for decades longer than the younger conspirators; they would be, despite their years, more cunning and more ruthless. He was, he realized, crumpling the scroll he had made of Kyel's drawings. He unrolled them, smoothed them against his knee and told the truth. "Paint."

He heard a breath. Greye Kestevan's hand rose swiftly to intercept what might have been a furiously aimed blow. "Then," Kestevan said, meeting eyes around the circle, "he will not interfere with us."

"He will betray us," Hilil Gamelyn protested, wrenching his arm out of Kestevan's grip.

"I can do nothing for you," Ducon said precisely. "I will do nothing against you."

"Paint." Gamelyn struck finally, at the drawings on Ducon's knee. They scattered. "Bastard. You have no name, no true place; you owe loyalty to no one. You will betray us, if you are forced, to save yourself."

Ducon stared at him, his face rigid. He said, when the veined eyes finally flickered, "My loyalty lies exactly where I pledged it: with the Prince of Ombria. You were there. You heard me. And I heard you."

"Loyalty to the prince is loyalty to the regent," Kestevan said softly, carefully. "You know that."

"I know what I said." He rose, pushed through the circle to pick up the drawings. No one stopped him. Half a head taller than the tallest, and possessing whatever it took to wander alone in the perilous streets, he made them wary. He added, retrieving a drawing out of a palm pot, "You are right about one thing: I am a nameless bastard without power. Why come to me?"

They watched him silently, until he picked up the last drawing and straightened. Sozon said bluntly, "Because no one knows you. What you want. What you might take, if you decided to take a risk."

"Ombria is a tree with fruit of gold," Kestevan said very softly, "guarded by a dragon. Whoever kills the dragon takes the gold. You don't need a name for that. Only the courage, the wit and the strength."

"Which is why I paint. I know the dragon too well. You must do what you must. But remember that the House of Greve is still very much alive and I have given my pledge to it. If you strike at Kyel, I will do what I must."

He walked out, leaving them to unravel whatever ambiguities they found in that. As he crossed the threshold, he felt himself breathe again. But for how long? he wondered. He was still shaken, torn between anger and fear, and seeing nothing very clearly. Moving quickly toward stairs leading to the upper chambers, he bumped into someone, and Kyel's drawings scattered again all over the floor.

Camas Erl, most likely on his way to find peace and quiet in the library, murmured an apology and bent to gather the drawings. He turned one over and then did not move, gazing at it. He did not speak. One by one, Ducon turned them all over on the floor and let them lie there; he knelt silently beside the tutor, studying them.

Each page held random impressions of the past days. A small white house with no windows and a black square for a door. A strange, limbless, shrouded figure like a cocoon; its human eyes were closed. A scattering of dark circles: pearls or eyes that did not close. The charcoal had pressed hard into the paper to render such black. A small crowned stick figure, whose face had huge eyes and no mouth. Other figures, one with hair falling to the hem of her skirt: Lydea. Another carrying a square and a twig: paper and charcoal. Black circles loomed over both their heads. In a final drawing, the black circle filled the paper, which was torn here and there with the pressure of the charcoal. At one lower corner outside the perimeter of the circle floated another shrouded figure, a little grub with a crown on its head, its face drawn and then smudged, eyes and mouth blurring into yet another pearl of black.

Ducon heard a sound. He didn't realize he had made it until he felt Camas's fingers on his arm. The tutor was sweeping the drawings together with his other hand.

"Not here," he said briefly. "The library. Nobody ever uses it."

Ducon rose, followed him wordlessly. Camas was right; the library, with its high, elegant shelves of rosewood and glass, was empty. The open books and paper on one table belonged to Camas; Ducon recognized the indecipherable scribblings. The tutor laid the drawings on the table. Ducon's hands closed hard on the back of a chair.

He said, "If I fight her, I die and Kyel is left with her. If I conspire with them, I will endanger Kyel. He is too young and vulnerable, they'll find a way to get rid of him — "

"Who?" The tutor's startled yellow eyes were close to his; his grip was bruising. "Ducon — Who?"

"You saw them," Ducon said very softly. "One group of them." He reached down, touched the little stick-figure prince who could not speak. His hand shook. "I thought the only danger was from her."

"Who? Who are the others? Ducon?"

"I have to think about what to do."

"But — "

"I have to think," he insisted. Camas let go of him finally, gazed down at the drawings. His eyes were still wide, owl-like; he seemed to be listening to Kyel's voice within the wordless drawings.

"Did you see the prince this morning?" he asked Ducon. "Is that when he gave them to you?"

"No. We have a secret place; I found them there. I think it's secret. That may be a delusion, too."

"I wish you would explain," Camas pleaded. "Who threatens Kyel? Who approached you?"

"If I don't act, I won't harm Kyel. If I don't speak, I will betray no one." He began to gather the drawings together again. Camas watched him, a line between his brows.

"Then what will you do?"

"Draw."

He left the tutor there, and went to his chambers. He made a rough sketch of their faces close together, his and the crowned prince's, like a promise. He made no reference to the Black Pearl in the drawing, in case she found it. He left it behind the mirror for Kyel. And then he left the palace to roam the streets of Ombria, where he painted shadows as he searched for light within them, painted thick, barred doors, as he searched in their hewn, scarred grains for what it was they hid, painted high windowless walls as if, rebuilding them stone by stone on paper, he could dismantle them and finally see the secret life behind the real.

He came back late, dishevelled and slightly drunk, his hands shadowy with charcoal and vague pastels. He went down to the servants' hall, where there were few guards, to open a door within the walls, then made his way to the mirror to see if Kyel had found his drawing.

The drawing was gone. But he stumbled over the message Domina Pearl had left for him: a man's body, his face covered with a palm leaf. Ducon, his own breath as still, his throat as dry as if he had swallowed his charcoal, lifted the palm leaf reluctantly.

Hilil Gamelyn stared at him, his eyes as furious in death, it seemed, as they had been in life. His lips were black. Ducon rose, took a lurching step back from him, swallowed an acid rush of wine. The paintings slid from under his arm, spilled like leaves over the dead: crazed images of Ombria, in silence and shadow, locked, barred, hidden from the eye.

He gathered them finally, knowing what he must do before Kyel opened the mirror again. He tucked the paintings in his belt, grasped Gamelyn's arms and pulled him, inch by inch, step by stealthy step, for seasons and years, until he finally reached the conservatory. He left the dead man there, hidden behind the giant fern for the gardeners to find, and for the conspirators to riddle over until they laid betrayal, if not death itself, on the bastard's head.

NINE

The Sorceress's Apprentice

If Faey noticed her waxling missing overnight and swallowing yawns through the day in an unusually ladylike fashion, she said nothing. Mag felt her eyes once or twice, and met a look as dusky and opaque as an old raven's back. But wherever Faey might imagine Mag had spent the night, it would sooner be in the pallid arms of the brewer's son than under the bed of the Prince of Ombria. So Mag thought, and let some days pass in the safety of the undercity while she pondered what she had glimpsed in the palace. Requests still made their way to Faey from the frightened courtiers, all for protective spells and wards, which kept Mag mindlessly busy and freed her thoughts for occasional conjecture. The palace itself had its secrets, its hidden doors and rooms. What, she wondered, did it hold at the heart of itself? Its past, most likely: ghosts, memories and dreams, guarded against time within passages as unnoticed as the silent, busy veins in the wrist. Then something more than past occurred to her one morning as she stirred a loathsome stew of dried, scaly creatures who were beginning to shift a wing, open an eye while Faey murmured over them. A place within those invisible passages, Mag saw suddenly, where Domina Pearl kept her books and objects of power, and did her spells. Entranced by the vision, she let her paddle idle. An ominous bubbling sigh from the cauldron and a baleful glare from the perspiring sorceress brought her attention sharply to the task at hand. They were making a potion, a distillation of the various venoms and excretions of the small, rare reptiles, which exuded such things each time Faey brought them back to life. The potion, glowing and stinking at the moment, would become imperceptible to the eye until, brushed on something of value or on a likely weapon, it adhered to human skin. Then it would glow for days, even in the dark, iridescent patches of guilt which spread as the thief or assassin tried to wipe it away.

The making was tiresome and difficult. At the end, after the liquid essence had been decanted into a small bottle and the creatures hung up to dry, Faey seemed to have forgotten her waxling's lapse. She sank onto a faded love seat, closed her eyes with a sigh, then opened them again and sniffed at herself disgustedly. Too tired to change her clothes, she changed her entire body. Mag, washing the cauldron, watched a blue-eyed, porcelain-cheeked lady in a wig like sculpted cream that was melting down around her haughty face transformed into a black-eyed, barefoot gypsy whose gaudy clothes seemed about to drop off her like petals off a blown rose.

Faey sighed again. "That's better. One more and then that's an end to it for the moment."

Mag was examining the residue in her mind of a third image that had formed, just for a blink, as the highborn lady faded and the gypsy began to emerge. There, within that blink, she thought she had glimpsed Faey's true form. But Faey's words startled her and the image vanished.

"Another? I thought we were finished."

"One more came, while you were above buying death's-head moths and lamb chops."

"From the palace?"

"Where else, these days?" Faey was frowning at something in the moist, shadowy air that even the scented candles Mag had lit couldn't clear. The narrow, focused stare Faey was giving the air seemed at odds with her blowzy body and her generous, painted mouth. Mag finished cleaning the cauldron silently. She knew that expression on any face Faey wore; it boded no good.

She put the cauldron away and waited. Faey spoke again finally, forgetting to move her mouth. "Go and change; I don't want to be distracted by that spell."

She was gathering her forces, Mag realized, preparing her mind for the place she needed to go to make death. "Yes, Faey."

"Bring the toad back with you, the one I keep in the cedar box. And all the ashes in the house."

"Yes, Faey," Mag said again, mystified. Faey, stirring, spared her waxling an absent glance and found her lips again.

"You see, I was right." She rose, to study the dying coals in her fire ring. "The bastard does go next. But I was wrong about who wants him dead."

Mag, collecting ashes before she washed, puzzled them and the toad together. The toad meant poison, but what did Faey intend with all the ashes from their morning fires? She pondered Ducon in memory, watched him draw the long line of her black veil. She drew in a sudden breath of ash and coughed a small flurry above the hearthstones in the breakfast room. Ash could be made into charcoal. In her mind's eye, she saw him smudge other lines lightly with his fingertips or the side of his hand. Poison from the plump, lethal toad mingled with the ashes on his skin. He leaned his forehead against his fingers, studying his sketch, leaving shadows of Faey's spell above his brow.

She swallowed drily, seeing with cold clarity the path that forked suddenly ahead of her. Along one road Ducon stood alive. Across the other, Ducon lay dead. Which? she wondered without answer. Which?

His life, it seemed, was a masterpiece of ambiguity. He was no one's son, therefore anyone could be his father. He had said neither yes nor no to the young conspirators who wanted to put him on the throne. They, suddenly wary, might have requested the poison themselves. He had spent a night beside Kyel without harming the child, but he had been watched at every moment by the Black Pearl's guards. Kyel had demanded his presence, the one person apparently whom Domina Pearl could not send away. Was that to Kyel's advantage? Or hers?

Mag found the other hearths clean and tracked the rest of the morning ashes to the bucket in the kitchen. She

added what she found and left them there while she went
to wash and change. Clean again, redolent of lavender instead of reptile, she made her way to the rooms at the top
of the house where Faey kept her menagerie, living and
dead. Most of them, being cold-blooded and scaly, were
slumbering. She opened the cedar casket cautiously, for the
toad, which hibernated in the dark, ejected poison if startled. It only looked at her out of the moonless night of its
eyes and asked her, *Which?*

She looked back at it, her own eyes as still, and knew,
for no clear reason she could give herself, that she would
not let Faey succeed with this one. She had no good reasons to trust Ducon Greve's motives, only disjointed,
meaningless ones: the way he moved so fearlessly between
the court and the city, the way he could draw a face, that
he had watched the long, dark hours while Kyel slept,
guarding the boy from nightmares. She closed the box gently, returned the toad to the dark. There would be some
moment when Faey, trusting her waxling, turned her back;
Mag would drop something into the spell to thwart it, or,
if asked, accidently substitute one thing for another. And
if subterfuge failed, one piece of charcoal looked very much
like another . . . When Ducon refused to die, she could suggest that perhaps the Black Pearl, for her own reasons, had
produced an antidote.

"Who wants him dead?" she asked Faey when she returned to the chamber, toad in one hand, bucket in the
other. The gypsy combing the ash in the fire circle for bits
of unburned wood, shrugged a shoulder; the loose neckline
of her bright silky blouse slid precariously down one arm.

"Some noble with a manticore on his seal. Or her seal.

The note was unsigned. The servant will return tomorrow for the making, and with the rest of the gold. Take these up, too, my waxling, and pour them all into that great cauldron."

Shovelling ashes out of the fire bed, Mag asked curiously, "Why do you need so much for something so small?" She wanted to snatch the words out of the air like butterflies and cram them back into her mouth as soon as she spoke. Faey gave her a look like the toad had, a fathomless, unblinking scrutiny.

"Thinking, are we?"

"It's a great deal of ash," Mag answered meekly. "It made me wonder."

"And where did your wondering bring you?"

"To charcoal."

"And how would you know that Ducon Greve draws?"

"I've seen him. Everyone has. He roams through Ombria, sketching or painting whatever catches his eye. I was trying to put the toad and the ash and Ducon together."

Faey made a sound through her nostrils like a restless horse and got up off her haunches. "I suppose I did encourage you to learn," she admitted. "Thinking becomes a habit. But be careful. It's a dangerous habit and I would not like to see it get in my way."

"No, Faey," Mag breathed, rolling the great cauldron across the flagstones. "Neither would I. Do you want this on the fire stones?"

"Yes." Faey opened the cedar box and stroked the toad lightly. It spoke a deep, organ-drone of a word and waddled onto her hand. "That's my beauty," she told it fondly. "You will have pearls and flies with jewelled wings to eat when we are finished. It's like the last spell," she added to Mag. "A distillation, a concentration. The charcoal must be fine enough for an artist to use, with no distracting hint of the poison in it." She paused a moment, gazing at the ashes, then snapped a fire alive beneath the cauldron with her fingers. She spat into the cauldron and liquid formed around the hillock of ash. "Now, we must give him a powerful incentive to use this particular charcoal . . . Bring me a dozen or so drawings off the walls, paintings if the sketches are not good enough. Only the best, my waxling. We'll add some magic to his charcoal; he'll draw himself to death."

Mag hurried breathlessly through the house, trying to choose with an artist's eye since Faey would only send her back if she brought the mediocre work that should have been burned. She could not guess what Faey might be doing while she was gone. Nothing more dangerous, she hoped, than stirring wet ashes. But the toad was on the windowsill when she returned, unrolling its long tongue at a glittering swarm of insects. Faey was so deeply immersed in her spell that the gypsy's face had smudged slightly. One eye was higher than the other; her nose had slid askew.

She saw quite clearly in spite of it, even into her waxling's head. "Yes," she said dreamily, as if Mag had asked, "the poison is in the ash. Take the pictures out of the frames and tear them up. Cut them if they don't tear. Put the pieces into the cauldron. They'll melt away soon enough, with what's in there. But they'll leave their images among the ashes . . ."

"What else is in there?" Mag asked in spite of herself. Faey, beginning to speak to the cauldron, did not answer.

Mag cut and tore paper and canvas, mingled cloud and city, tree and child and dying knight into the brew. What lines they might make for Ducon as they came out of the charcoal, she could not guess. When she finished, Faey handed her the paddle.

"Gently, my waxling, gently. It will sear if it splashes on you."

Mag stirred. The mess turned various colors from the paint, then no color at all, so deeply black that the cauldron seemed to be filled with night. Faey watched it without blinking, still murmuring, her drifting eyes hooded. Her voice grew smaller and smaller; so did her brew, ebbing toward the bottom of the cauldron. Finally she whispered a word. The last of the inky liquid shrank together and hardened. A rounded stick of artists' charcoal lay at the bottom of the cauldron.

Faey loosed a sigh; her eyelids flickered open. She reached down briskly, picked up the charcoal and tossed it lightly in her hand. "There. Now we can get some rest." Mag's eyes followed the charcoal as Faey turned to lay it gently in a plain wooden box. "Don't touch this," she warned Mag. "It will poison you as easily as Ducon Greve."

"Yes, Faey."

The sorceress dusted charcoal off her hands and stretched, popping a bone or two back into place. Then she rearranged her face and yawned.

"Clean up, my waxling, and take the toad back up." She slid the wooden box into her skirt pocket. "I have the perfect case for the charcoal in my room. Gold with ivory inlay. It's worth giving away for what I'm being paid to kill the bastard." She paused, blinking, then touched her eyes with her fingers, and added with an unaccustomed hint of regret, "Well, the Black Pearl would have been the death of him sooner or later. This is just sooner."

Mag lay awake later, listening for Faey's snores. The gypsy was unusually quiet for hours. Finally, when the Watch on the streets cried midnight, Mag heard a delicate, sea-shell snoring echoing through the house. She slipped out of bed, walked barefoot to Faey's room, avoiding the slats and steps that creaked. The door was open. Faey had fallen asleep with a candle burning. An *Illustrated Book for Gardeners* lay open across her face. The room, untidy at best, was a formidable chaos of half-visible things: furniture that could not possibly fit in it, great wardrobes, the corners of massive tables, other beds. Clothing or fabric was strewn everywhere; shoes from several centuries lay piecemeal and without partners all over the floor. The skins of slain animals along with their heads hung across mirrors, upside down from wardrobe doors. They watched Mag, tiny candle fires in their eyes. Even the grate seemed full of oddments, illusions, as if every painting from which Faey had ever borrowed her bedchamber were all crowding into the room at once.

The charcoal in its gift box could be anywhere: stuffed into a shoe, in a bear's mouth, lying on a table like an illusion in yet another room. Mag felt an odd prickling of panic, though there was still time. She could intercept the messenger or the box in the morning, exchange ordinary charcoal for the poisoned. Even if the box eluded her hands, Ducon would not drop dead immediately upon receiving it; it would take its time. On the bed, the gypsy gave a sudden snort; the book slid. Mag pressed herself against the wall outside the door, breathless and motionless as wallpaper. She could simply warn Ducon, or better, return to the palace, find his chambers and steal the charcoal. That way he would not see her face.

The gypsy had stopped snoring.

Mag closed her eyes, held her breath, and fashioned her thoughts into the peonies and peacocks flaunting their glories on the wall behind her. Something crashed onto the floor. The candle in Faey's room went out.

Faey heaved over, muttered a word or two, and began to snore again. Her waxling slunk quietly away like a cat avoiding the other boot and found her own untidy room.

TEN

The Magic Shop

Lydea, still working for her father while she waited impatiently for her feet to heal, felt worry sharpen itself on the whetstone of each passing day. The child-heir of Ombria had been crowned; afterwards, he might have simply disappeared, as far as anyone knew. So had Mag, apparently, and no amount of wishing could produce her. Perhaps she had spoken the Black Pearl's name once too often, in the wrong company. What Lydea wanted her for might be just as dangerous. But Mag's curiosity was already snared by people and events governing Ombria, to the extent that she could meddle in subtle and eerie ways with who lived and who died, so Lydea might as well make use of her. She had thwarted Domina Pearl at least once already by saving Lydea's life. In the fearless and cold-blooded way of the young who have not yet learned what they could lose, she was weighing Ducon Greve's life in her balance. If Lydea could persuade her to apply her peculiar talents to the palace, perhaps she could discover some role for Lydea to play in Kyel's life that would give comfort to the child without attracting attention or suspicion.

But where was Mag?

She found herself finally moving without pain through her mundane tasks, though she was no less distracted. All the noisy, sweaty, hairy faces blurred together; she would gaze at them helplessly with a tray of mugs and cold meat in her hands, wishing the air would ignite into letters over their heads, telling her who wanted what. Her father complained little, though she glimpsed, a time or two, a wistful memory of sapphires in his eyes.

One morning she found herself trying to remember the name of the sorceress with whom Mag lived.

Underground, she had said. Not an easy place to find. Lydea, washing mugs piled up after a late night, paused to frown down at the damp floorboards. People found her, evidently, this sorceress who could unmake life and who didn't approve of Domina Pearl. The difference between the two of them eluded Lydea, but it had seemed clear to Mag. If Mag didn't come to Lydea, then Lydea would go to Mag. Underground couldn't be that difficult to find. It was as simple as not breathing; everyone found their way there in the end.

She blinked back the sudden sting of tears. Fate, she thought.

Faey.

"I'm going out for a little," she told her father when

she finished. She had not, she realized with some surprise, been out the door since she had flung herself, bruised and bloody, through it into the path of her father's broom. He remembered, too; she saw the sudden darkness in his eyes.

But he only said, thinking she meant to look for work, "Perhaps it's best." He bent, reached into the petrified boot behind the bar where he kept his money. He handed her a coin. "In case you see something you need." He added gruffly, at her expression, "I'd pay anyone else to do what you do."

"You'd show anyone else the door," she said wryly. "I'll be back before it gets busy in here."

"Be careful."

By daylight the narrow streets were as ragged, noisome and lively as she remembered them. She dodged cows and sheep led to market or slaughter, stepped through skinny urchins playing intense and mysterious games with a stick or a ball of rags. She resisted urges to catch hold of a hank of hair or a dirty ear and demand: *Did you try to run me to death that night? Did you swallow my ring?* By day, their watery, shifty eyes looked around her, through her. She existed in some other world; if they had pursued her, it had only been in a dream. Smells changed with every breath she took: great waxen wheels of cheese in a shop, a puddle of piss, a waft of green from a piebald patch of grass in front of an inn, perfume, a billow of brine from the sea. She was looking for something, she realized after a time. She didn't remember what, but she would recognize it when she saw it. Some childhood memory: a dusty window, the door into an empty house left ajar for so many years that it had taken root in the floor. A place that led into, and then down into an echoing darkness that smelled of water. Or had she dreamed that?

She stopped her headlong ramble into childhood. She had never found a sorceress then, and it didn't seem the best way to find one now. She looked at the shop signs around her with a clearer eye than memory. Might a baker know where a sorceress lived? Unlikely. An apothecary? Possibly. A purveyor of fine quills and bound blank books for divers and sundry purposes? She could not venture a guess about that one, but since most could barely write their names in that part of the city, she could make a shrewd guess about the state of the purveyor's business. The dust was so thick on the window panes she couldn't tell if anyone was inside. The window had been cobbled together from the bottoms of glass bottles, thick, whorled circles shaded green, blue, amber. The sign above the door, a quill letting fall three drops of ink like blood in a fairy tale, was so old it had cracked.

She blinked and remembered it.

She had opened the door long ago and gone in . . . but there was no inside. That had frightened her; she had fled back into the sunlight. What exactly had frightened her? she wondered curiously, and wrestled with the warped door until it opened. She heard a bell ring somewhere, though there was none on the door. She closed it and stared, astonished, at the place where the back wall of the shop should have been.

There was nothing. The walls and ceiling and floor framed a square of darkness. A breath of moist air and earth came out of the dark. She moved cautiously toward it, hoping that the floor was not balancing on a precipice.

It seemed solid enough. She held onto the edge of one wall and looked down.

She caught a brief, puzzling glimpse of a black river far below, outlined and illumined by softly glowing lamps along its banks. The lamps and the water seemed to flow forever into the distance. Then the door opened behind her, and the bell clanged again, a jarring, tuneless note like a cowbell somewhere down in the dark.

She turned, startled, expecting anyone, anything other than the portly woman in voluminous black, the bun on the top of her head wearing two jet skewers and a white, starched frill around it. She studied Lydea silently, her hands clasped demurely in front of her.

Lydea said dazedly, "I'm looking for a sorceress named Faey. Is this—Do you know—"

The woman nodded. "It's one of my doors." She had an opulent, husky voice that seemed at odds with the plump, prim face and the servant's garb. As though sensing Lydea's confusion, she touched her own face, feeling at it like someone blind. She gave a sudden snort of laughter. "I've tangled with my housekeeper. She's not quite alive. You are—?"

"Lyd—" Her voice would not come; she cleared her throat. "Lydea. I'm—I was—I—"

"Come in," the sorceress said graciously. And suddenly they were in, somewhere within the cavernous dark, Lydea guessed, standing in a small, cozy room. Its yellow walls were sprigged with painted violets; plump chairs seemed to have wandered through it and stopped at random beside potted plants spreading great fans of leaves as sharp as swords. The sorceress had evidently returned the body to her housekeeper. There was a chaotic tussle of color and image where she had been. Lydea watched, her mouth hanging indecorously. Finally a complete woman appeared, flushed and patting her hair as if she had been fighting her way out of a small whirlwind.

"Sit down," she said, with the same fascinating mix of rich and raucous in her voice. It did not match this face either, which was made of ivory and roses, the lines beside eyes and mouth as faint as cobweb yet, the hair an indeterminate hue between white-gold and white. Her eyes flicked over Lydea's beer-stained homespun, the sleeves still rolled up from washing, her creased cap, her wooden clogs. She took a guess. "Love, is it?"

"Love?"

"You want a potion? To make someone love you?"

"Oh. No. He's dead." She hesitated; Faey watched her curiously. "I'm looking for Mag," she said finally. "I want her to do something for me. Maybe I'm wrong to ask."

The fine, arched brows rose as high as they could go. "You want to use my waxling?"

"I didn't know—She doesn't seem at all waxlike to me. She helped me once before in odd ways, so I thought of her for this."

"How did she help you?" The rich voice purred; the wide green eyes watched like a predatory cat. There was no way out, Lydea realized; no way but into, through.

"She saved my life. When the Prince of Ombria died, Domina Pearl threw me out of the palace in the middle of the night for being the prince's mistress."

Both voice and eyebrows quivered at that. "You."

"Well, I wasn't dressed like this."

Faey leaned back with an unladylike thump, her eyes trying to piece together the spell that Lydea had cast over the prince. Lydea pulled off her cap to help; her hair fell limply, still damp from steaming dishwater. But the sorceress was nodding, illumined. "I remember. The red-haired tavern girl. I heard rumors. But what do you think Mag can do for you? If you're looking for revenge against Domina Pearl, you don't want Mag and you can't afford me."

"No. I'm not that much of a fool."

"Well? People don't find their way here because they lead sensible lives. What kind of fool are you?"

"I suppose it is a matter of love. I want a disguise, to get back into the palace. It's for Kyel's sake. I can't bear to leave him alone in the Black Pearl's care. I've known him since he was born. You might say we grew up together."

Faey made a noise in the back of her throat. She broke a spray of leaves as long as peacock feathers off the plant beside her and fanned herself. Her eyes had narrowed. "And you wanted Mag for — ?"

"To spy in the palace, find some likely disguise for me. I never paid enough attention while I was there. I only looked at the surface of things within the palace. Not at how they were all kept working together. I thought of shoes, not about where they went to be cleaned, and satin sheets, but not who changed them. I thought Mag could — I know it's dangerous — maybe I'm not thinking — "

Faey was. A trickle of smoke or mist came out of one

nostril. Lydea's throat dried. "And you think she will do this for you?"

"Well, she seems — She has an eye on what happens in the palace. She said she dislikes Domina Pearl."

The fan in Faey's hand folded suddenly with a rattle of leaves. Lydea gripped the arms of her chair nervously. The sorceress rose, paced, the leaves twitching like a cat's tail. Chairs shifted out of her way, Lydea saw with amazement. The sorceress's eyes had turned black as charcoal.

"Would Mag do this for you?" she asked abruptly.

"I think — I think so." Lydea swallowed, tried to steady her voice. "She is so curious, and so fearless. She came to me at my father's tavern to ask about Ducon Greve."

"Ask what about him?"

"Where his loyalties lie. In case you — " She faltered. "If — "

But Faey only waved him away with her leaves. "Ducon Greve is taken care of," she said with chilling disinterest. There was a hard furrow between her brows. Her face was changing, the elegant lines loosening, sagging, the brows growing coarse. Her neatly coiled hair fell down suddenly. She tossed it impatiently out of her face and pinned Lydea motionless with murky, smoldering eyes. "When did you last see Mag?"

"The day," Lydea whispered, "they buried Royce."

"Not since."

"No."

The sorceress flung herself back into a chair and touched her face here, there, tightening, adjusting, refining. The frown went and came again, a fainter line. "I warned her to stay away from the Black Pearl."

Since she was trapped anyway and apt to be turned to cinders by those eyes, Lydea risked a question. "What is she? Domina Pearl?"

The sorceress only nibbled a palm leaf between perfect, white teeth. She seemed to be listening to something within herself, or in the dark beyond the pretty illusion around them. After a while, Lydea ventured another. "Do you know where Mag is?"

Faey picked a fleck of green from between her teeth. "I have no idea." She looked at Lydea, her eyes like molten stone. "Of course you're welcome to wait with me. Tea?"

ELEVEN

The Stranger

The death of Halil Gamelyn, following so closely the death of the Prince of Ombria, had a stupefying effect on the court. It seemed a portent of things to come, that the powerful minister and councillor of the buried prince had so suddenly breathed his last among the potted palms. Very little was said about the matter. He had felt his heart fail, it was expediently decided, and had stumbled into the conservatory looking for help. Why his lips and tongue had turned black, no one ventured to guess. But conjecture cast an eerie, frightened silence throughout the palace. For a day or two afterward, Ducon moved through his life with the expectation that it might unexpectedly and ruthlessly come to an end at the next moment. The Black Pearl had heard a whisper of conspiracy within the palm trees; she must have known Ducon had been among them. He refused to leave the palace for the streets, where he might have been paradoxically safer. Her malevolent eye would turn to Kyel next, if she thought Ducon had betrayed her and fled.

But she simply sent the body back to Gamelyn's family, and made no further reference to the matter. Her small, erect figure in black silk moving quietly across a room could transfix the courtiers, pare conversation down to meaningless, safe noises. She did not mention conspiracies to Ducon, or secret hiding places behind mirrors. She had, Ducon realized with growing uneasiness, effectively rid herself of a man who had threatened them both, and had cast suspicion on Ducon at the same time.

"Odd," Marin Sozon remarked to Ducon, distracting him a moment while the regent was introducing her chosen ministers and councillors to the court. Half were pallid, elderly nobles who could barely stand straight and seemed miserable; the rest looked as if they had borrowed shoes for the occasion and had wandered in from the docks. "Where Hamil died."

Ducon, thinking of the secret door behind the mirror, was startled. Then he remembered where he had dragged the body. He looked at Sozon silently; the bloodshot blue eyes were bland now, hiding thoughts. "Perhaps," Ducon answered softly, "he thought he might find you there."

"Someone found us there," Lord Sozon breathed, shrugging lightly. "Evidently." He shifted a step away from Ducon as Domina Pearl sent an opaque glance in their direction. He added, after a moment or two, "I thought, at the time, that he was wrong."

"About?"

He gave Ducon a brief, equivocal smile. "About you."

"He was," Ducon said tightly. Sozon did not answer. Ducon turned to watch Kyel, seated beside the regent. There were dark half-moons under the child's eyes, but he looked more weary than frightened as the officials bowed to him. His eyes widened at the size of the knife one of them wore. The man drew it out, said something about gutting sharks. The regent spoke sharply; her councillor sheathed the massive blade and Ducon breathed again. When he returned his attention to Sozon, all he saw was the embroidered manticore guarding the back of his jacket. Its wild, hungry face bore an odd resemblance to the armed councillor bowing unconvincingly to the prince.

The aging conspirators said nothing more to Ducon about Gamelyn's death. Domina Pearl said nothing at all. But he heard their unspoken words everywhere, even in his dreams. The tension, unbearable as a storm that refused to break, drove him finally into the noisy, unpredictable streets. Paper under his arm, a box full of charcoal and pastels in a pocket, he listed like a broken boat into the murky backwaters of Ombria. Scattering sketches and stubs of charcoal in his wake, he drifted through changing light and shadow, in one tavern door and out another, drawing whatever caught his eye, until the streets darkened and he found himself standing in gutters, drawing by lamplight the fire-limned faces passing restlessly through the night.

He walked carelessly, without direction, his body carrying him into puddles now and then, in which the sickle moon floated and splintered under his foot. He was wondering how many moons there were to shatter when someone came up behind him. A hand caught the neck of his shirt, twisted it roughly. He felt the prick of a blade at his back.

"What gold have you got, my fine beauty, in your pocket?"

"My gold turns to coal," he answered. "See for yourself."

The hand loosed his shirt, snatched the box out of his pocket. After a moment, the thief cursed; the box hit the cobbles, raining watercolors and charcoal. Ducon used his elbow and the metal-rimmed heel of his boot. He heard the knife drop; the man limped moaning into the dark of an alley. Ducon, still clutching drawings under one arm, set them down carefully and picked colors out of the debris in the street. One unbroken piece of charcoal he discovered in a shadow. It was glowing slightly, awash with faint, elusive color. The better to find you with, he thought, dropping it back into the wooden box. The world spun when he straightened. He caught the corner of a wall for balance, wondering if he were about to spend the night in the gutter along with all the moons. But the dizziness passed; he began to walk again.

Some time later, he found himself sitting at a battered table, gazing at the face that had come out of his charcoal. It seemed vaguely familiar. He rubbed a shadow under the eye, blurred a line beside the mouth, then contemplated it again, chin resting on his blackened palm. He raised his head after a time, studied the morose, untidy faces around him. None of them had inspired this drawing; they were all strangers. He looked at his paper again, absently rubbing his brow, leaving dark streaks across it. He had seen those fearless, curious eyes before, the long, taut mouth, the pale hair and brows that spare lines of charcoal barely suggested.

He started; his elbow slid off the table, nearly taking the wine with it. He had drawn himself. He took a closer look, frowning to focus. Not exactly himself. There were faint lines beneath the eyes, beside the mouth, that suggested himself in the future, after a couple of decades of Domina Pearl's rule. But this face was not grim, simply thoughtful; the man might have been gazing back at his younger self. Who was sitting, charcoal in hand, looking at him. Ducon felt a sudden vertigo. He closed his eyes, left a shaky smudge of black between his brows. Someone pulled out a chair beside him noisily. A whirl of color, scents of sweat and lavender and beer settled beside him, pulled the drawing from under his hand.

"Are you ill, my lord Ducon?" a woman asked. He blinked at her. She had a young, pock-pitted face and a sweet smile; he wanted instantly to draw her. "If you're going to show us what you had for dinner, don't lay it out on your picture."

"How do you know my name?" he asked.

"Everyone knows you."

"What does that look like to you?"

"Looks like you've drawn yourself." She picked absently at a tooth, studying the face, then protested, "No, you've made yourself too old. Who is this, then? Your father?"

He felt the world lurch; sweat stung his eyes. He put his hand over his mouth, though the recognition left him hollow, empty, as if even his name had vanished. The woman's fingers closed gently around his wrist. She spoke again. He was on his feet, gathering things. She gave him back the sketch, and rose, clinging to his arm, still talking. But when he reached the door she was no longer with him. Time and memory had blurred; he was leaving a different tavern entirely.

He woke in an unfamiliar room later that night, or maybe the next; he was unsure. A silver branch of candles softly lit the face of the young woman who watched him. She wore a loose confection of raspberry silk and lace, soiled where the hem dragged. Her bare feet, propped on the bed near his face, were dirty.

She smiled. Her triangular cat's face with its golden eyes was lean and hollow, the milky skin marred by a jagged scar across one cheek. He recognized the smile, if not the face or the place. He caught a glimpse of darkness through the threadbare velvet curtains behind her.

He asked huskily, "How —"

"You wandered in here and fell into bed, my lord Ducon. Fortunately, I found enough in your pockets to satisfy the gentleman already in it."

"You know my name," he said tentatively.

She gestured at a chair in answer, where the pile of drawings lay on top of his clothes. "You're easy to recognize. And no, you've never met me."

"I thought not. I would have drawn you if I had."

Her smile changed for an instant, became genuine. He started to sit up. The fruit bowl colors of raspberry silk and cherry velvet swirled together; the bed tried to float. He dropped back, his eyes tightly closed. He felt her fingers against his cheek.

"You're cold," she said, startled. "Cold as death. Are you ill?"

"I can't be," he murmured reasonably, "if I am dead."

But she had lost her smile; her eyes grew apprehensive. "I'll send for a physician, my lord."

"I don't need one. Most likely, I'm just drunk."

"Then let me get you some broth to warm you."

"No," he said, his throat closing at the thought. He reached out blindly, caught a frill of lace and then her arm. "Just lie beside me. Please. Did I have enough in my pockets for that?"

She hesitated, still wary; then he felt her arm lose its tension. "Not with that charcoal all over you," she grumbled. In another shard of time he felt her washing his face and hands, the warm, scented water almost as soothing as her touch.

The Black Pearl's gaze cut into his dreams and he woke abruptly, before sunrise. The woman snored softly beside him, buried in faded strawberry satin. He stroked a single, visible curl but she did not stir. He drew himself up carefully; the room stayed still. Kyel crossed his mind then. The child had no idea where he had gone or why. He would blame Domina Pearl, since she caused people to disappear; she would be forced to silence him. . . .

He dressed as quickly as he could, losing his balance now and then. If he hurried, he could enter the palace, leave a drawing for Kyel before he woke. Something he would recognize: a flounder, perhaps, crown askew, dancing on the waves as a pale-haired man drew it. He wandered for some time through the corridors of the silent house before he found a door to the street. By the time he reached it, the sun was pushing through a cloud bank at the end of the world, and the silvery air was damp with brine. A ship gliding away from the dock toward the open sea seemed to sail on light. He reached for charcoal.

It dropped from his shaking hand; he bent to pick it up and fell briefly into a dark, whirling vortex. He had to lean against a wall while he drew. The ship's masts tilted at peculiar angles on his paper. He finished it, stood a moment rubbing his eyes with smudged fingers, trying to remember where he needed to go so urgently and why. Sun broke through cloud; he wandered away finally, following the light.

Later, he woke with his face against a charcoal face. Tavern noises droned and buzzed around him. He raised his face from the paper, found a cup of wine, apparently untouched, near his paint box. Glancing dazedly around him, he saw the startling face he had drawn a day or two or five before attached to a body and gazing back at him.

He rose quickly. Then he sat down again to wait for the sudden darkness to recede. When he could see again, the tall, pale-haired figure had turned away and was heading out the door. Ducon gathered his drawings hastily, swept charcoal and brushes back into his pockets, and took his first swallow of wine to clear his head.

It was as though he had drunk fire. He could not breathe; he could not make a sound. He sagged against the wall, blinking away tears of pain. When it ebbed, he moved again, impatient with his strange malady, intent on his quarry: the man who wore his older face.

Outside the light burned him; he could scarcely see. The man lingered at the next shop window to study a pair of fencing foils. He turned abruptly, but not before Ducon glimpsed his face, with its level brows and grave, sea-mist eyes. Ducon felt his heart pound. They were of a height, as matched as the foils in the window. He tried to speak; the wine had burned his voice away. The man moved quickly through the crowds. Ducon, his pace slower and helped along by walls and idle wagon wheels, kept the light, trimmed head in sight. Sometimes it was the only thing in the world that he could see.

He had no idea where he was going. Streets he had known all his life looked suddenly unfamiliar; he could no longer understand language. When the pain ran through him again, finding its way into every vein and the marrow of his bones, he finally saw the cool, silvery eyes turned back to look at him. He closed his own eyes, and fell through a sunken window into nowhere.

TWELVE

Mirror, Mirror

After the charcoal had begun its deadly journey without her, Mag spent her spare time searching for Ducon Greve in every tavern she could find between the docks and the palace. When that failed to unearth him, she threw caution to the winds. She abandoned her shopping basket, which Faey had ordered her to fill with eels for supper, in the middle of a busy street and went underground at the sunflowers. Encumbered by an ancient green silk gown that shed thread and seed pearls at whim, she decided upon a quest for clothes. As she moved swiftly and noiselessly through the vast palace cellar, odd noises weltered toward her. Voices and echoes of water rippled through the air as if, in some magic chamber, whales and dolphins cavorted among young maidens in great tanks of water. When she reached it, all the fish turned into laundry, stirred and beaten in steaming cauldrons by glum, limp-haired women as wet as mackerels. She snatched something dark out of a dry pile and retired behind the wine racks to change. The dress was plain as shadow and made for a beer keg. But it covered her from neck to wrists and ankles; at a cursory glance, it would go unremarked.

She found the narrow stairway down which the laundry travelled, and flitted up. It led to a huge room full of cloth. Hillocks of laundry were being sorted into other hillocks. Sheets and hose and hemlines were being mended, caps and collars ruffled and starched. Flatirons heated like tiny furnaces sizzled as beads of perspiration rolled off the reddened faces of the ironers. Clean clothes were sorted, folded, hung, and delivered to prim maids who appeared like clockwork figures, precise and relentless, at the door. It was a busy place. Mag slipped behind a massive cupboard where linens, folded and stacked, waited for bed and bath.

Gossip turned for the moment on sheets. They could be read, apparently, like tea leaves; their stains predicted fortunes. Mag caught vague and mysterious allusions to those who slept on satin.

"She must have lost it, with all that blood. They'll never be washed clean."

"Then she won't need to worry about who it looks like."

There was a click of shears, a hiss from an iron on damp cloth.

"Blood on satin is easier than red wine. What's worst of all, I think, is mustard. Lord Picot must have been rolling in it last night."

"Chocolate," someone muttered. "That's far worse."

"Charcoal," someone else suggested. "When Ducon Greve falls in bed drunk after a night out drawing, he gets it everywhere."

There was a laugh. "You can tell whose bed he's been in."

"I wouldn't mind the charcoal."

"Who would? He's welcome to leave his fingerprints all over me. And I'd wash his sheets for him."

"I wonder who—"

"I wonder—"

"Watch the sheets. He wasn't under his own last night. Neither was she."

The voice dropped low on the last word. There was a brief, tense silence. Then someone ventured, just as softly, "It's hard to tell with her. She doesn't leave signs behind her."

"Maybe she doesn't sleep."

It was Domina Pearl they spoke of in their hushed voices, Mag realized suddenly.

"I think she sleeps elsewhere. Somewhere secret. That's why her sheets are never rumpled, and there's never a hair or a crumb among them. Not even the outline of her body. She won't even leave that behind."

"But who washes her secret sheets?"

Who, indeed? Mag wondered. And where might her secret place be? But no one guessed; they were back to stains again, the most stubborn—"use salt"—the most peculiar—"crushed garlic everywhere"—the most disturbing—"she wrote his name in blood right there where he had slept." But nothing more about Ducon Greve or the Black

Pearl. Mag caught herself yawning. She could not leave
until they did. She leaned her face against the back of the
cupboard and wondered if they ever slept. Then brisk footsteps came across the room toward her. The cupboard
doors banged shut, jarring her.

"There. That's tomorrow's sheets in order. And just in
time for supper. Go and call them up from the washing."

Cramped and drowsy, Mag was forced to wait until
the damp and grumbling women from the waterworld below changed into dry uniforms. They drifted out, leaving
a taper burning for the evening's work.

Mag lost no time. If Ducon Greve had not been found
dying in his bed, then perhaps he was somewhere in the
secret chambers within the walls. If he were ill and visible,
gossip would have veered away from sheets to him. She
hadn't found him on the streets; he must be in the palace
somewhere. Covered with charcoal, stricken with some odd
raging in his body, in a place where no one heard him call.
Fluttering batlike in the voluminous dress, she ran down
dim, silent servants' hallways until she found the huge urn
behind which she had lost him before.

This time, she discovered the small white rosette carved
into the molding that could be felt if she slid her hand
between the wall and the urn. She pressed it. The narrow
door opened soundlessly. She picked a candle out of the
sconce above it and entered the secret palace.

Another silent maze of passages it seemed, unguarded
and empty. She walked slowly, wary of creaking floorboards. Doors opened to small, plain rooms. Servants'
quarters, she guessed, and long disused. Dust and cobwebs
furnished them, and the odd forgotten adornment: a silk

pincushion, a watercolor of a child, a swan whittled out of soap, seamed and yellow as ancient ivory. But none of them held an artist facing death by charcoal.

She wondered if secret stairways led upward to larger, rich rooms strewn with memories of fine lords and ladies instead of servants. Perhaps Ducon had become confused by the poison. Lost within the labyrinth of those forgotten halls, he might have dragged himself upward, trying to find his chambers.

She looked for stairs. The toad opened its dark eyes within her heart, watched her search. Despite her habitual calm, her hands grew oddly cold; her thoughts kept darting and fluttering like blown leaves. Ducon's face, vivid with candle fire, haunted her. He might be anywhere or no-where, having no place left in the world to go. Like her, he belonged everywhere and nowhere; he had uncertain origins and no true name. Like her, he wandered fearlessly and had a penchant for secrets. They might have been kin, though he lived in the palace above the world, and she beneath it. She had never felt so like anyone human before. And now, despite all her intentions, he was dying some-where, most likely helpless, alone, and completely bewil-dered. When she finally found stairs hidden behind a warped, flecked mirror in the back of a room, she lost all caution. She ran up, shielding her shivering flame with one hand, into the dark at the top of the stairs.

Words leaped out at her, gold, silver, red. She turned; the shifting candle illuminated manuscripts, massive bind-ings, all speaking to her in familiar and unfamiliar lan-guages. Other candles emerged under her flame; she lit them all, and saw what she was standing in.

The brewer had one like it: a room completely full of books. Tomes, he called them, and showed her pictures of witches, alembics, elaborate diagrams that revealed, symbol by symbol, the path to the perfect element. Like his, this one smelled old. Unlike his, this one was guarded.

The guards looked real enough, standing among the shelves in the little oval room. The fine, polished surfaces of their buckles and sheaths and the silver embroidery on their sashes kindled cold stars from the candlelight. Their grim faces warned Mag that in the next moment their swords would slash the air into ribbons of silver; she should escape, hide herself, quickly, now. But she had grown up with ghosts, with their eyes always looking at the past, with the frail flickering embers of their thoughts. These were strangely passive; they never even blinked. They told her not that she was in danger, but that the books were, from the likes of her. They wore the uniforms of the palace guard; they were not ancient ghosts, simply no longer alive.

They would belong to Domina Pearl. Mag felt again the dry, butterfly pulse of a vein in her throat. She had chanced across the Black Pearl's library. The knowledge she found important, her spells, perhaps her history. But Ducon Greve had no time for history; he must be somewhere near the end of it. She turned quickly to resume her desperate search, then stopped again and allowed the nagging, slippery thought that she was trying to drown in the bottom of her mind finally surface. If she found him and he was dying, what could she do? Take him back to Faey?

"Here," she whispered, "there are spells."

Caution, left idling at the bottom of the stairs, caught

up with her. She wrapped her hands in the wide black skirt before she touched the books. If it glittered later with a stardust of guilty fingerprints, the dress could remain in the palace; Mag's hands couldn't. She read the faded bindings carefully, hearing what they promised before she dove heedlessly into them. *Maps,* one said, *of the Known World, Useful Plants From the Hindmost Islands and What to Do With Them, The History of Ombria From the Beginning of the World, How to Maintain Hair, Teeth and Nails After Accidental Death.* She nearly opened that one. But she had no time now for Domina Pearl. Finally, a likely title in gold ink on a pale leather binding caught her eye. *Natural and Unnatural Poisons,* it said, *and Antidotes.*

She pulled it down and heard steps in the hall below.

She was moving, blowing out candles and eying the shelves for a place to hide, almost before she caught her breath in surprise. Ducon, she hoped fiercely, and remembered to put the book back on the shelf. She slipped through one of the guards and hoped she left nothing of herself in his shade. There was room for her between the wall and the overladen shelves. She shifted two scrolls and looked through them, like spyglasses. Then she heard the Black Pearl's voice in the room below and closed her eyes.

"Look at this door," she demanded. "And that mirror. Both wide open. He wanders through these passages; he disturbs things. What does he do, what is he looking for, if not my secrets?"

A man's voice, thoughtful but not servile: "I don't know, Domina."

"Ask him. He has always trusted you. I want him watched. I want to know where he goes at all times. No one can find him now; he hasn't been seen in days. He is either out on the streets, or within these walls. The child is beginning to fret again."

Mag, her breath stirring the scrolls, heard them coming up the stairs. She willed herself boneless, a shadow, less than a ghost, nothing. The Black Pearl stepped into the room. Mag opened her eyes suddenly, wondering if she could smell the smoke and warm wax of blown candles. But another burning taper floated into view within the circle of the scroll.

The man carried it, apparently, for Domina Pearl came between the light and Mag's eyes. She closed them again, thinking: *Nothing. No one.*

"Where is that book . . ." The Black Pearl seemed to be speaking through a tube of parchment. She was close enough to smell. "He comes here, looks through my books. How does he get in here? What doors does he know besides that mirror in the nurse's room? Has he shown you?"

"No."

Mag heard an impatient breath. "I put it here, on this shelf, after I killed Halil Gamelyn." Her voice grew thin as a fly's wing and Mag's skin shifted. "If he took it, I will blind him. He is clever and far too secretive. He could kill us in our beds. If we slept in them."

"He doesn't mention anything more dangerous than art. That and the young prince are all he seems to care about. You must not harm him needlessly. We may need his eyes. Tell me what you're looking for; I'll help you search."

"*Natural and Unnatural* — Ah! Here it is." The book slid off the shelf, revealing a swath of dark that was Mag's sleeve. Domina Pearl turned away, and Mag saw the man's face, lean and intent, his chestnut hair threaded, here and there, with silver. In the candlelight, his eyes flared yellow as a cat's.

"Who, now?" he asked curiously.

"Kyel," the Black Pearl said with chilling composure. "Nothing to kill him, just to subdue him, dampen his spirits, produce a melancholy more appropriate to his loss than temper tantrums. You will find him far more docile when you begin to tutor him."

The man's thin mouth tightened slightly, but he said nothing. He turned to follow the Black Pearl out. The light receded down the stairs. Mag's eyes clung to it; all her thoughts, mothlike, danced after it. At the bottom, the Black Pearl spoke again.

"I'll set a spell on this lock. No one but you or I will open this door."

She murmured something. Mag heard a faint click. Steps and voices faded. Mag stared through her paper spyglass at the dark.

THIRTEEN

The Jewel in the Toad

L ydea, drinking an endless cup of tea in the sorceress's leafy chamber, realized occasionally, in the buried part of her where time still moved, that she was spellbound. Somewhere, hours passed during a single sip; night fell as she replaced her cup in the saucer; the sun rose when she lifted it again. The sorceress, or an illusion of her, spoke lightly of the weather, though there was none, and of people whom she seemed to think that Lydea knew, while her terrible eyes smoldered and fumed boiling pitch and fire. Sentences echoed through time, repeating themselves. Now and then, Lydea, her mind as tranquil as a summer afternoon, heard the echo, felt her mouth move to say appropriate words that she must have said a hundred times between the moment she began to raise her cup and the moment it touched her lips. She never tasted the tea; she might have been drinking cloud.

"How fortunate we are that the morning rain has ended," the sorceress commented, though neither night nor day was visible around them. "We will be able to go after all to—" She stopped abruptly. Lydea felt perfunctory words leaving her lips like bubbles. The sorceress interrupted her harshly. "There is a stranger below."

Lydea, about to make her usual reply to that, realized that she had none. As if a glass dome over her had shattered, she sat in shards of time, bewilderedly trying to piece fragments together. She stared at the teacup halfway to her lips. The tea was stone-cold and had grown a tiny, floating garden of mold.

She dropped it back into the saucer, feeling dizzy, frightened. "What—Where—"

Faey had risen and was pacing. She looked as if she were scenting the air with her ears, or trying to see with her mind. Lydea stood up. The plants whispered around her; she caught at a chair back, lightheaded and oddly stiff.

"How long have I been here?"

Faey ignored her. The room was changing around them, walls growing sheer, the sharp-bladed palms withering in their pots and vanishing. The chair in Lydea's hands fell apart; its parts turned into pebbles or little, many-legged things that scuttled away toward the river. She stood on its bank, a wall of earth rising behind them toward the light of some day or another high above her head. Only the teapot, a strange crockery animal with legs like tree trunks that poured tea through its long snout, refused to vanish.

"Odd," Faey remarked finally. "Very odd."

"I have to go home," Lydea told her, wondering if she could climb the cliff of earth to the light. Faey flung her a glance that left a burning streak in the air.

"I need you," she said succinctly. "My waxling is no-where to be found. Come with me."

"But my father — He'll be up to his ears in dirty beer mugs."

"I'll send your father a note."

"He can't read."

"Well, he'll have to wait," the sorceress said irritably. "Mag doesn't argue with me. I need someone human to deal with the body when it fails. I wish," she added, be-ginning to move quickly along the river, "that people wouldn't die down here. I can usually send them back up before they get too far, but I was busy searching for Mag . . ." She turned, gestured at Lydea, who could not seem to find her feet. "Do you want to walk or fly?"

Lydea caught up with her.

They found the man lying facedown within the rubble of a shattered room. The window he had fallen through had mostly sunk below the street. Lydea gave a cursory glance at his white hair. Then her eyes rose desperately to the scant feet of freedom that led into the noise and light of Ombria. If he had gotten in, she could get out. . . .

The sorceress, standing beside the body, was murmur-ing something with her eyes closed. Lydea heard a sharp, anguished groan from the dying. He lifted his face blindly. His skin was gray with old mortar and bloody where he had scraped himself, rattling down among the broken slate. He opened one eye and one blackened hand as if to drag

himself away from Faey's voice, and Lydea felt her bones
try to leap out of her skin.

"No!"

The sorceress's eyes opened. She broke off a word,
stood with a curious stillness, gazing down at the man.
"No," she agreed softly as Lydea knelt beside him. She
recognized him in piecemeal fashion: the silvery eye, the
charcoal on his hands, the bone-white hair. Several drawings lay crumpled beneath him; others had drifted into the
shadows. She rolled him over as gently as she could. He
was still breathing. His other eye opened; he gazed at her
senselessly.

"Ducon." She touched his hair lightly. "Ducon. It's Lydea." She heard his breath catch as she glanced in wonder
up at Faey. "It's Ducon Greve."

"I know it's Ducon Greve," the sorceress said. "I was
paid to kill him." Lydea stared at her. Faey bent, gripped
Ducon's wrist briskly and rolled him up over her shoulder.
She wore him as easily as a scarf trailing down her back.
"I can't send him up in this condition."

"What are you going to do with him?" Lydea whispered. She got to her feet as Faey began to move, and
caught at Ducon, forcing the sorceress to stop. Her voice
rose to a scream that echoed down the dark river. "What
are you going to do?"

Faey turned to look at her. Her eyes, beneath the
arched, elegant brows, had grown blue again. Lydea could
not read the expression in them; they hardly seemed to see
her at all. "I'm not sure," the sorceress said finally. "But
since my waxling is gone, you must take care of him."

She began to walk toward the distant, graceful line of

lamps lighting the crumbling faces of houses that rose like fragments of dreams along the water. Lydea followed with one hand on Ducon's back. She asked, her voice trembling in the aftermath of the scream, "Where are you taking him?"

"To my house."

"Why did — Who wanted him killed? Domina Pearl?"

"I have no idea. Someone very rich, whose servants wear a manticore."

Lydea lost a step in astonishment. "Lord Sozon? I wonder why." She heard Ducon murmur something. She bent to hear, but he said nothing more. She stayed close to him, talking so that he could hear a familiar voice in that eerie place. "You won't now, though. You won't kill him."

"No."

"Why?"

"That's a good question."

Lydea, waiting, gave up finally and asked another, tentatively, "What did you do to him? It would help me to know, if you don't want him to die."

"It was in the charcoal."

"What was?"

"The poison."

Lydea heard another incomprehensible word from Ducon. She lifted her free hand, touched her closed eyes with icy fingers. "Do you have an antidote?"

"Yes," the sorceress said. "Me. He'll be very weak afterwards; he'll need someone to care for him. If that woman has my waxling, I'll make a broth out of her bones."

"I wish you would," Lydea said fervently. "Then there would only be one of you."

Faey was facing Lydea so suddenly that Lydea's puzzled eyes were still trying to see her turn. The sorceress's well-bred face was a mask of frosty displeasure. "I cannot imagine why you would insinuate that we are in any way alike."

"I do not believe," Lydea said in her best courtly manner, "that I have insinuated any such thing. I said it. You're a pair, you both are; I can't tell the difference between you. You're the one who tried to kill Ducon, not Domina Pearl. Living down here, safe in magic, you don't have to care about anything or anyone. If you had killed Ducon, it would have broken Kyel's heart. He may be only a child, but he is the Prince of Ombria, and if his heart dies so soon, so will Ombria. Not that it would come to your attention if the city over your head vanished. It would have to be dead a century or two before you'd notice."

The blue eyes stared at her without expression. Then the sorceress was moving again, toward a sprawling mansion that might have sunk under the weight of the immense cream-colored urns balanced on its portico. Her voice drifted back to Lydea. "I do care about something. I care about my waxling."

"Her name," Lydea said coldly, catching up, "is Mag."

"I know. I named her."

"She's not just something you made out of candle drippings. Who is she? Is she your child?"

Something snapped out of the sorceress, as if she had spat lightning. Ducon gave a sudden cry of pain. Lydea pushed her hands tightly against her mouth.

"Do not meddle," Faey said softly without turning, "between me and my waxling. She belongs to me and does my bidding. That's all you need to understand."

"I don't understand anything at all," Lydea whispered, but only to her hands.

She recognized the plump, prim housekeeper who opened the door to them, and who betrayed, not even with the flicker of an eyelash, no surprise at the man dangling across the sorceress's shoulder.

"The peacock room, I think," Faey said. The housekeeper nodded without speaking and picked up a branch of candles to light them up the marble stairway.

In a room colored the indigo and green of peacock feathers, the sorceress let Ducon fall among velvet cushions on a bed, and drew breath to call. She loosed it, said incomprehensibly, "I forgot; she isn't here to get my toad. See to him while I'm gone."

She left abruptly. Lydea grappled a moment with the idea of an urgent need for toad, then gave up. She was undressing Ducon when the silent housekeeper returned with water and linens; she waited, while Lydea washed the charcoal and dirt and blood off him. He was unconscious again, his breathing shallow and erratic. The housekeeper was helping to settle him beneath the sheets when Faey returned.

She opened the small casket she carried, and slid her hand beneath the toad in it. She lifted it out, raised it to eye level. Silently, eye to eye, the toad and the sorceress conversed. So it seemed to Lydea, who was beginning to recognize Faey's methods. The toad's eyes closed to hair-fine slits of darkness.

The sorceress set it on Ducon's forehead.

She brought a forefinger to her lips as Lydea, her heart hammering at the strangeness, opened her mouth. She closed it. Faey lowered her finger and touched the toad very gently between its eyes. She closed hers.

Lydea shifted close to the fat corkscrew of ebony that supported one corner of the canopy over the bed and clung to it tightly. The toad never moved; neither did the sorceress. After a while, Lydea realized that Ducon's breathing had slowed, grown deeper, rhythmic. The sorceress's breathing had slowed to match his. So had Lydea's.

The toad spoke. Its word formed a bubble of milky liquid between its jaws, like a great pearl. Faey opened her eyes, quickly moved her hand to receive the pearl. She let it fall into the box. The toad opened its eyes, shifted a splayed foot. Faey opened her hand again, and let it waddle onto her palm.

"My beauty," she murmured and kissed its nubbled back lightly before she set it into the box. "Thank you. I must take him back and feed him," she said to Lydea, who wondered for the first time since she had opened the sorceress's door, if she were lost in someone else's dream. But there was Ducon, in it with her, his stiff face beginning to relax, lose its frightening pallor. "Tell the housekeeper what you need for him. I am going to find my waxling."

"Please," Lydea begged desperately. "Please. Is there someone you could send to tell my father not to worry about me? He'll think I've died in the streets, or left him again."

Faey glanced at her housekeeper. "Send someone from the kitchen," she said briefly. "Someone alive."

"The Rose and Thorn," Lydea said faintly, as the housekeeper bowed her frilled and skewered head. She lingered, her eyes going to questioningly Ducon. "Oh. He'll need a little broth," Lydea added, "when he wakes."

"Feed her as well," the sorceress told the housekeeper. "And now I do not wish to be disturbed by anyone, living, dying, or dead."

Alone with Ducon, Lydea pulled a chair to the bedside and sat, her eyes on his face, her thoughts stunned by magic and coincidence. The housekeeper returned with a tray. She drank a little wine, nibbled a bread roll crumb by crumb until her head sank back into the soft tapestry bosom of the chair and she napped. She dreamed something had slipped out of her grasp; she had lost it. She started awake. Ducon was still asleep. The bread had slid out of her hand. She rose, feeling spellbound again, this time by sleep. She lay down in the wide bed beside Ducon and closed her eyes.

When she opened them again, he was awake and staring at her.

"Lydea?" he whispered. He looked incredulously past her at the rich, unfamiliar chamber. Then, with painful slowness, he lifted a few inches of velvet and glanced at his own nakedness. He turned his head again, studied her stained apron, the crumpled cap on her head, askew and trailing strands of her hair. He swallowed. "I don't understand." His voice sounded husky, weak and groggy with sleep. "How much did I drink last night? I've never felt so terrible in my life. Where are we?"

Lydea felt words as rich and unexpected as jewels fill

her mouth: *Magic, spellbound, illusion, ghost, toad, sorceress.*
She got up after a moment, and brought Ducon the cooling
mug of broth she found on her tray.

"We're in the underworld," she said. "Drink this."

FOURTEEN

The Labyrinth

The owl-eyed man returned first to the Black Pearl's library. Mag, slumped on her feet behind the book shelves, her face against a musty pile of manuscripts, blinked senselessly at his taper light. She was thirsty and disoriented; she had no idea if an hour or a day had passed in that silent, changeless room. Accustomed to adjusting in peculiar situations, she did not betray herself with so much as a mouse's rustle against the manuscripts. The man lit more candles and began leafing through a book from the shelves on the other side of the room. The door at the bottom of the stairs, whose lock had resisted every barbed pin in Mag's hair, stood open. She felt her body tense, preparing to emerge unexpectedly through the nearest armed ghost. In the second that the man stood transfixed and staring at the apparition, she would run down the stairs and slam the door behind her.

That would imprison him in her place. Or would it? Would he simply burst out and chase her down the halls, shouting for Domina Pearl? During the moment she wondered, he slapped the book abruptly shut and blew out candles. He was careless; one wick sprang to life again as he clattered briskly downstairs. The door clicked shut behind him. Mag slumped despairingly. Then she realized that she was no longer in the dark.

She stepped out cautiously, noiselessly. Two spells demanded solutions now instead of one: the locked door, and Ducon Greve. One precluded the other; both were imperative. She pulled books down hastily, searching at random for either spell: to unlock a door, to unpoison a man. She left careless fingerprints everywhere, knowing with cold certainty that Domina Pearl would more likely find her first.

Despite her urgent tasks, odd things in the books snagged her attention, clung to memory. She found hints of complex and extraordinary aspects to the history of Ombria, as well as tantalizing suggestions of what strange brew of exotic succulents and insects might keep Domina Pearl alive, or something resembling alive, long past anyone's memory. When the candle began to sputter, she put the books hastily back on the shelves and crept behind them again. She did not dare light others; she might as well toss books onto the floor as leave a ring of melted stubs around the room. The candle died. Again, she waited. In the dark, one persistent image came to mind and refused to budge: Ducon dying in a back alley or among the weeds

on an abandoned pier, while she, equally alone and powerless, stood trapped by books and unable even to open a
door.

She heard steps in the room beyond and readied herself
to spring out and run past whoever came up. But the door
opened and locked again before the steps came up. She
swallowed a brief, startling stab of tears. She leaned gently
against the shelves, quieting the sharp-winged dragonfly of
fear that darted and hovered and darted through her.
Domina Pearl's ancient, dead-moon eyes would not miss
her twice.

But it was the man again, his steps anything but fur-
tive. Again, he did not stay long; again he left a candle
burning, as if he intended to return soon. She watched him
choose his book and turn to go. She moved soundlessly
behind the shelves, her hands rising to find a suitable pin.
She would follow him down, force herself through behind
him; the barb at his throat would persuade him to silence.

She saw what he had left on the floor as she passed
through a ghost. The blood shocking through her brought
her to a halt. He moved quickly in that moment; she heard
the door shut as she stood staring at the floor. A plate of
cold roast beef and bread lay beside the lighted taper on
its stand, along with a pitcher of water and a glass.

Eat me, they said. *Drink me*. She swallowed, startled and
wary. The Black Pearl had seen her, and had sent him with
spell-riddled food and drink. Only that could explain it; he
would not dare risk secrets from Domina Pearl. And Mag,
her mouth as dusty as the old tomes, did not dare drink.

She didn't. But neither did she hide when he came up
again. His quick, noisy tread told her clearly how lost she

was within the secret palace, how far from help. She sat on the floor next to the untouched food and water, her face withholding expression as his flame fell over her. She felt his own surprise like a touch on a web between them. Whatever he expected, she thought, it was not her.

He said, "She doesn't know you are in here. I brought the food and water from the kitchens, not from her."

Mag was silent, studying him, wondering if he truly hid things from Domina Pearl. She gave him a little piece of herself, the sound of her voice. "Who are you?"

"Camas Erl. I often work in libraries. A misplaced book, the scent of melted wax catches my attention. Domina Pearl had other things on her mind." He settled himself down on the floor, grunting a little as he folded his long legs. His yellow eyes, rayed with streaks of hazel, were curious as a bird's, "I am the prince's tutor. Before that, Ducon Greve's."

"Ducon," she said hollowly, remembering. "He is dying."

"What?"

"I've been searching for him everywhere."

"Who are you?"

"I'm Faey's waxling," she answered impatiently. "The sorceress. If you are close enough to Domina Pearl to share secrets with her, then you must know the sorceress who lives underground."

His eyes refused to say if he knew her or not. "But why does she want to kill Ducon?"

"She was paid to, by a manticore. She made a poisoned piece of charcoal."

He whispered something, running fingers through his

hair, dragging a strand out of the tie at his nape. "Charcoal. That would do it. He fairly eats it when he draws. Are you sure about the manticore?"

"I didn't see it. Faey recognized it."

"Does this Faey know a manticore from an apple core?"

"If it's worth knowing."

He grunted softly. "Why don't I know her? Domina Pearl is aware of her, you say?"

"Domina Pearl has sent to her for spells. Please," she begged, "if you let me go, I can look for him."

"Domina has her own ways of finding people. That might be simpler."

Mag's skin chilled at the thought. "She would ask how you know Ducon is dying. You would have to tell her. She'll unmake me if she lays eyes on me. She warned me once before. I've been with Faey long enough to know what that means."

He grunted, still gazing at her, uncertain and uncomfortably probing. "You have no reason whatsoever to trust me," he said abruptly. "I wouldn't. Except, for the moment, two things. Domina Pearl does not want Ducon dead, and neither do I. The second thing is this." He tore a piece of crust from the bread, washed it down with a swallow of the water from the pitcher and wiped his mouth. "It's harmless. For now, I'll keep all this from Domina Pearl. Where have you searched?"

She told him.

He refused to set her free, even after she described in vivid detail the places Ducon frequented. He only promised, "I'll find him. He must be out there. He's nowhere in the palace."

"Please—"

"Domina Pearl won't find you. She rarely comes here. In this palace, libraries are the most private places." He seemed to see the sudden, raw determination behind Mag's eyes. He rose quickly, picked up the single burning candle from the stand, and walked backward as he spoke. "If you stay quiet, I'll leave this lit for you on the bottom step. If you move, I'll leave you in the dark, and I will summon Domina Pearl."

Her fists tightened, but she did not move. "Just hurry," she said tersely.

She unclenched a little after he had gone, enough to eat something, and resume her incessant reading, for nothing about Camas Erl indicated he might know how to reverse death by toad.

The manticore, she learned in her random, harried leafing through the Black Pearl's books, belonged to an ancient family, close kin to the House of Greve. Evidently the lord or lady bearing the name Sozon had it in mind to whittle away secretly at the heirs to the crown, which did not entirely explain the attack on Ducon, who would not have inherited anyway. She had paused briefly to ponder the elusive logic of that, as though it were some mathematical problem, when her head snapped backward against leather bindings worn as soft as lambskin with age. She slept without moving, without dreams.

Camas Erl walked into her sleep and woke her. The candle he had left her had burned out. She made some sort of noise, a broken question, as she gathered her complaining bones together. He shook his head.

"I didn't find him."

His face was patchy, sagging tiredly. The flame lit stubble, chestnut and salt, along his lean jaws. She pulled herself into herself, suddenly cold, huddling within the shapeless wool. She gazed at him, her eyes stunned, luminous.

"Then he's dead."

"How do you know?" He touched her when she did not answer, shook her a little, lightly. "What was the poison in the charcoal?"

"It was from Faey's toad. I have been trying to find an antidote in the books."

"How long ago did she make it?"

"I don't know, anymore. Days."

He rubbed his eyes wearily, baffled. "No one in the palace has seen him in days. I looked everywhere you told me to look and a few places you didn't. A woman in a brothel told me he had been there a night or two ago. He seemed ill, she thought. He said he was only drunk, but he was cold as death, and he would eat nothing."

Mag shivered. "Cold as toad," she whispered. She reached for the pitcher, drank from it; water sloshed, waking her further. She washed her face with her wet skirt, and straightened the pins in her hair. Then she said with grim desperation to Camas, "Domina Pearl will kill me if she finds me here. She told me so once before when she caught me spying on her. You must let me go before you tell her about Ducon. Unless you're angry with me for helping Faey with this, and you want me dead."

"You helped her?"

"I couldn't stop her. So I thought I could find Ducon in time, exchange the magic charcoal for an ordinary piece. But I couldn't find him, I couldn't, though I've looked everywhere—"

"What," Camas Erl asked, his wide eyes no longer an owl's, but fiercer, fixed and predatory, "exactly are you?"

"I don't know," she answered, reckless with the truth. "What are you? You know Domina Pearl's secrets and yet you hide things from her. What does she want? What do you want? What is the Black Pearl?"

He was silent, thinking, a furrow trowelled across his forehead. "The Black Pearl," he said finally, "is a piece of the underside of history. The dark side of the moon. The shadow it casts across the earth when it eclipses the sun. She is, shall we put it, something that should have vanished long ago, but didn't. I have a passion for the history of Ombria, which leads me in strange directions, because it is not simple. You are one of the stranger things I've run across in my journey through the labyrinth of history. You and your sorceress who lives underground. She made you, you say? You are her—what? Her waxling?"

"So she says."

"And you? What do you say?"

Mag was silent. She held herself tightly, motionlessly, her arms around her knees; the tutor held her eyes. After a long time, she heard someone, herself and not herself, answer, "I don't know. If I say I am human, then where do I belong? And if I am not human, then where did I begin?"

"I will let you go," he told her very softly, "if you tell me how to find you again. And how to find Faey."

"What do you want with her?"

"To know her. She is part of Ombria. To learn what she is, where she comes from."

"She won't like being studied."

"I can be very discreet. There's little time to talk now. I'll give you a chance to leave the palace before I suggest to Domina Pearl that she should search for Ducon. If you find him alive, send word to me. I'll tell her that I found him. She'll do what she can to heal him, even if she has to pay your sorceress to undo her own spell."

"Faey has done that before," she answered heavily. "It will cost."

"Domina Pearl will pay."

"Why? Why would she care that much about the bastard son of the House of Greve? Faey thought she would be the one to kill him."

But he finished his instructions without answering her. "If Ducon is dead—" He hesitated, then said flatly, "If you find him dead, tell anyone. It won't matter."

She nodded, rising stiffly, and waited for him to lead her down, unlock the door. But he wasn't finished with her yet. He held his taper between them, lighting both their faces, and asked curiously, "Why weren't you afraid of them? The ghosts in here? Why didn't you run the moment you saw them?"

"They're only ghosts. I was raised among them, down in Ombria's past."

She saw the light and longing flood his eyes, as though she had told him of some great treasure buried deep beneath the city. He asked sharply, "How will I find you again?"

She told him. He said nothing more as they went down the steps; he unlocked the ensorcelled door and set her free.

FIFTEEN

Charcoal and Wax

Ducon dreamed, and woke remembering.

In his dream he followed a tall white-haired man through the crowded streets of Ombria, whom he always seemed about to overtake, and who always eluded him. Shop doors opened; people pushed between them; street urchins being chased by an irate confectioner for the sweets in their hands careened wildly across his path. A duel fought with sudden, savage intensity in front of him forced him to stop. He watched the pale head move farther and farther away from him with never a backward glance while the duellers whipped mercilessly, relentlessly at each other, their rapiers weaving patterns of silver that froze in the air across his path into a shimmering wall of blades. He cried out desperately to the distant figure, "Wait!" He found himself alone, walking the maze of hidden rooms within the palace toward the place where, he knew with absolute certainty, the stranger who wore his face waited.

He woke before he reached it.

He remembered, before he opened his eyes, the face that had formed unexpectedly on his paper, as if it had come out of the charcoal instead of him. The face had been one of many unpredictable sketches. Where was it now, this charcoal that glowed in the dark?

Where, for that matter, was he?

He opened his eyes finally. Lydea, whom he had last seen lying beside him in a hideous cap and a beer-stained apron, was sitting in a chair beside his bed. Apparently, her clothes had also offended the eye of the mistress of the mansion; she now wore a gown of rich green velvet, of a stark simplicity that hadn't been fashionable for a hundred years or so. Only her face and fingers were visible. She seemed to be in the midst of contemplating her fate, but she turned quickly as though she had felt him wake.

She touched his face, then lifted his head a little and held a cup of water to his lips. His mouth tasted of charcoal, he thought as he drank; he wondered if he had swallowed it.

"Explain to me again," he begged, "why we are here."

She had told him once before; it had been like listening to a vivid, improbable dream. This time, he kept his attention on the path the charcoal took from the sorceress's cauldron to Lord Sozon's servant, and somehow into the box he carried with him when he drew.

"The poison was in the charcoal," Lydea said. "It seeped into your skin."

He nodded. "I'm told I get it everywhere. I never notice." The simple movement, the few words, took their toll. The pain, a drowsing beast, began to stir in his head. He tried to ignore it. "Where is it now?"

"Where is what?"

"The charcoal."

She looked bewildered. "I don't know."

"There was a wooden box. In my coat pocket." He formed words with infinite care, trying not to disturb the beast.

She opened her mouth, then rose without asking why. He saw his torn, bloody clothes lying across a chest. She picked up his coat. One pocket held a lump of rubble; the other, hanging by threads, was stained with an explosion of colors.

"What was in the box?"

"Paints. Pieces of charcoal."

"It must have been crushed beneath you when you fell." She put the coat down and came back to him. "Don't worry. You're safe from it."

His eyes filled with tears of pain, of impatience at his weakness. He whispered, "I loved what it drew."

He slept again. This time, in his dreams, a monstrous and beautiful sorceress slung him over her back and carried him across the arid wasteland of some immense cavern. Upside down, breathing in the cloudy fabric of her sleeve, he tried to bargain with her for that piece of charcoal.

"I'll draw your face with it," he offered at one point.

"Which face?" she asked him. And then her raucous laughter echoed off the stones around him and he woke.

Or thought he woke: the sorceress still loomed over

him. He recognized her, though she wasn't wearing the face in his dreams, or even the face he had glimpsed above Lydea's when she had knelt beside him in the rubble and said his name.

The sorceress wore her power like a great cloak of many colors, only visible if he did not look straight at it. It flowed and billowed all around her, in the corners of his eyes; it filled the chamber and spilled beyond the door, beyond her house, he guessed, like a second river beneath the world, like wind. The face she wore, tempestuous and beautiful, was a mask, nothing.

He whispered, "No wonder you laughed."

She was silent a moment, while the colors pulsed and shimmered around her. Her dark eyes seemed enormous. "What do you see?" she asked him. He knew that voice: it had hunted down his breath, the rhythms of his blood, to kill him. But here he was, safely in bed in her house; for no apparent reason she had changed her mind.

"You," he answered simply.

The wild power faded, hid itself. He was left with only her disguise, fascinating enough with its proud bones, its dark, untamed fall of hair, its ever-changing expressions. But it only made him wonder: if he drew that face with the charcoal she had made, would her hidden face emerge instead?

She asked abruptly, "Do you know my waxling? Mag?"

"I don't think so."

"You wouldn't have to think about it if you did. She goes places, does things for me. She likes secrets. Lydea said she was spying on you."

"Me."

"Is that possible? Are there places she could have gone within the palace, where she could watch you without you noticing?"

He started to nod, thought better of it. "The palace is riddled with secrets," he said. His voice sounded frail, reedy as an old man's. "Some are Domina Pearl's secrets. Others are left from the past. Others — I don't know what they belong to. Who."

She breathed something sharply that made the bones in his head vibrate like a bell. He flinched. She touched him; he saw the boring worm of pain, bright, throbbing, cling to her fingers. She shook it away absently.

"Sorry," she said. He stared at her, amazed. She whirled, paced a step or two, her lovely eyes narrowed, so dark they refused to reflect a spark of light. "I've lost her. I warned her and warned her to stay away from Domina Pearl."

His head pounded again, just at the thought of her. "Kyel," he whispered suddenly, and tried to sit up. The pain swung a well-aimed hammer between his eyes; he dropped. Through the haze, he saw Lydea lean over him, felt her cool hand. He heard himself say with dreamlike clarity, "Give me back the charcoal and I will find your Mag."

He heard, within the silence, the unspoken questions leaping into the sorceress's mind. Then she spoke and he heard nothing at all.

He drifted into the world after a long time, following a scent. Rosemary, he thought drowsily. Or orange. Opening his eyes, he found himself alone. Lydea had gone elsewhere, maybe into another dream. But the food on the tray beside the bed was real enough: roast chicken sprinkled with rosemary and stuffed with slices of orange and lime, bread still hot from the oven, a bowl of figs and purple grapes. He sat up cautiously. The pain in his head had gone; he felt scoured, hollow, and hungry for the first time in days.

The door opened as he broke into the steaming loaf. He paused to watch what still seemed an impossibility: Lydea, closing a door, crossing a room, as though she thought she were still alive. He saw the relief on her face at the sight of him wielding a butter knife over the tray on his knees. She sat down on the bed, and poured a little wine into their cups. She looked hungry, too, he thought; her lovely face, which he had rarely seen except in formal circumstances, seemed hollow and worn. He buttered bread for her; she carved, and passed him a plate. They ate silently for a few minutes with their fingers, too impatient for the fine, heavy silver lying on the tray.

He tired quickly, leaned back, wiping his hands on linen and watching her eat. He said softly, "I never thought I would see you again after Domina Pearl escorted you out of the palace that night."

"Mag helped me cross the city. She saved my life."

"Mag."

Her mouth crooked. "The sorceress's waxling. That's what Faey calls her."

He nodded, enlightened. "The lost waxling who was spying on me. Why would she spy?"

A complex expression, both wry and troubled, crossed Lydea's face. She touched her lips delicately with her napkin, as Royce had taught her, and took a sip of wine. Her voice, when she spoke, was very low. "To see if you were worth saving."

"From—" He stopped himself before she shook her head. His eyes widened; he felt a crazed urge to laugh. Then he glimpsed the twin-headed danger that threatened Mag in her odd pursuit: the sorceress betrayed, on the one hand, and the Black Pearl on the other. He said slowly, trying to understand, "She must have thought I wasn't. She's not the only one to come to that conclusion."

"She's missing," Lydea reminded him somberly. "Perhaps dead. Maybe because she thought you were."

He was silent, musing over the faceless waxling bound to Faey, who kept an eye on his life without his knowledge. He glanced down streets in his memory, into taverns, and came up blank, without a likely face, not even one he might have drawn on impulse. "What does she look like?"

"She's young, midway between Kyel and me. Between knowing too little and knowing too much, you might say. She wears pins like skewers in her hair, which is the color of gold and looks like a pile of straw. She's tall, wiry, and not afraid of anything, not even of what she should fear."

He shook his head, trying to conjure her up and failing. Lydea stripped a cluster of grapes and held a handful out to him. "Eat," she advised, "if you want to get out of here."

His hand slid over her hand, closed. He said, "Thank you for finding me, and taking care of me. In this most improbable place."

She smiled a little, turning their hands over so that the grapes fell into his palm. "I didn't realize how invisible I felt since I left the palace," she said slowly. "As if I had died there. And then you recognized me, and brought that Lydea back to life."

He swallowed a grape to please her, and dropped the rest on his plate. "I understand what I'm doing here. But how and why did you find your way here, wherever here is?"

She told him. *Kyel*, she said, and again, *Kyel*, reminding him, filling him again with a weary impatience at his helplessness. Then he began to hear what she was telling him.

"You'd do that?" he interrupted incredulously. "You'd put yourself under Domina Pearl's nose to watch over Kyel?"

"It was hard enough losing Royce," she answered painfully. "I didn't understand at first how much I would miss Kyel. I can't do anything more for Royce; he's safe where he is. But I have nightmares about what the Black Pearl might do to Kyel."

"Whatever you dreamed, she will do." He pushed his hands against his eyes, trying to think. "I know of places to hide within the palace . . . She rarely lets him out of her sight by day . . . Except—" His hands slid down; he gazed at Lydea without seeing her. "He will begin to study soon; his tutor will have him for several hours a day. Perhaps, then . . ." She came clear under his eyes: the long red and bronze sweep of her hair, her smoky eyes, the fine, elegant bones of her face. He shook his head restively. "No. It's too dangerous."

"What?"

"Cutting your hair would be easy. But you would have to change the expression in your eyes."

It changed as he spoke, became fierce with longing, hope. "I'll do that," she promised. "I'll do anything. What —"

"If you could disguise yourself, pretend to assist Camas somehow — He might take the risk, for Kyel's sake."

"Camas?"

"Camas Erl. Perhaps you never met him. He was my tutor."

"Perhaps I never paid attention to him," she said steadily, "if he was only a tutor. After all, I was the prince's mistress." The bitterness in her voice surprised him. She stood, hefting the ornate tray off his knees, and added, "It's strange that the more clearly you can see yourself, the clearer other things become."

"Do they?" he asked. "I wouldn't know. The only time I glimpsed myself was in a dream."

He saw the dream again, the face that was his and not his, and felt again the shock of recognition and his thoughtless longing, that had not made the world around him any clearer as he followed the stranger through the streets of Ombria, but had changed it at every step until, when he had finally fallen out of it, the world had become completely unfamiliar.

"Sleep," Lydea said gently, settling a pillow under his head. "Neither of us can leave until you're well."

He saw the sorceress just before his eyes closed. She stood at the foot of the bed, holding something small in her hand. Around her the bewitching tides of her powers eddied and gathered and ebbed into distances.

"I found your charcoal," she said. "The toad has taken

the poison out of it." In the fragmented time of dreams or sorcery, she was beside him suddenly, laying the charcoal next to his hand. "Now you must find Mag."

It was still there when he woke.

SIXTEEN

Here and There

Lydea, roaming through the mansion in search of the sorceress while Ducon slept, felt that she moved backward in time, wandering haphazardly through layers of history that changed at random and were never consecutive. A certain garment worn by one of the taciturn ghosts evoked an entire epoch of Ombrian past; a change in the style of a chair leg signalled a death or a coronation in the House of Greve. The fashions and supercilious faces in paintings reminded her of other ghosts in other paintings who had watched her nervous passage through the halls of the palace. Family, Royce had called them with easy familiarity. The earliest of them were painted on wood, and wore their weight in furs and pearls. Here on Faey's walls hung art that seemed earlier still, and verged upon artless. Strange landscapes and animals, the suggestion of a city's

streets, an even vaguer, blurred face glimpsed in a glittering fog, were depicted on what looked like the round tops
of wine barrels, or on stretched hide. Older than anything
Royce had shown her, they seemed. Older than the House
of Greve, though that could scarcely be possible. Ombria
and the House of Greve had been born together, twin children, bloody and ignorant, who had made the world
around them as they grew.

So Royce had told her. His memory shadowed her as
she searched. The age and richness within the sorceress's
mansion, the changing glimpses from room to room of
older times, the antique velvet Lydea wore, made her feel
ghostlike, as if she were haunting her own memories of life
within the palace. She listened futilely for Royce's confi-
dent, good-humored voice explaining this and that to her:
an odd, obsolete weapon, the curdled expression on an an-
cestor's face. Strange, she thought, how such assurance,
such perception, could not foresee its own abrupt end. She
took comfort in the thought that he must have believed he
would live unchanged forever.

A face hanging at one end of a long ballroom stopped
her. Surely Faey had worn those blue eyes, that pale, dis-
dainfully arched brow. She still did, it seemed. The pursed
lips opened suddenly, and the sorceress's husky, impetuous
voice came improbably out of them.

"I'm in here," the lady in the painting said shortly.

"Where?" Lydea asked, after a hiccup of surprise.

"Go through three doors without turning."

The moving lips melted back into paint. Lydea, thinking it best not to think too much in that upside-down place,
grasped the two door latches in front of her, pulled the

ballroom doors wide, and walked across the hall to open what looked like a cloakroom.

The sorceress, surrounded by brass hooks knobbed with porcelain, was sitting on a small gilt chair. A single cloak hung behind her: wine silk, lined with snow hare. Faey, also in wine silk, her unruly dark hair coiled neatly around white rosebuds, looked as if she had shut herself up in a closet as punishment for having misplaced her waxling.

She fixed a dark, humorless eye on Lydea and said, "I told you I do not wish to be disturbed. You're disturbing me. What is it?"

"I'll help you," Lydea said steadily, "if you'll help me. And I can pay you."

The sorceress regarded her dourly, but with slightly more interest. "With what?"

"With all I have left. I have shoes with sapphire heels —"

"So do I. And ruby. And emerald."

"And I have —" Lydea's voice faltered, strengthened. "I have this ring."

She pulled it from under her gown: the opal inset between pearls that Royce had given her. Faey leaned forward to study it. "Pretty," she said absently. Her eyes had narrowed. "You should hang it on something besides that dirty ribbon."

"I tore it out of my cap."

"Why do I see my waxling within the opal?"

Lydea blinked. "Because she rescued it for me?" she suggested. The black, abysmal gaze moved to her again.

"You will help me. How?"

"You can change your face at will. Give me another face so that I can return to the palace and watch over Kyel. If you do that, I can search for Mag there, too, with no one being the wiser."

"What makes you think that the Black Pearl won't see beneath any mask you wear?"

"It's she who pays you for your magic. How could she see through any mask you would make?"

The dark brows, angled upward like crows' wings, flew higher. Faey seemed to slump for a moment into herself; her neck disappeared; her backbone began to meld with her knees. Then, as Lydea's eyes widened in fascinated horror, the sorceress shook her body back into its beautiful proportions.

She said grimly, "I'm not sure anymore what that woman can or cannot do. I thought she was some ghost of the House of Greve, who refused to die and kept herself upright with a lacquer of beetles' wings and amber. But I haven't paid enough attention to her. I don't know how powerful she has become in the past century. Looking back, I see now that I have always done her bidding." She contemplated the Black Pearl in silence a moment, then added, "I sent Mag out for eels for supper. That's the last I saw of her. She may be nowhere near the palace. She might have run away, been abducted by pirates, fallen in love—"

"Would you know if she were dead?"

"Of course I would know," Faey said imperiously. "She is my making." But her eyes, uncertain, brooding, suggested otherwise. She did not look at Lydea when she asked, "Wouldn't you know if your making—or if some human child you had taken to, Kyel for instance—had died?"

"No."

The sorceress turned a stony face to her. "You don't know that. You have never made a child."

"No," Lydea sighed. "Which is why I want to be near Kyel. Will you help me?"

The sorceress held out her hand.

Lydea untied the ragged ribbon looped through the ring. She dropped memories into Faey's palm, a priceless treasure of them, along with love and rue, jewel and gold. The sorceress, sliding the ring onto one long finger, saw only the face of her making within the opal.

She studied Lydea with a practical eye. "The child," she said with unexpected perception, "would take cold comfort in some stranger who tried to persuade him to believe that she was you. You must keep your own face."

Lydea agreed reluctantly. "You're right. He probably suspects I'm dead; after all, I vanished like his father, and on the same night. If I wear a strange face, he might think I'm just something Domina Pearl made to confuse him. But how—"

"Oh, there are things I can do," Faey murmured, turning Lydea's face with her jewelled forefinger, "to disguise you from other eyes. Unless you come face to face with Domina Pearl. I have no idea how well she sees, if she would recognize my magic. I've been sending my makings to her for years."

"Why?" Lydea asked recklessly. The sorceress, contemplating her past, seemed to wonder herself.

"She needed; I made. It was business. I never thought

anything of it, except that I disliked her. But I never questioned anything she wanted. She seemed inconsequential, until now. I have lived a very long time; I've seen minor powers come and go. I kept expecting her to go." She paused, her eyes growing lightless, flat; Lydea guessed that she was, at least in imagination, helping the Black Pearl along her way. "I suggest that you do nothing to attract her attention. Don't search for my waxling. Ducon can look for her. If that woman has her, I will search the palace for her myself. And not even Mag will recognize me when I do." Lydea nodded wordlessly. "But before I permit you to leave my house, you must make Ducon well." She gestured dismissal, then added as Lydea turned to go, "It's odd, don't you think, that he wanted that deadly piece of charcoal back? Did he tell you why?"

"Only that he loved the drawings that came out of it. I think he was delirious. Did you put something besides poison into it?"

"Just some old paintings . . . He made his death into art."

"You nearly killed him—"

"You do dwell on details."

"But something stopped you. Something in him. What was it?"

The sorceress, contemplating a brass hook, seemed to see again some mystery, an unanswered riddle. "He sees," she murmured, "more than he should. More than human."

Lydea, trying to imagine what someone more than human might see in the commonplace world, found herself standing outside the cloakroom door without realizing that she had moved.

She found her way, or the sorceress found it for her, back to the room where Ducon lay sleeping. She studied him. Beyond the mystery of his coloring, or lack of it, he looked as human as anyone. His eyes opened; at that moment they seemed to see nothing at all. He muttered something, stirring; his hand shifted from beneath the bedclothes to grasp her wrist.

She leaned closer. "What?"

"Paper." His eyes drifted closed, opened again. "I need paper."

"Of course you do," she sighed. "What else?"

"Drawing paper."

"Well, I didn't think you wanted to wrap up a mutton chop." She touched his face; it seemed warm with fever. Better than the icy chill that had seeped into him from the toad, she thought. But still not good enough to free them. She held water to his mouth. "You must get well," she pleaded. "What will Kyel think?"

The silvery eyes saw her clearly then: someone real, standing in time, not in a dream, with a face he recognized and thoughts that he could guess at if he had to. How strange, she reflected. How strange to be in a dream one moment and in the world the next, and to know the difference in the blink of an eye.

"You have a very peculiar expression on your face," he commented drowsily.

"I was just thinking."

"About what?"

"About how we know what's real. How we wake out of a timeless place and recognize time. How you know me here, now, even when nothing or anyone else in this place is familiar. I might have been wandering through your dream, but you knew immediately which of me will bring you paper."

He was silent for so long, still clasping her wrist, that she thought he must have fallen asleep without knowing it. He said finally, "Say that again."

"I can't," she answered helplessly. "It was just a thought. I gave it to you."

"Something about dreams coming to life —"

"That's not what I said."

"That's what I heard." His fingers loosened; he smiled up at her, his eyes as translucent as rain. "No wonder my uncle loved you."

She made very little of that; an effect of fever, she decided. Just as feverishly, he clung to the idea of paper: she must find it now, so that he could see if the magic were still in the charcoal, or if it had vanished with the deadly poison. She left him lost in a meandering discourse about death and art, and went to find the housekeeper.

Not all the artists in the house had been dead and hung on the walls. She and the housekeeper found a cache of fine, heavy paper among a pile of unfinished canvases in an attic room. The paper had been nibbled through the years by worms and mice, but Ducon did not seem to mind. Lydea made him eat before she gave it to him. Then she sat quietly beside him, outwardly emanating patience, but inwardly chewing her nails and wondering if they would find anything at all familiar in the world above their heads when the sorceress finally let them go.

Ducon drew for hours. Random sketches slid off the bed, made a paper island around Lydea's feet. They seemed, upside down and otherwise askew, everything he remembered about the streets and taverns of Ombria. Winding cobblestones, ships' masts, shops, carriages, barefoot urchins, merchants, roaming animals, ale-drinkers in the midst of ardent arguments, covered the floor at first. They became slowly layered, as time passed or did not pass within the sorceress's house, with sketches of the palace, rich rooms, exquisitely plucked and painted faces, even, Lydea saw with wonder, the occasional plain, half-averted face and sturdy hands of someone carrying a coal scuttle or a tray. He saw everything, Lydea thought, more than she had ever noticed, though so far nothing more than human. The stick of charcoal, which should have been worn down to a splinter by the time it began its journey through the palace, never changed its shape.

He drew her, while she drowsed for a few moments. The face he showed her was from memory: she almost did not recognize it. Some lovely, foolish young woman looked back at her, a crown of pearls around her elaborate hair, her smile careful, stiff. One graceful hand was raised to touch a jewel hanging at her throat. The nails were bitten to the quick.

She drew a quick, startled breath, half laughing, half wanting to cry. "Was I so transparent?"

He nodded indifferently, already beginning another drawing. His hands and face were smudged dark; he was beginning to resemble one of his drawings. He seemed obsessed, spellbound; the magic charcoal would not let him stop. "That's the expression I always saw. My uncle would have seen something very different. But you never showed me that face."

"It seems so long ago," she murmured, letting the drawing fall to carpet the floor with the others.

"It seems long ago because you have come so far since then."

"From palace to tavern to the sorceress's house . . . You should rest," she begged, suddenly fretting again, imagining disasters in the upper world: her father furious and in despair, Kyel enthralled by the Black Pearl, recognizing no one. "Please. Stop."

He did not seem to hear her. His drawings changed again. This time they depicted rich, empty, crumbling rooms; not even ghosts flitted through them. The sorceress's mansion, she guessed at first. But the chamber he lay in was all he knew of it, and those long, silent hallways and ancient rooms, she herself had never seen. He seemed to work backward through time. Walls and ceilings showed their underpinnings; paints chipped; torn wallpapers revealed other patterns, which yielded to gashes of lathe and plaster. Where, she wondered, uneasy and fascinated, had he seen all that, where had he been?

He had stopped before she realized it. He sat quietly, gazing at his final drawing, while she waited for it to flutter to the floor, another page turned in a story he was telling. When it did not fall, she leaned over his shoulder to look at it.

It was a door in a wall that seemed to be weeping rain. But where the door should have been there was nothing, darkness, charcoal. Except . . . She looked closer, and saw the lines emerge from the blackness: the suggestion of a face, a vague nimbus of pale hair.

The charcoal slid out of Ducon's fingers. He leaned

back, his eyes heavy, still watching the drawing as though in the next moment the shadowy figure might show its face clearly, step into the light.

"There," he whispered; he had finally reached the place where the mysterious tale the charcoal told ended or began. "There."

His eyes closed. Lydea caught the drawing as it fell.

SEVENTEEN

Blood and Roses

M ag spent a day or two on the streets of Ombria searching for Ducon, listening for rumors, for a single, random memory of him in anybody's head. No one had seen him but everyone knew him, therefore he must be around somewhere: Had she looked in the Whistling Swan? The Panting Hart? The King of Flounders? She had crossed the sprawling, erratic web of cobbled roads between docks and palace so often that her feet finally stopped midstride on their way to yet another improbability. The sky was growing grey. A wind from the sea, sharp and blustery, was driving threadbare urchins to their lairs, and whirling scraps of refuse into vague, ragged forms that walked the gutters a moment and then collapsed. A briny edge of wind caught her eyes. She blinked away sudden tears and thought wearily: *Either Camas Erl has found him or he is dead.*

She slipped down the nearest entrance to the underworld and trudged through the dark toward the distant, serene lamps along the river that illumined her path home.

She did not immediately recognize the woman who opened the door to the sorceress's mansion. A new housekeeper, she guessed; the old one must have drifted completely out of life. This one was dressed from throat to heel and wrist in black taffeta. She looked slightly demented. Her black hair hung loose; her delicate oval face was powdered dead-white; her red-rimmed eyes glittered feverishly. She stared at Mag; Mag stared back. Then a tiny frog leaped into Mag's throat and she put her hand over her mouth.

"Where have you been?" The sorceress's voice seemed to come from everywhere at once: out of the river, out of stones, out of the muddy banks and far, cavernous depths. "I sent you out for eels! From the fish market, not from the next kingdom! And why are you wearing that—that pavilion?"

"I'm sorry," Mag whispered behind her hand. She could not see where truth would get her, but it seemed even more dangerous to lie to those furious, reddened eyes. Faey could not have been weeping. She was too old to have any tears left. She was too old to remember what they were for. "I went—I went to look for Ducon Greve."

The black eyes did not flicker. "Why?"

"I didn't want him to die."

Faey was silent, her arms folded, gazing at her waxling.

There was a curious expression on her face. Mag, expecting swords and lightning bolts to leap from the sorceress's mouth, was stunned when Faey finally spoke. "No. Neither did I, when I found him. I just sent him home."

Mag's voice barely got past the frog. "He was here?"

"He fell through from the street. Lydea took care of him, since you were nowhere to be found."

"She was here?"

"You are echoing yourself. You were on the streets above all this time?"

Mag shook her head, both hands over her mouth now. "Not all the time. Not exactly."

"So." Cold blue eels of fire swam for an instant through the sorceress's eyes. "She did find you."

"Not —"

"Exactly."

"May I come in?" Mag pleaded. "I am so tired."

"You deceived me."

"You deceived me," her waxling said recklessly. "You told me I am wax, and that you made me. You taught me how to lie. I'm not wax, you did not make me, I've known it ever since I swallowed that heart. But you never wanted me to know. So what else could I do but lie?"

"I don't think," the sorceress said slowly, "that I am the only one you deceived."

Mag started to answer, stopped. She bowed her head, feeling exhaustion drain through her, weighing on her bones, dragging at her until she didn't know if she had the strength left to lift a foot across the sorceress's threshold. "It seems," she heard herself say, "that I tried to deceive us both. For a long time I didn't want to be human."

"What changed your mind?"

"You," she whispered, "with that toad and that charcoal making Ducon Greve's death. I don't want to be like you, either."

Faey was silent, her powdered face as white as porcelain and as expressive. She moved finally, opening the door for Mag to enter. Her fingertips, falling lightly on Mag's shoulder, stopped her as the door closed behind her. A crack appeared here and there across the porcelain. "I'm older than you can imagine," the sorceress said. "And I think I have forgotten a few things I knew when I was young. I realized that when I remembered how to weep."

Mag stared at her, feeling the frog again in her throat, swelling and about to speak. "You cried for me?"

"I wouldn't have wept over wax."

She moved; Mag followed after a moment, too amazed to speak. Now that she seemed irrevocably human, human questions began to swarm in her, things she had, in her amorphous state, overlooked for years. *Who am I?* she wondered silently, and as intensely, she asked the sorceress's back: *Who are you?* Nothing seemed certain any longer; she felt that if she stopped to think about it, she might forget even how to walk.

Maybe I should have stayed wax, she thought confusedly. *I wasn't frightened then.*

"I don't know who you are," Faey said, answering her unspoken questions. "Someone left you on my doorstep." She turned, as Mag stopped again in wonder. "Literally. You woke me with your crying."

"Here?"

"On the steps outside."

"So someone knew to come here. Was I sold? Did you pay for me?"

Again the sorceress heard what was unspoken. "Many women knew their way to me; they bought spells for love, and revenge, and for doing away with unborn children. You were not the result of a spell that didn't work, but of one that did. Love can make a child, but not keep it fed or unharmed in the streets. You know that. You were brought to me and left deliberately, not for money but in hope. Of what, I'm not sure. That I would find a home for you, I suppose, or keep you myself. Which I did. I thought you might be useful. I never thought—" Faey gestured wordlessly, scattering possibilities in the air between them. "I thought you would always be my waxling. That with me to think for you, you would always be safe. I didn't realize until now that despite all these years as my waxling, you had learned to meddle with my heart."

Mag swallowed. Still her voice came out edged and scratchy when she spoke. "How can you assume that I was—that I was left here because I was wanted? I was abandoned on your doorstep—"

"You were given to me," Faey said. Somehow, without moving, she seemed closer, her shadows, cast by various candles on the walls around them, all stretched across the floor toward Mag. "You know what happens to unwanted newborns. You've come across them. They aren't dressed and warmly wrapped in wool and silk; they don't wear mysterious lockets around their necks containing three drops of dried blood and a flower petal."

Mag took a step toward her. "A locket?" Her voice shook. "She left me a locket?"

"On a chain around your neck. It's a wonder you didn't inhale it; you were bellowing enough. I never saw so many windows lit up in those old houses along the river."

Mag took another step. Her entire body was trembling now; her hands rose, clasped. "Please. May I see it?"

"You can have it," Faey said, "when I remember what I did with it." She waited while Mag bridged the distance between them, step by uncertain step. "Remember," she said softly as Mag reached her, "I am not human. I raised you as if you weren't, because myself and ghosts and Ombria's past are all I know. You'll have to find your own way into the human world. If that is what you want."

"I don't know what I want," Mag said helplessly. "Except that this is the only home I know. Don't force me to leave just yet."

"I can't promise that you will want to stay. You know what I am."

Mag's mouth crooked. "And you know what I am. I don't know if I would have a place in the human world. I don't behave like anyone human." Ducon's face drifted into her thoughts then, unexpectedly. He might be eccentric, she reminded herself, but his place among humans, while on the edge, was still within the border.

"You'll find your way in it," Faey said. "You found your way out of here." She touched Mag again, lightly, tentatively. "Go and wash. And find something less hideous to wear. You can tell me where you've been while we have supper."

They charted the paths of Mag and Ducon Greve together over turtle soup. Over fish, Mag listened, astonished, as Lydea found her way into the sorceress's house.

Over roast beef, cold and heavily peppered, Camas Erl first appeared in the Black Pearl's library. Faey set her fork down then; her eyes never left Mag's face. They looked oddly muddy, Mag thought, as though they had picked up something of Camas Erl's yellow during the telling. A salad roused the sorceress.

"This tutor—he does the Black Pearl's bidding?"

"I think," Mag said, "he does what he wants. He let me go. If he had told her I was there, I'd be there still. Or as likely dead. He has his eye on something; I don't know what."

"And yet Ducon Greve trusts him."

Mag felt a prickling down the back of her neck, as though one of Domina Pearl's ensorcelled guards were staring at her. "Did he tell you that?"

"He suggested that Lydea become Camas Erl's assistant, pretend to help him tutor Kyel, so that she could be with the boy. I gave her an aura that might deceive the Black Pearl if she doesn't look too closely, and sent Lydea to the palace with Ducon. She gave me this in payment."

Faey spread her jewelled fingers; Mag recognized the dead prince's ring. There was a peculiarity within the opal. She looked more closely at it and started.

"That's my face."

"Indeed."

"How did I get in there?"

"You must have made an impression."

Mag studied herself, marveling. Faey had given Lydea a spell in return for her waxling's face; her waxling, considering that, felt the unfamiliarity of suddenly becoming human diminish a little. "Would you have come to find me," she asked uncertainly, "if Camas Erl hadn't freed me?"

The sorceress's eyes changed again, hard as diamond, black as coal. "I don't remember how to be subtle in the world above," she said obliquely. "I would have come to get you if the Black Pearl had you, but I might have destroyed too much. There is a mystery in the House of Greve. Domina Pearl sees it; Ducon Greve is part of it; I think this Camas Erl, who wears one face for the Black Pearl and another for Ducon Greve, glimpses it also. He seems a foolhardy man, juggling bare blades with his bare hands —"

"What mystery?"

The sorceress shrugged an ivory shoulder. "If I knew, it wouldn't be a mystery."

Mag took a breath, held it, then said precipitously, "Camas Erl wants to meet you. That's why he let me go."

Coffee and chocolate interrupted the sorceress's immediate comment. She lifted her cup daintily as the door closed, then returned it to the saucer with a clatter, sloshing coffee. "Why?" she asked drily. "Who does he want me to kill?"

"He seems more interested in people already dead."

"Does he?"

"He wants to know where you came from."

"Does he." She lifted the dripping cup, stared into it a moment, puzzledly, as though she were trying to remember herself. Then she took a sip. "I would like to know where he came from. He sounds reckless and dangerous, and I didn't spare Ducon's life just to have him betrayed by the tutor."

"He said that he and Domina Pearl want Ducon alive — "

"But for how long, I wonder? And what of Lydea and the child? Will Camas tell Domina Pearl about Lydea?"

"Perhaps," Mag suggested, "you can bargain with him for his silence. He likes past. You have one. You have enough down here to keep him busy for years."

Faey considered that for a moment, dipping a chocolate into her coffee. "Why," she wondered, "did I never let you think before?" She smiled a guileless smile at the invisible tutor before the melting chocolate disappeared between her fine white teeth. Mag felt a pinprick of sympathy for Camas Erl.

Later, she watched from the doorway as Faey surveyed the chaos of her bedchamber. "Now, where . . ." she murmured, stepping through a tide of mismatched shoes, around mountains of garments, scarves, cloaks, moth-eaten drapes, small tables cluttered with sea shells, a set of wooden teeth, a crab carapace, endless strands of amber, pearls, gold wrapped around tortoiseshell combs and perfume bottles. "Where would I have . . ." It seemed impossible. But after looking in several bowls and boxes, a few satin slippers, and under the bed, Faey moved with sudden inspiration to the marble mantelpiece. There she picked up a red glass vase and upended it. A thin gold chain slid into her palm, pulling a little locket of ivory and gold behind it.

She gave it to Mag, then shifted a sagging cheekbone into place and stifled a ladylike yawn.

"I'm going to bed," she said. "I must be up at moonset."

Mag lifted her eyes from the locket, looked a question. Faey shook her head, patting Mag's shoulder, turning her adroitly out the door to avoid her gaze. "Nothing I need help with. You should rest; you're beginning to look like one of the household ghosts."

But I'm not, Mag thought with a fierce, burning triumph, as she lay in her own bed with the locket in her hands. Neither ghost nor wax . . . My bones belong to me.

The locket, carved of ivory and rimmed with gold, was rectangular and thick, like a tiny book. She pressed the catch; it opened easily. She held it flat, scarcely breathing lest she disturb what lay inside. Three minute pearls of red as dark as dried roses lay on a tiny piece of parchment cut to fit one side. The other side held a faded white rose petal behind the thinnest oblong of glass. She gazed at both sides, her lips parted. Whose blood? she wondered. Whose rose? His blood, she guessed, and the rose that he had given her. It seemed as likely as any other tale, and more comforting than most.

Then she saw the third side of the locket, another page in the book, outlined in gold behind the petal. She pressed the latch again, very gently, and it flicked open.

She stared at the darkness for a very long time before she touched it. Still potent, a little cloud clung to her fingertip. Absently, she rested her head on her hand, studying the locket, and transferred a streak of ashy black along one raised eyebrow.

Charcoal.

EIGHTEEN

What the Manticore Said

Ducon, reappearing after days of mysterious absence, produced, in various circles, such a confusion of responses that he thought he might as well have come back from the dead. Marin Sozon, who had spent a small fortune trying to kill him, greeted him easily enough, but turned so white he seemed to be trying to fade away completely under Ducon's eyes. The Black Pearl, whom he thought would be unmoved, actually produced an expression beneath the brittle lacquer that held her face together. He had fallen ill, he explained smoothly, and had been recovering in the house of some friends.

"I searched for you," she said, perplexed and suspicious. "I have my ways, and even they could not find you. You must tell me who these friends are so that they may be properly thanked."

"I'll thank them very properly," he answered, managing a hint of private amusement, "when I see them again."

She had no blood left in her to produce a flush, but even her hair seemed to stiffen. "They might have sent a message," she complained. "We have all been very worried."

"I should have thought. Perhaps I should reassure my cousin."

Her hesitation, the flicker of an eye, was so subtle that in anyone else he would never have noticed it. "Yes. He has been asking for you. You might find him somewhat subdued. Melancholy. The physician assures us that it is a natural response to the great changes in his life."

Ducon felt a familiar, tangled knot of dread and anger tighten in him; for a moment he could not speak. Domina Pearl didn't wait for a response. Moving past him, she added, "He has begun his studies with Camas Erl. They will be busy all morning. You may see the prince for a moment or two when they finish."

He didn't wait.

He found Camas Erl and Kyel in the library, where the prince was staring listlessly at a chart Camas had hung from a cabinet knob. The massive family tree of the House of Greve dangled names as thick as crabapples from its branches; Kyel's name on its trunk seemed a lonely, insubstantial support for it. The prince turned his head as Ducon entered. For a moment the wide, indifferent gaze encompassed even Ducon, and transfixed him with its apathy. Then the prince rose wordlessly, went to him.

Ducon knelt, held him closely. He felt Kyel's arms finally, closing limply, hesitantly, around him as though he had forgotten how to touch. Ducon stared over his shoulder at Camas Erl, who was still holding a pointer on a contentious bit of history: the twin heirs born to Kasia Greve a couple of centuries before. Camas, staring wordlessly back at Ducon, finally put the pointer down.

"Welcome home."

Ducon nodded, and drew Kyel back to look at him. His face was very pale; there were shadows like bruises beneath his eyes. He blinked under Ducon's scrutiny as though he had just wakened.

"Ducon." His voice sounded strengthless, fragile. "Where were you?"

"I was taken ill; I couldn't come home for a while. I'm sorry I wasn't able to tell you."

"I thought you died," Kyel said with chilling calm. Then expression stirred in his eyes; he found the past again, remembered what death was. He looked at Ducon almost accusingly, found him still alive, and a little color rose in his face. "I thought you went where Lydea and Jacinth went, and my father —"

"No."

"I thought Domina Pearl —" The prince stopped abruptly, his eyes widening, and swallowed the name. He turned his head slowly, as if he expected to see her looming behind him, summoned out of his thoughts. Ducon's jaw clenched. He stood up so that Kyel would not see his face, and took the prince's hand, led him back to the table.

"Tell me what Camas Erl is teaching you."

"He is teaching me the history of the House of Greve," Kyel answered without inflection and without interest. He sat down again; his eyes went to Camas with perfunctory attention. But he still clung without realizing it to Ducon's hand.

Ducon freed himself gently; Kyel did not seem to notice. Camas went to the boy, gave him paper and a pen.

"Practice your letters, my lord," he said. Kyel dipped the pen obediently, without answer, and bent over his work. Ducon lingered, watched him a moment longer. Then he took Camas's arm so forcibly the tutor winced, and strolled with him to the far end of the room.

"What has she done to him?"

Camas shook his head, answered softly, "Some potion or another, to make him passive. I don't know how or when she gives it to him. Ducon, where have you been? I've searched everywhere—"

"You missed a place. Listen to me. I have found an assistant for you."

"For what?"

"To assist you while you tutor Kyel."

The tutor gestured incredulously. "Look at him! He's barely conscious of me. The only thing that holds his attention is making letters, and I think that's only because he remembers the drawings he did for you. I don't need an assistant; I need a pupil."

"You will need this one."

"Ducon, you're making no sense. I've never had—" He stopped then, hearing something in Ducon's inflexible argument. "Why? Who is he?"

"She."

"Who?"

"Never mind who. Unless you take her, I will go to

Domina Pearl and demand to know what she is poisoning Kyel with—"

"All right," Camas breathed, patting Ducon's shoulder anxiously. "All right. You'd disappear so fast no one would know you ever came back."

"What you yourself don't know, you can't be held accountable for."

"That's reassuring," the tutor said drily. "And in this place, hardly true. Ducon. Just tell me what you want."

"I want her to watch over Kyel. Domina Pearl wouldn't permit me to, you are in no position to, and this is—this is someone whom Kyel will trust."

The owl's eyes, wide and watchful, glimpsed the trembling in the grass, the secret glide of some living thing through the world. Camas ran splayed fingers through his tidy hair, pulling tendrils loose. "Not—"

"You won't recognize her. No one will but Kyel."

"But how will I explain to—"

"Think of something."

"But how can she—Ducon, where have you been?"

"In the underworld," Ducon answered. Camas was suddenly, oddly, without questions.

Ducon went to speak to Lydea, whom he had placed in the discreet care of the prince's pretty chambermaid in the silent, unguarded lower floors of the palace. The chambermaid, having other arrangements, had offered Lydea her own bed for the night. Ducon tapped lightly on one of the indistinguishable closed doors lining the hall, and hoped he had remembered the right one. It was opened by a prim, elegant stranger; he stepped back, murmuring an apology.

"Ducon," she said. He took a closer look at her face, and remembered that he had last glimpsed it within the folds and shadows of a deep hood on the voluminous silk cloak which the sorceress had pulled out of some forgotten century to protect her spell.

"It's not," he commented slowly, walking a circle around her, "so much that your face has changed. It's what meets the eye in that first glance at you. Someone poised and very proper, sure of her place in the world, calm and unassailable. Whatever you gave the sorceress for this was worth it."

"That doesn't sound like me at all," Lydea said shakily.

"But it's what you seem."

"I can't even bite my nails." She showed him long, graceful fingers tapering into perfect ovals. "I don't know what she made them out of. Old boot soles, maybe."

The height, the coloring, the slender figure had not truly changed, he saw. Her hair was pulled back into a coiled braid. Something about the plain style seemed to diminish its brightness; its color didn't draw the eye. Nothing about her did, except an impression of calm intelligence which, in that palace, would attract no attention whatsoever. The dark gown she wore, unadorned but for black ribbon at the wrists and neck, gave her an odd air of authority that she had never possessed in five years as his uncle's mistress.

"You look very scholarly."

"That's fortunate," she said grimly, "since I barely know more than how to read and write."

"That's more than Kyel knows."

"Did you talk to Camas Erl?"

"Yes."

"What did he say?"

"What could he say? I didn't give him a choice." He touched his eyes, feeling a flickering shadow of pain behind them. "The Black Pearl is giving Kyel something—some potion, Camas guessed—that leaves him passive. Spiritless." He glimpsed her familiar face then, very clearly, vivid and flushed with passion. "Don't do that," he warned. "Don't look like that."

"Like what?"

"Don't feel. It's a stronger spell than the sorceress's. Do what you can for him. Think for him. Think for us all."

She looked at him closely, an unfamiliar woman who seemed to know him oddly well. "Ducon, are you all right?"

He nodded absently. "A lingering reminder . . . Camas will find a way to explain you to Domina Pearl, and I'll bring you to meet him tomorrow." He glanced around the spare, neat room, furnished with a narrow bed, a chest, a pitcher and basin. "Where will you stay? Will they give you all you need?"

"I am told that my status will allow me to have a private room, exactly like this, if I am accepted as assistant to the prince's tutor." Even her voice could sound scholarly, he thought, precise and reserved. "It's another world down here, with its own rules and its own structure. Not unlike what goes on in the court above our heads, just not so gaudy or well fed. I don't have to share a bed, and I may have a tray brought to my room, just like a lady-in-waiting or a nurse." She sat down on the bed, at which Ducon gazed in appalled fascination.

"I didn't know they made them that small." He turned

restively. "I'm going to see if Kyel left me any drawings, and then I'll begin to search for Mag." He paused, his hand on the doorknob. "Straw-colored hair, you said?"

"A lot of it."

"Eyes?"

"An unusual pale brown. The color of walnut shells."

He grunted, struck. "I wonder why I've never painted them."

"You've never seen them watching you. Ducon," she pleaded as he opened the door, "be careful."

"If I find her," he said, "I'll let you know." The sedate, composed face he saw did not seem to need reassurance, but he smiled at it anyway. "I'll come for you tomorrow."

He was walking quickly through the light and airy upper corridors when he realized suddenly that in the stretch of hallway where his chambers were he saw no guards anywhere. He froze instantly, thinking: *Kyel. Something is wrong.* The knife that should have struck him at his next step sailed past him and into the benign eye of his grandfather, who was hanging, as large as life, on the wall beside him.

He heard a pithy curse and whirled. Someone drove into him from behind, pinned him to the floor, breathless and gasping. Before he could shout. A heavy boot grazed the side of his head; another slammed into the back of his knee. He went limp for a moment, dizzy with pain. His wrists were caught, his arms twisted ruthlessly behind his back. A hand pulled at his hair, wrenched his head up. He saw the manticore then, the fierce, mad human face on the lion's body rearing above a pair of crossed swords in gold and silver thread on white livery. Beyond it, Marin Sozon stood watching, with Greye Kestevan beside him.

Something glinted at the periphery of Ducon's vision; he felt a cold, thin edge of metal against his throat.

The manticore said softly, "You should have died the first time." He nodded briefly without taking his eyes from Ducon. "End it."

The hand holding his hair loosed him abruptly; the floor smacked against his face and he tasted blood. Then a bulky, cumbersome darkness dropped over his head and shoulders. His arms were suddenly free; someone stumbled across him as though he were part of the carpet. He heard the chaos around him then, a tempest trying to be as quiet as possible, grunts, thuds, a hissed shout. He tried to shrug off the dead weight that had fallen on his head. His arms were caught again; exasperated, he tried to shout and breathed in a mouthful of silk. Someone rolled the darkness off him and he saw the manticore of thread again, a knife neatly severing the bloody swords where they crossed.

Sozon and Kestevan had vanished; his one-eyed grandfather gazed cheerfully down at another liveried thug groaning at the foot of the painting. Ducon, pulled ungently to his feet and freed, finally saw his rescuers.

He had last seen them on the end of a rotting pier: cousins and the sons of Sozon's dangerous faction. Since then, the expressions on their young faces had hardened, become desperate. Four guarded the stairways at each end of the hall; the others clustered in a tight circle around him. They were scarcely bruised; they must have overwhelmed Sozon with numbers and surprise.

"Thank you," he said shakily. "How — where are the Black Pearl's guards? Did she plan this?"

The cousin he remembered most clearly, with the burning, visionary's eyes, explained briefly. "Sozon planned a disturbance in another part of the palace. When the regent pulled the guards away from here, we guessed he might attack you here." He gripped Ducon's shoulders, shook him a little. "We don't have time for this. We are supposed to be fighting the Black Pearl, not each other."

"I told you —"

"You told us nothing. You told us: Wait. You told us: You'll let us know when you need us. As what? Drinking companions? You said you would choose."

He tried to answer. Lightning struck behind his eyes; he staggered. They caught him, not without some frustrated cursing.

"He's hurt."

"He looks like he's been dragged through the gutter," someone added disgustedly. "Get him to his room before the guards return."

"What about the bodies?"

"What about them? They're Sozon's — let him explain them to the Black Pearl."

"You don't need me," Ducon commented dazedly as they dragged him down the hall. "You're doing fine by yourselves."

"We need you," the visionary said between his teeth, "to help us destroy the Black Pearl. You see her constantly; you know her better than anyone."

They drew him into his chambers, dropped him onto the bed. Someone, with a kindness he hardly expected, pulled off his boots. They looked down at him, their blurred faces seeming alike, an endless circle of twins.

"Should we send for the physician? We can't just leave him like this, bleeding all over the sheets."

"Why not? He must be used to it, the way he lives his life. Let him sleep it off. And then—" Ducon felt fingers cup his jaw, shaking him to regain his fading attention. The blue eyes held it: his uncle's eyes, but fierce and scalding with impatience. "Let him think. We'll be back. You owe us your life. We'll tell you what to do with it."

He opened his eyes much later to taper fire and a gentler touch. The conspirators, in the magic way of dreams, had turned into the physician and Domina Pearl. The Black Pearl, her words brusque, clipped, flames seething across the icy barrens in her eyes, seemed as furious as he had ever seen her. He wondered how many of the conspirators would be left in the palace by dawn.

He drank what the physician gave him and slept again. He woke at dawn and saw, in the opaque grey light slowly rediscovering the world, a little scrap of cloud that had been pushed beneath his door.

He rose slowly, stiff and aching in every muscle. He limped to the door to pick the paper up, thinking as always at any anomaly, and feeling the knot of love and fear tightening in him at the thought: *Kyel.*

But Kyel could never have written, not even three short words, especially not formed as they were from dripping candle wax. He stared at them until they made sense. And then he opened the door abruptly, trying for a glimpse of her walnut eyes, but only finding guards everywhere that somehow she had eluded.

I am safe, said the wax.

NINETEEN

Mistress Thorn

Lydea, also awake at dawn in the chambermaid's windowless room, had no idea what hour it was. Dreams had wakened her. When she closed her eyes, she saw Domina Pearl watching her; when she opened them in the dark, she heard Kyel weeping. Slowly the sound would turn into a soft, lonely sobbing that came from behind one of the endless lines of closed doors along the silent hallway. She thought of Royce Greve, and of his pampered, nervous mistress, who had chewed her nails among the satin sheets in one of the rich, high, light-filled chambers with a view of the gardens and the sea. Now she was buried beneath the palace, on a meager bed in a room like a cell in a hive and her fingernails so hard you could drive them into a plank with a hammer.

She waited, sleepless and frightened, until someone

tapped on her door. She opened it and found hot water, tea, bread and fruit. She washed and dressed, drank the tea and ignored the food, then sat tensely on the bed until she heard another tap on the door.

She opened it, stared at Ducon, just as he was staring at her, startled again by the face she wore.

She put a hand to her mouth. "What happened to you?" He had a bruise near his temple as big as a fist, a cut lip, and a taut, puckered set to his mouth, as though it hurt him to move. He only shrugged a little, which he had second thoughts about afterward.

"Politics." He tried to smile and was sorry about that, too. "Don't worry."

She composed herself. "Do I look suitable? I feel like I'm going to my own hanging."

"You look very calm, very self-possessed for a woman about to be hanged."

Camas Erl did not recognize her. He thought he would; she could tell by the sudden, puzzled expression in his eyes. There was a moment's confusion for them all when Ducon, about to introduce her, remembered just as she did that she had no name.

"Rose," she said hastily, wondering if she would live to see her father's tavern again. "Rose Thorn."

"Mistress Thorn," the tutor repeated curiously. He must have buried himself in the library for the five years she had lived in the palace, for she did not remember him at all. "I asked Domina Pearl's permission to have you teach the young prince the rudiments of reading and writing, so that I can spend the time on research for my history of Ombria. I will instruct him in mathematics, languages and history. You will assist me with that as necessary."

She bowed her head sedately, appalled at the thought. "As you wish, Master Erl. Though my skills are some-what—"

"I'm sure they will be adequate for our purposes," he interrupted quickly. "My lord Ducon, you will be some-what of a distraction for the prince, wearing that face. I suggest you take your leave before Domina Pearl brings him here. She should perhaps have no reason to assume that you and Mistress Thorn have ever met."

Ducon made himself scarce. Lydea, her heart thudding at the imminence of the Black Pearl, stood quietly as Camas Erl studied her.

He asked abruptly, "You can read and write?"

"My mother taught me," she answered carefully. "She only knew enough mathematics to make change."

"It's astonishing."

She met his eyes, surprised. "Master Erl?"

"She did it, didn't she? That sorceress who lives un-derground. Tell me how you met her."

She hesitated. "Master Erl—"

"If we go down under the Black Pearl's eye, we go down together. Ducon will have to rescue us. I've spoken with the sorceress's girl—the one she calls her waxling."

She drew breath. "You've seen Mag? Recently?"

"She sent me a note last night to leave under Ducon's door, telling him that she is safe. I met her while she was searching for Ducon. She said that the sorceress dwells in the ruins of Ombria's history and that she would take me to see her. You've been there." She did not answer, only watched him narrowly, astonished and disturbed without knowing why. He did not seem to need an answer; he continued, his strange eyes wide, alight with visions of the city's past. "I have only one passion in my life and that is the history of Ombria. Have you heard the story of the Shadow City?"

He was not afraid, she realized suddenly. That was what she found disturbing. In that palace where a scion of the House could be all but murdered in broad daylight on the way to his chamber, Camas Erl did not have the sense to be afraid.

He was waiting for an answer this time; she said tardily, remembering the question, "Yes. I used to tell — " She stopped in time. Babbling like he is, she thought. But he didn't seem to notice.

He said very softly, "I believe it."

"Believe — " she began bewilderedly, and then fell silent again at the sudden flatness in his eyes. She turned.

The Black Pearl entered with Kyel beside her. She kept a hand on his shoulder, but her eyes were on the stranger standing next to Camas Erl. Lydea felt her face freeze. Luckily she could not see Kyel clearly; he walked with his head lowered. A trifle belatedly, she remembered that the Black Pearl and Kyel were also regent and prince; she swept her skirts and herself immediately into a deep curtsey, hiding her eyes from Domina Pearl's scrutiny.

"Mistress Thorn," Camas Erl said with a proper measure of briskness and indifference. "My lord Kyel, she will teach you to read and write."

Lydea risked a glance at the child beneath her lashes. He still had not looked at her; he made no reply to Camas.

"At no time will the prince be left alone with Mistress Thorn," the Black Pearl said tersely. "Especially not after yesterday's events."

"No, of course not."

"I have doubled the guard outside; call them in if you must leave him. She'll be useless if there is any trouble. I assume, Mistress Thorn, that you are not a skilled swordswoman?"

Lydea gave a brief dance-step of a curtsey. "No, my lady."

"Don't bounce up and down like that when I speak to you. Look at me."

Lydea raised her eyes reluctantly. The cold, black eyes had changed, she realized, in the brief time since Royce's death. They looked harried, dangerously driven. She had smelled blood, this woman. She would not have bothered to escort the dead prince's mistress to the streets; she would have tossed Lydea out the nearest window instead.

"You look intelligent enough," Domina Pearl said after an ominous silence. "I trust Master Erl's judgment. And it may be just as well not to allow the prince to become too attached to his tutor. You will teach the prince only at Master Erl's direction; you will see him at no other time, and in no other place. Outside of this room, you do not exist."

She turned. Lydea curtseyed again. Kyel, the weight having lifted from his shoulder, went to the table where paper and ink and books lay scattered, sat down and gazed at his reflection in the polished wood.

Lydea straightened slowly. She glanced uncertainly at Camas Erl; he flicked a feathery eyebrow toward the prince and went to a far table so laden with columns of books and pyramids of scrolls that he all but vanished behind them.

Lydea pulled out a chair beside Kyel. He did not look at her, though an eyelid flickered and he shifted slightly when she drew her chair close. She said gently, "My lord, will you show me what letters you have learned to write?"

He drew a piece of paper out of the clutter and picked up a quill. She opened the ink for him. He dipped the nib and produced an egg with a tail, and then an egg lying at the foot of a post.

"Shall I show you how to write your name, my lord?"

He did not answer, simply waited while she printed his letters on the paper. Even to herself her face seemed a cold, dispassionate mask, while her heart was busy growing thorns, one for the pallor in his face, another for his listless silence, another because the spell had failed. He could not hear beneath the calm, precise voice of the stranger who meant nothing to him. How do I reach you? she thought in despair as he dutifully copied his name. How do I tell you who I am? How do I make you see?

Talk to me, said the King of Rats while the Prince of Ombria lay dying, and those who loved the child had begun to disappear. The goose whispered, her throat aching at the memory, "Shall I tell you a story?"

His pen stopped. He sat without moving, at the fork in the Y, so still he seemed spellbound. Waiting, she thought. Waiting. If he turned to look at her, the woman he waited for would disappear; there would be only this stranger.

"Shall I tell you the story of the fan?"

Still he waited, frozen, his eyes on the paper, the ink melting out of the nib into a black pool over his name.

"This is Ombria, my lord," she said. "The oldest city in the world."

His lips parted, silently shaped a word.

"The most beautiful city in the world."

She heard his voice finally, frail and hesitant, picking up the thread. "The richest city in the world."

"The most powerful city in the world."

"These are the ships," he whispered. "The ships of Ombria."

"These are the great, busy ports of Ombria."

His face was turning finally, his eyes enormous, shadowed. "This is the palace of the rulers — This is the world —"

"This is the shadow of Ombria."

He stared at her. She smiled, her mouth shaking, and two tears spilled out of him, fell like rain among his letters. He leaned toward her, let his brow fall against hers; she cupped the crown of his head in her hand. She whispered, "I am your secret. Your secret Mistress Thorn. Remember when we played with the puppets?" He nodded against her; she felt him trembling. "I was the goose and you were the falcon."

"The King of Rats."

"Yes. Only now I am Mistress Thorn. You will only see me here, and you must not say my name outside this room. I will teach you how to read and write."

"She sent you away," he whispered, his voice no more than the scratch of quill on paper.

"I came back."

"She'll find you again."

"She doesn't remember who I am. So you must not remind her. Say my name." He breathed it against her cheek. "No, my lord. Not here in the other side of the story. We are in the Shadow City, and I am Mistress Thorn."

He drew back from her a little. "Then who am I?"

She touched his face, swallowing, drew his hair back from his eyes. "In the Shadow City, you are my heart."

They got very little done in the hour Camas Erl allotted for words and letters. But he did not seem to notice. He had drugged himself with past, Lydea thought; ghosts stared out of his eyes. He studied Kyel's drunken row of letters without seeing them and murmured, "Good, good." In the time he spent writing numbers and puzzling over the grammar of an ancient language, Kyel's eyes grew vague again. Pointer in hand, revealing the muddled lives and politics of Kyel's ancestors, Camas Erl grew lucid, passionate and frustrated over his pupil's indifference. By the time Domina Pearl came to take Kyel away, both seemed much as she had left them. To Mistress Thorn, hovering in a corner with her hands demurely clasped in front of her, the Black Pearl gave no thought whatsoever.

"I wonder," Camas Erl said to Lydea, "if you might do something for me. Domina Pearl says that you do not exist beyond this room, which reveals an imprudent failure of imagination on her part. Those whom we think beyond notice are those who do what we might never dream. You have a room; you will go to it; what will you do there?"

"Have nightmares," Lydea said succinctly.

"You don't embroider? Or some such?" She looked at

him incredulously. He indicated the book in his hands. It
was old and tired, with a cracked leather binding, a sagging
spine and gilt-edged pages crammed with an endless flow
of words. It looked dry as a rusty bucket. "You might," he
said, "consider this. And take these, too. And this." He put
the book into her hands, piled paper, pens, an ink pot on
top of it. "To write down whatever you consider signifi-
cant."

"About what?" she asked distractedly. She was already
missing Kyel and fretting over him, anxious about what
the Black Pearl might come up with next to keep him docile. Would he think Lydea had been a dream? Would he
forget and say her name?

"The story you were telling the prince. About the
Shadow City."

She gazed at the book, hugged the paper and ink close
so that she could open it. There seemed no shadows in it
anywhere, just words packed as thick as cobbles in a road,
and all looking alike. "This doesn't seem like any story I've
ever heard."

"It might be there, it might not." He watched her, his
odd, intent eyes yellow as a street dog's. "If you glimpse it
in here, write down what you see for me. There's no time
left to hunt through everything."

"No time?" she repeated puzzledly. "What do you do
now? Darn socks?"

"No time," he answered obscurely, "in the world.
Please. I can pay you."

She shrugged a little, righting the ink pot before it fell.
"I don't know. I'll see how far I can get. It may be more
complicated than I could possibly understand."

His thin mouth twitched upward. "You understand a great deal, Mistress Thorn. You have been high above the world with the Prince of Ombria, and beneath it with the oldest sorceress in the history of the city. You were going to tell me how you found her."

"Was I?" she asked evenly, perplexed by him and still disturbed. "I went down a street until I recognized a sign, remembered a shadow I had run from once . . . and I opened a door."

"And there she was," he finished softly. "You walked into the oldest story in Ombria."

Still puzzled, trying to understand what he was telling her, she carried the magpie's nest of words and paper and quills to the tiny, silent room allotted to her station.

She read for the rest of the day, and lit a candle to read into the night.

TWENTY

City of Ghosts

Mag met Camas Erl one afternoon a few days later in a small, leaf-choked courtyard surrounded by empty buildings. A century ago they had been an inn and its stables and carriage house. Now, roofs were sunken under the weight of moss and rain; shutters dangled; not a shard of window pane big enough to throw a stone at had been left unbroken. It was yet another door into the sorceress's world. The casual passerby found no reason to linger there. Those who needed Faey made their way through drifts of leaves and shadows and fallen roof beams to the cupboard door beneath the stairs.

Mag opened the door for Camas. A bell rang faintly in the undercity. The tutor, who had been silent until then, his birds' eyes flicking everywhere, looked at Mag incredulously. "A shop bell?"

"It's business," Mag answered.

They stepped through the cupboard door into the sorceress's house.

Faey, whose assessment of her visitors was astute and unpredictable, welcomed them accordingly. She had decided to give Camas Erl the last thing he expected: that seemed to Mag the only explanation for the languid, violet-eyed beauty draped across a couch who extended a lily-pale hand to him from out of a cavern of velvet cushions and filmy shawls. He accepted it uncertainly, still looking for the sorceress, trying, it seemed, to see into the lady's bones.

"How can I help you?" she asked with polite indifference.

He was at a loss himself, until he found the word he wanted. "Illusion," he murmured, studying her intently, as though she were something nameless and tropical that had floated in on one of Domina Pearl's ships. "Everything with you is illusion. Even your waxling. May I see your face?"

She sat up, scattering cushions. For a moment Mag, holding her breath, thought Faey would give him what he asked. But she only said, "Actually, I can't remember which face I had first. And if I show you what I am now, it would cost you more than you would ever want to give."

Sensibly, he yielded to that with a nod. She flung a few cushions over the back of the couch and patted the seat beside her. He joined her without a qualm that Mag could see. "Tea?" the sorceress suggested, and slid her insouciant, flower-petal eyes to Mag. "Perhaps?" she added doubtfully, as if she were not capable of wringing a stream of tea out of thin air. Mag left her alone with Camas. She waited until the sorceress summoned her silently. Then, laden with illusions of propriety in the shape of a tea tray, she returned to the room that Faey had composed like a mood around her, with its shadows and sultry purples, its whiff of scented wax and ash. There she found Faey pacing and Camas sitting on the couch, passionately discussing the history of Ombria with the fair, indolent illusion who nodded encouragingly from time to time but never spoke.

Mag put the tray down and listened.

"There are pieces to the puzzle missing," Camas said. He was tugging at his hair; his eyes glowed eerily in the red light from a stained-glass lamp. "And pieces that don't yet fit. What, for instance, precipitates the shift from city to shadow city? Is it sorcery? Has it to do with the precarious state of affairs in the House of Greve? The powerless heir, the bastard who cannot act? What secrets are hidden within the secret palace? What is there to gain by anticipating and surviving the shift? Domina Pearl believes that it is possible, if one can remain aware during the transformation, to amass enormous knowledge and power. To rule the shadow city when it emerges, since no one else will remember the previous city, and who ruled then. All will be accepted as it is revealed. All of which is why I am so eager to speak with you. You live in Ombria's past, its ghosts and memories. How far back do you remember? Were you alive before the previous shift? How many transformations have there been? Many? One? None at all? How old are you?"

The illusion of Faey inclined her head gracefully; Camas continued without listening for answers. Faey spoke then, her voice sliding within, beneath his words. "What do you expect to gain from what you call the transformation?"

Camas interrupted his own sentence with a word. "Enlightenment. And the power that comes with an unbroken memory of the history of the city. Domina Pearl's knowledge of sorcery may not survive the transformation if she herself is not aware of the shift. I want to stay alive, be aware of the shift from city to shadow, and I will ally myself and my abilities to anyone powerful enough to maintain the integrity of existence, knowledge, memory and experience through the transformation."

"Such as Domina Pearl?" the sorceress suggested. She kept her voice light, careless, but her eyes were very dark.

"Domina Pearl," Camas agreed. "Or you. Or perhaps even Ducon. He is another puzzle piece, I think. He is drawn to the hidden palace, and to the odd, unnoticed places in Ombria where the boundaries are visible between the city and its shadow. He draws them constantly."

"So you would pledge your loyalty to him or betray him, depending on the moment?"

"Or her. Or you," Camas answered, nodding briskly. Mag stared at him with wonder. "Exactly. Depending on the moment."

Faey raised a white-gold brow. Undeterred by her silence, Camas picked up the thread he had dropped some moments before and continued his conjectures about Faey, the past that surrounded her, and its connection to the shadow city.

"Is it true?" Mag asked her softly. "That the city is on the verge of change?"

The sorceress twitched an indolent shoulder. Her eyes, still on Camas, had narrowed. "Who knows? Who would know? This is a very foolish and very dangerous man."

"What will you do with him?"

She answered simply, "Give him what he wants. Let him walk into the past until he no longer remembers the way back." She eased onto the couch to merge with her illusion and poured Camas a cup of tea. The tutor, suddenly quiet, blinked at her confusedly.

"What — what were we saying?"

"You were telling me of your deep interest in Ombria's past. When you have finished your tea, Mag will show you the undercity." She offered him confections of whipped sugar, egg-white and chocolate; he swallowed one whole in his excitement.

"I cannot tell you how invaluable this would be to me. Nor how grateful I am. And will be in the future, and can be, if all goes as planned." He paused, sipped tea, then sat frowning at it without knowing why. His eyes went to Mag, questioning. She gazed back at him composedly, without pity. He said hesitantly to the sorceress, "You haven't asked me for anything in return. I thought that all magic has its price."

"Magic does," Faey said. "But let us consider this an exchange of knowledge. I'll tell you what you want to know and you'll tell me why you want to know it."

The tutor's eyelids drooped; his thoughts drained out of his face like water seeping into earth. "A fair exchange," he said equably, and raised the cup to his lips.

Mag showed him through Faey's house, from the high attic rooms where she kept her menagerie, to the spell-steeped chamber where she worked over her cauldron. He examined everything with interest, but murmured, "This is now, not past. Where does she keep her past?"

He found it in her ghosts.

Being a historian, he recognized some of them from old paintings: the immensely fat, warty and befurred merchant who had built many of Ombria's docks for his fleet of ships; a tiny, long-nosed woman who had painted three generations of the House of Greve; the balding, ferociously mustached duke who had forged an army out of the city's surprised citizens and defended Ombria from the closing maw of barbarian hordes attacking at once by land and by sea; the stripling in a long, moth-eaten robe who had written the first history of Ombria. Mag had never seen any of them before in her life. They all spoke, which startled her as well. The household ghosts she was accustomed to were a ruminant lot who could understand the present but spoke only to the past.

Faey was making them, she realized suddenly, as visions from the past kept wandering across Camas Erl's path, passing through doors without bothering to open them, or rising up from the depths of chairs that had been empty a moment before. Camas spoke to them all eagerly, amazed with his good fortune; each answered his questions willingly so long as it was alone, and held all his attention. The moment he became distracted by another, the one he was speaking to began to fade. As if, Mag thought, they existed only when he saw them.

They were leading him slowly, ghost by ghost, to the front door. He did not seem to notice. A tall, bronze-haired woman with close-set green eyes, dressed in a long tunic of hide and deer fur, a sword in a leather sheath hanging from her belt, walked him out the door as Mag opened it for them. Mag lingered on the steps; Camas Erl, his long fingers seeming to pluck his words out of the air as he gestured, strayed toward the river. Across the bridge another ghost waited, one less incongruous against the background of sunken mansions. Their opaque windows softly brushed by light from the river lamps, they looked as if they had opened their dreaming eyes to watch.

Camas crossed the bridge to the elegant lady in lavender silk who took his arm. Behind him, the warrior vanished. Mag sat down on the steps. The ghosts had him well in hand; he had forgotten her. She wondered how far Faey would send him. Parts of the undercity were impenetrable, even by Mag. They were so old, they seemed little more than visible memories, and no matter how she had tried to reach them, they remained always in the distance.

She toyed with the locket around her neck and wondered if Faey could conjure up her mother's ghost. If she were dead, she reminded herself. But she had never come to retrieve her child, and the three drops of blood in the locket had belonged to someone. Perhaps both parents had died, and a grieving friend had brought the baby to the sorceress. "Perhaps" could be spun endlessly into different tales; even telling herself all of them, she would still be none the wiser. She opened the thin leaves of the locket, one after another: blood, rose, charcoal. All she knew of the tale was those three words. Watching for Camas Erl and listening for Faey, she strung the words together in highly improbable ways. It doesn't matter, she told herself at last, coldly. It doesn't matter. I have always done without.

The door opened behind her. A ghost sat down beside her, or so she thought until she smelled its sweat. Faey's hair had fallen down; it looked more white than gold now. The perfect, listless oval face had grown pallid and seamed; her violet eyes sagged with weariness. But a smile clung to the still flawless lips, a small, wicked thing like an imp that had crawled out of the sorceress's mouth.

Mag felt a ghostly hand flutter down her backbone. She asked, "Will he come back?"

"Perhaps. When he gets hungry enough. But he will continue to see ghosts for as long as he desires them. We are the insubstantial ones to him now."

"Domina Pearl will miss him. He is supposed to be tutoring the prince."

The sorceress snorted. "I've done her a favor, if she only knew. That man would betray his own shadow. And for what? A child's tale."

"Is it?" Mag looked at her. "Is it only a tale?"

For a moment, the purple eyes grew dark, black as the little rags of shadows that Mag saw on empty streets or patches of barren ground, attached to nothing, seemingly blown at random from some place adrift in light.

But Faey only answered, "How would any of us know? The tale promises nothing. Camas Erl has been trapped in his own illusion."

"What will happen to Lydea if he doesn't return?"

"I suppose she will become the prince's tutor until Domina Pearl finds another. At least she can read and write." She drew limp, damp hair away from her neck and

waved away Mag's next question. "Not now, my waxling—
It was exhausting, remembering all that history."

"You remembered it?" Mag breathed.

"Well, yes. I was young once, you know." She dropped
a hand on Mag's shoulder and pushed herself up. The
darkness had faded from her eyes, but a certain grimness
lingered. "Stay out of the palace. If Domina Pearl truly
sees what Camas Erl says she does, then she is as mad as
he is. Without any help from me. Come in to supper now.
Camas Erl will likely eat illusions and get drunk on history
for some time before we see him again."

"Yes, Faey," Mag said absently, following the sorceress
in, her hand closed around blood, rose, charcoal, as though
the locket were a talisman. Ducon has his mysterious charcoal, too, she thought curiously. I wonder what he sees
with it.

"Mag."

"Yes, Faey."

"Don't 'yes, Faey' me. Listen to me this time."

"Yes, Faey."

TWENTY-ONE

This or That

D ucon stood at the edge of the shadow city, drawing. Deep within the hidden palace, he had been pulled like some perverse moth to the place that no light could penetrate. The doorway with the bare wood on one post, the painted irises on the other, held a darkness so palpable that it seemed, like the charcoal in his hand, a crucible in which anything might form. When he held a candle across the threshold, the black swallowed the fire completely. When he tried to step across it, he felt nothing beneath his foot. Sometimes he heard rain, a bird-cry, wind soughing through tall trees; mostly he was aware only of an intimation of vastness, silence, as though he stood at the edge of a world.

He saw nothing. So he let the charcoal imagine what might lie on the other side of the door. Faces came out of it, and fantasies of airy palaces, endless woods and frothy seas upon which sailed ships with bowsprits like the spiralling horns of unicorns. One face in particular it drew at random. Ducon found it on a figure riding through the wood, or standing on the top of one of the high towers. Once or twice the man wearing that face walked the streets of a city that might have been Ombria, if Ombria could harbor an entire forest of ships' masts, and the windows overlooking its twisted streets were filled with flowers.

Wishes, he thought. Dreams. That's all the charcoal held: a child's prosperous, perfect world, a city of ceaseless delights. Still, it seduced him, kept him coming back to that worn, silent, rain-riddled room, that doorway full of nothing.

He had to be very careful moving through the palace. Domina Pearl insisted that he be guarded at all times, not only for his own sake, he suspected, but for the sake of her growing curiosity about what he did when he vanished into the secret palace. He had not seen Sozon or Kestevan again, but Domina Pearl had not frightened all of the conspirators away. He glimpsed the younger ones now and then, and knew they watched him. He found ways of eluding his guards when he wanted to, but though his secrets remained safe, he did not.

Neither, it seemed, did Camas Erl, who left the palace one afternoon after tutoring Kyel and had not been seen since.

The Black Pearl seemed inordinately incensed over the loss of a tutor.

"First you vanish," she snapped at Ducon when she summoned him to the library to show him the lack of

Camas. Kyel and Lydea were waiting for the tutor with
her. Both seemed indifferent to his absence, though Ducon
suspected that but for her disguise of calm and composure,
Lydea would have been tearing at her fingernails. "And
now Camas Erl. Where would he have gone?"

"I am at a loss," Ducon answered, which was true: he
would first of all have suspected Domina Pearl.

"You are close to him. Where does he go? What does
he do?"

"He comes here," Ducon answered blankly. "He reads
and works on his history of Ombria. Perhaps he went to
research something."

"When he should be with the prince? And without telling me?"

"It does seem unlikely."

"Does anyone want him dead?"

"For what?" Ducon asked, startled. "Why would anyone kill a tutor? Perhaps he ventured into the streets,
though it's not his habit. He might have been hurt."

"You know the streets better than anyone in this palace. Look for him. No." She closed her eyes, touched them
with fingernails as curved and dark as black beetles' backs.
"You must stay here with the prince. Tutor him yourself
when the girl is finished with his letters. I don't want them
left alone in here, not even under guard. Go and look for
Camas when you've finished. You'd know the odd alleys
and rat holes to search, I'm sure. Arm yourself and do not
leave the palace without a guard. Try to be careful."

He inclined his head and watched her leave, amazed
that she did not precipitate a furious wake of fallen books
and scattered papers behind her. Lydea sat beside Kyel,

who was gazing listlessly at the paper and ink in front of
him. She said his name softly, and then hers, in what must
have been a ritual greeting between them.

"My lord Kyel. I am Mistress Thorn."

He lifted his head, looked at her. The change in his
face, hope flowering out of the mute, weary despair in it,
made Ducon's throat close.

"I am the Prince of Ombria," Kyel whispered, "and you
are my secret Rose."

"Yes, my lord." She lifted her head, met Ducon's eyes;
he searched, fascinated, but could not find the secret Rose
at all within the cool, proper face of Mistress Thorn. "My
lord Ducon," she said, "do you have any idea —"

"None at all."

"I fear that if the regent examines my education too
closely while Camas Erl is away, she will not be entirely
pleased."

He put a finger to his lips. "The ink pots may have
ears. You don't look as though you are afraid of anything,
Mistress Thorn."

"If you leave," Kyel said abruptly, "I will go with you."

"My lord," she answered carefully, "I do not intend to
go anywhere until you learn enough to write the story of
the fan in several languages."

"Will that take a long time?"

"A very long time," she whispered, "since I will have
to learn them first. Now. Perhaps, as your cousin is here,
you could practice writing his name in case you ever need
it."

He bent willingly over the work. Ducon watched him
a while, soothed by the tiny island of peace they made for

themselves in the troubled and dangerous place. It would end soon enough. But for that moment at least, the child remembered that he had a heart.

Ducon stayed with them, teaching Kyel randomly about scorpions and tidal waves and such, trying to keep the struggling recognition alive in his eyes. The Black Pearl returned for Kyel in the early afternoon. Ducon walked to his chambers, guards flanking him at every step, to get his paints and paper and the sword he never bothered to wear except at court. Then he went through a door beside the fireplace in his bedchamber, and made his way alone through hidden corridors to the cellar and down a vaulted passage beneath the back gardens to the street.

Where to look for Camas Erl eluded him completely. But Lydea was right: if Domina Pearl was forced to look for another tutor and questioned Lydea too closely about her background, the sorceress's spell might unravel completely under her probing gaze. Lydea would be found under a pier with a broken neck and Kyel would become a living ghost. Therefore, Ducon had to find the missing tutor.

He made inquiries among the taverns and brothels he knew best, but without great hope. If Camas had wanted to visit such places, he would have asked Ducon to come with him. The tutor was retiring and abstemious; the idea of him walking alone through the door of some ale-soaked den called the Mackerel Smack and quaffing down a tankard seemed ludicrous.

Twilight brought Ducon back to the palace, certain that Camas would more likely have lost himself in the maze of the hidden palace before he found trouble in the streets.

He returned to his room the way he came, left his drawings there, and stuck his head out the door to check on his guards. They were too ensorcelled to be embarrassed or furious with him, but they were confused and very reluctant to admit to Domina Pearl that they had misplaced Ducon Greve. They hadn't, his presence assured them. He vanished back into his chamber and went from there into the secret palace.

He was making an erratic, impulsive path toward places he thought Camas might have found when he began to hear voices.

He stopped to listen.

There was a rustling in the walls, an occasional word, squeals from the floorboards. He started to say Camas's name and didn't. There were too many feet. They seemed to be moving down a parallel corridor, or through chambers opening into one another on the other side of the wall. Guards, he thought, searching for Camas. But Domina Pearl's guards did not move furtively or whisper. His mouth tightened.

It was easy for him to elude the young conspirators; they had no idea where they were going in the labyrinth of forgotten rooms and hallways. Ducon retraced his steps, slipped through a door or two and blew out his candle. He saw them ahead in the hallway, their faces lit by their own tapers, absorbed, eager, as they opened doors, thrust their fires into dark rooms to search them, then closed the doors again, trying to make no noise beyond their breathing and occasional, muffled arguments.

Ducon followed cautiously, wondering if they could possibly lead him to Camas. He couldn't begin to guess what they were looking for. They separated at one point, scattered through what he knew to be rooms empty but for cobwebs and mice and his own dusty footprints. He hid himself where they agreed to meet and heard their whisperings when they regrouped.

"It must be in another part of the palace. There's nothing here."

"Ducon might know."

"We can't ask Ducon; he'll want to know why. Besides, what if he betrays us to Domina Pearl the way he betrayed Hilil Gamelyn?"

"He hasn't yet. And I don't believe he would betray anyone to her. He hates her."

"She hasn't taken anything from him."

"He's a bastard; he doesn't have anything. No lands, no title worth anything, nothing to lose except a bed in the palace and an allowance that the regent controls. Unlike our fathers."

Ducon, behind a door in a room they had already searched, heard a sharp, bitter explosion of breath. "I can't believe what she's taking. She told my father yesterday that any ship docking in Ombria henceforth will be considered the property of the Prince of Ombria, and all the goods therein. She has already appropriated the docks and the harbor fees for her pirates. Now she's stealing ships. My father has half a dozen on the open sea; there's no way to get word to them."

"She took lands from my uncle that have been in our family for generations," someone else said as vehemently as was possible in a whisper. "She showed him a map drawn centuries ago when the land belonged to the House of Greve. It was given to my family! She said the land was improperly deeded and should have been reclaimed a hundred years ago. She wants the timber on it, my uncle said, for more ships."

"Why not? No one will dock here after this but her ships. Ombria will be completely dependent on her stolen goods."

"We have little time to waste searching, and none of us knows anything about poisons. I say we disguise ourselves as guards and smother him in his bed."

"Poison is more subtle, and would make the Black Pearl immediately suspect."

"We could poison her instead of Kyel."

Ducon felt his heart clench like a fist and hammer against his ribs. He bowed his forehead against the door, cold sweat beading along his lip, his hairline. The unaccustomed weight of the sword at his side caught his attention, tempted him. He forced himself to listen.

"We discussed that. We agreed." Their timbreless whisperings made them all anonymous; he could not match faces to their voices. "She is too unpredictable. Ducon might be knowledgeable and cunning enough to kill her, but he refuses to act against her. If he thinks she killed Kyel—"

"He'll kill her. So. End of the Black Pearl's reign. And no one will ever suspect us."

"What if—"

"There are no what if's."

"She could blame Ducon."

"No one would believe her now; she's gone too far already."

"What if she kills Ducon when he attacks her?"

There was a brief silence. Ducon, gripping his sword hilt so hard his fingers might have turned to metal, held his breath while they pondered.

"Then we are lost," someone acceded in a tendril of sound. "We flee with the rats out of Ombria. This is our only hope."

"But where in this maze does she keep her poisons?"

Ducon opened the door.

He had drawn the sword before he realized; it was just there, a long flare of silver from the taper light, rising in a slow, strangely elongated moment during which every stunned, mute face turned to him etched itself indelibly in his head. Then the tip of the sword came gracefully to rest on bare skin just above the fine embroidered collar of the most fervid conspirator. His eyes changed. Ducon, staring at him, felt himself moving and watching from a distance, for the blink of an eye, the shifting muscle in the throat beneath his blade that would make a decision for him. The young man was motionless, his face the color of his candle; around Ducon no one breathed.

The sword trembled in his hand, fire rippling down it. He felt the fury then that he had not dared feel before, that had separated him from himself. The young man, his blanched face going slack, his eyes closing, tried for a word.

"Be quiet," Ducon advised, his own voice barely enough to cause a flame to flicker. The sword, like his rage, still had arguments of its own; neither would yield yet. He freed it finally, drew the blade back and drove it with all his strength into the wall. Blood from a thread-thin nick in the

side of the young man's neck flicked like a scatter of gar-
nets against the paint. He reeled abruptly, doubled up, and
retched.

Ducon sheathed the sword, his hands shaking. No one
even tried to speak. The man who had almost died straightened slowly, painfully, leaned back against the wall, facing
Ducon again. The passion had gone from his eyes; the expression in them, weary, hopeless, reminded Ducon of
Kyel.

Ducon breathed suddenly, his voice catching, "If Kyel
dies, I will kill you. One by one. I have drawn all your
faces."

"My lord—" the young man whispered helplessly.

"Leave the Black Pearl to me."

TWENTY-TWO

Tutors Minus Two

Lydea saw the change in Ducon when he came to her door early the next morning. Like hers, his true face had vanished; the mask that hid it was rigid, unsmiling, its eyes guarded. Mistress Thorn received a stranger into her chamber, who said tautly to the stranger that she was, "I can't find Camas Erl, and Kyel's life hangs in a very precarious balance."

Lydea felt the blood startle out of her face; Mistress Thorn only folded her hands tightly and asked gravely, "What can I do?"

"Don't leave his side while you're with him. Especially if anyone you don't expect enters the library."

"You'll be with us," she reminded him, suddenly unsure even of that. So was he; he put a hand to his face, rubbed the fading bruise absently and winced.

"Domina Pearl confers in the mornings with her advisers," he murmured. It was a polite title for what found its way out of the streets and docks to her council chambers. "She won't know I'm gone."

Lydea swallowed drily. "Where?"

"There's a secret place I want to find," he said very softly. "I'll search as quickly as possible, and return before she comes for the prince. If anyone enters the library while you're alone with him, call the guards in. If Domina Pearl returns there before I do, suggest to her that I might have heard a rumor of Camas Erl and have gone to investigate."

"What—what should I teach the prince?" she asked, panicked at the thought.

"Anything. It doesn't matter." He stooped, picked up a book from the clutter on the floor beside her bed. "You've been studying. What is all this?"

"Histories and tales. Camas asked me to read them and write down references to the story of the fan."

"The what?"

"The shadow city. What he calls the transformation. He thinks it's real."

Ducon looked at her silently a moment; she could not fathom his expression. "Do you?"

"I don't know. How does anyone know? If it truly happens, no one remembers. And yet you can glimpse the tale there in all those books. It slips out unexpectedly like sun on a cloudy day, a shimmer of light across the world. And then it's gone, but it never fades that quickly from your heart. The heart remembers. And so the tale worked its way into history."

He was still gazing at her. She saw the light pass

through his eyes, turn them silver, and then stark again, metallic. "Strange," he whispered, then found his voice again. "Maybe that's what happened to Camas Erl."

"What?"

"He was transformed."

"Ducon." Her fingers, still locked together, felt icy. "I'm very frightened."

"Yes." You should be, his face told her. Then he went to her, took her hands. His own were not much warmer, but his voice became less distant. "You," he said gently, "are the prince's Mistress Thorn and she is a woman of remarkable strength and ability. She is where Kyel has hidden his heart, and she will yield that to no one."

"Where are you going?" she asked him. "What are you searching for?"

But he would not tell her.

He met her in the library later; they waited together for the regent and the prince. The Black Pearl, her mouth clamped so hard she looked lipless as a tortoise, let loose a few terse words about Camas Erl's absence. Lydea expected the fuming air around her to rumble with sullen thunder, snap minute bolts of lightning. To Lydea's relief, she did not linger. She had urgent business, she told Ducon with exasperation; he should stay to tutor Kyel and then continue his search for Camas.

She left. Lydea sat close to the prince, gave him their private greeting, and was rewarded with the rising sun of recognition in his eyes. When she turned her head, glanced around for Ducon, he had already gone.

Mistress Thorn kept her voice calm; Kyel noticed nothing amiss. But when, after an hour or so, she strayed from letters into history, she felt him fidget. Hers was not the voice of history, and Ducon was the other safe stepping-stone above the angry current of it that was flooding through Kyel's life. He turned his head toward the table behind them, where Ducon would have sat drawing while he waited for them to finish.

He turned back, said with curious composure, "Ducon teaches me this."

"Ducon is busy, my lord. I will tutor you today. Do you mind?"

He shook his head without perceptible distress and shifted closer to her, to lean over the book she read from and watch her moving finger beneath the words.

Ducon returned so quietly she did not realize he was with them until, struggling through some rudimentary math, both of them counting on their fingers, she glanced back in despair at her ignorance. There he was, reading quietly, his long legs crossed on a chair, one elbow propped on the table, his hand shadowing his face. Lydea wanted to melt with relief. Mistress Thorn in a thicket of numbers and no way out, opened her mouth to request help.

There was a step at the threshold of the far door. A shadow intruded, a faceless figure falling starkly across the polished floor. Lydea, the words catching in her throat, watched it. Ducon did not move, except to lift his pale head slightly, his fingers repositioning themselves along his cheekbone. She saw him in profile; his back was to the door. But he had stiffened; despite the languid pose, he was aware and listening. Whoever stood at the door did not enter. The shadow watched him for a while; Lydea watched the shadow.

Then it turned and was gone in a quiet step or two. Kyel touched her hand. "Mistress Thorn," he said in the careful voice he had learned for his survival, "may we use our thumbs?"

"I always do," said Mistress Thorn. She watched the prince count and then form his answer with pen and ink: an egg with a tail curling over its back like a lap dog. Quick, light steps startled Lydea again; Mistress Thorn turned with graceful composure, an uplifted brow. But it was only Ducon coming back; the tutor felt even Mistress Thorn's prim face ease.

Then she stopped breathing. Ducon, glancing at the open book on the table, asked swiftly, "Is Camas back?"

No, her mouth said without sound. She found her voice with an effort and rose. "Practice your numbers, my lord, while I speak to your cousin."

Ducon waited for her to join him on the other side of the room, his face closed again, tense, his fingers splayed across the open pages.

"Someone was here," he murmured.

"You were," she said helplessly. "You were sitting there and reading." His hand rose from the book, closed on her arm. "Someone tried to come in. Whoever it was saw you and left."

She saw his face turn as pale as paper. He loosed her slowly, sat down on the table. He tried to speak, swallowed. His eyes turned molten suddenly, she saw with astonishment, silvery with unshed tears.

"It wasn't me," he whispered.

"It looked like you."

"Did you see his face clearly?"

"No. You had your—he had his hand—" Her throat closed, burning, though she did not know why. "Ducon, who was he?"

"He came out of my charcoal. I saw him in the streets; I've seen him in dreams. I see him in the absolute darkness at the heart of the secret palace. On the boundary between shadow and light."

"Is he you?" she asked incredulously.

"No. If he had let you see his face, you would have guessed, even without knowing either of us, that he might be my father."

Her eyes widened; she felt the spell fraying like cobweb across her face. Ducon touched her again in warning. Her hands rose to her waist, clasped tightly; her face quieted itself, firmed within its mask.

"My lord," she said softly, "perhaps you could show the prince where your father might be placed on the family tree."

"I think, Mistress Thorn," he answered unsteadily, "that we would need a different family tree entirely."

When the regent came for the prince, all was as she expected it to be: Ducon leading Kyel through some tangled patch of grammar, and Mistress Thorn reading at the far end of the room while she waited to be dismissed.

She took the book with her when she left. It was the one the stranger had been reading: a collection of children's tales. It seemed a peculiar choice for a man who had wandered between worlds in response to his son's need. Ducon's father, she thought wonderingly. The unsolved mystery of the court of Ombria. Who was he, in his own world? And how had Royce's sister caught his eye, drawn him across the elusive boundaries between light and shadow and time? Or had she gone to him?

Or had they met at the conjunction of their worlds, the place where air and water kissed, and the white-hot blaze of fire streaked out of the sky to ignite the earth?

Ducon's mother had never said. She had just borne her white-haired child who, if Ducon guessed correctly, was heir to both worlds, one impenetrable and the other all too likely to be the death of him.

Lydea tried to imagine, as she ate her solitary meal in her room, where he had gone that morning, what he was plotting that he would not tell her. Then she continued reading the book the stranger had chosen. She was completely unsurprised when she came across an archaic version of the story of the fan.

The Black Pearl was no happier the next morning with the prolonged absence of Camas Erl.

"Come with me," she said brusquely to Ducon. "You have wandered through my private rooms, tried to pry into my secrets, tried to discover what I know and what I can do. I can find Camas Erl, but I need help from someone with intelligence, strength and discretion. He is not here to help me with this; you must take his place."

Ducon started to speak, faltered. He stared at her, the bruise on his face suddenly vivid against his pallor, as if she had struck him. She gave him her feral smile.

"You trust too easily. Like your uncle did. I taught Camas all those years while he was teaching you. I find him helpful and I do not wish to lose him. But if he has betrayed me as well, then you will help me kill him. I have my ways."

Still he could not find words. Lydea, her heart pounding, resisted every impulse to draw the listless Kyel close to her. Even Mistress Thorn was blinking rapidly, discomposed. Ducon spoke finally, huskily.

"Why me? Anyone off the streets would do for you. Why reveal your secret powers to me?"

"Because," she said contemptuously, "you have shown me that I have nothing to fear from you." She summoned guards into the room to watch over the prince. "Let no one enter," she ordered. "Hold anyone who comes here." Her baleful gaze swung to Lydea then, boding no good to Mistress Thorn. "Camas chose you; I must trust that, for the moment. But if you speak of this I will tear out your voice and drop it down the nearest drain."

Mistress Thorn bowed her head speechlessly. The Black Pearl eyed the young prince. But nothing in his blank face told her that he had paid the slightest attention to anything she had said. She gestured imperiously to Ducon. His face rigid, he followed her out of the room without a backward glance.

Mistress Thorn found herself trembling. She sat down beside Kyel, silent until she felt the imperturbable mask of the spell conceal her thoughts. He had understood something, she realized; he leaned against her for comfort even before she said her name.

To her relief, Ducon came to her at some black hour of the night. He brought a taper in with him, and lit her candles while she pulled her dishevelled hair out of her eyelashes and her mind out of nightmares. She searched his face silently; it looked very pale, hollow with weariness and vaguely stunned. She sat up; he sat down beside her, ran his hands through his hair until it spiked.

"She opened the door for me," he whispered incomprehensibly, "and I went in. I've been searching everywhere for that door."

"To her secrets, you mean?"

"The place where she works. She sleeps there, too," he added. "In a kind of cocoon. I think it makes nightly repairs on her raddled carcass."

"Did she find Camas?"

"After a fashion. He seems to have wandered into history. He was talking to a lot of ghosts. I had to shift some heavy mirrors for her, and tell her what I know about the sections of Ombria they saw."

"What part of Ombria has so many ghosts?" she asked bewilderedly. Then she answered herself, with a suck of breath. "The undercity."

"Yes."

"Is that where he is? With the sorceress?"

"After a fashion. He's lost to the world and babbling to ghosts. You met him. You saw how he is. Temperate and predictable. So I thought." He rose suddenly, not before she glimpsed the cold flare of anger in his eyes. "He lied to me and he would have betrayed Kyel. I can't forgive him that. His clothes are torn and dirty; his hair falls across his face; he looks as though he eats whatever ghosts eat. Domina Pearl had no idea where he could be in the undercity; she has never been there. She couldn't tell if Faey had anything to do with the ghosts haunting Camas. If he knew they existed, he would easily have found them irresistible and gone looking for them on his own. She tried to summon him back here."

"He wouldn't come?"

"He didn't seem to hear her." He paced a step or two restively, then turned back to Lydea. "She wants me to go there and bring him out. With Faey's help, she said, if I needed it. She said the sorceress bore her no ill will and always did what she asked."

Lydea thought of the sorceress striding down the riverbank with Ducon dangling over her shoulder, brought to a halt mid-pace by the notion that she might in any way be compared to Domina Pearl. "Really."

"So she thinks. I wanted to tell you now so that you'll know where I am tomorrow."

A pulse of fear beat in Lydea's throat; she swallowed. "Leaving me alone—"

"To tutor Kyel."

"With a woman who wants to tear my voice out and me having to count on my fingers to multiply."

He sat down on the bed, shifted a strand of hair from her face with his fingers. "Even now, you manage to look like the poised and decorous Mistress Thorn. Domina Pearl has far too much on her mind to remember that you exist."

"I hope so," she whispered. Then somehow the dispassionate Mistress Thorn found herself gripping his wrist. "But, Ducon, Camas knows who I am! He told me so! He'll tell her—"

"No, he won't," Ducon answered quickly. "He knew and didn't tell her; he would be caught in his own lie. I'll remind him of that when I find him. I'll be back as soon as I can; I don't dare leave Kyel long."

"Be careful. Don't get lost with Camas."

"I don't intend to."

Something in his voice made her look sharply at him. "What do you intend?"

"To ask him a question. To ask him what he wants so profoundly that he would destroy the House of Greve and the city he loves for it."

He rose. His hand hovered an instant near her cheek, but he turned and left without touching Mistress Thorn.

TWENTY-THREE

Thrice a Fool

Mag, returning to the palace in the silvery light of dawn along with the milk and carts from the market, slipped into the kitchens with a couple of groaning baskets of squash in her arms, deposited them in a likely place, picked up a bucket and cloth along the way, and left through a different door. For once she had dressed carefully, in something plain and dark. She endured the bleak stares of what seemed endless lines of Domina Pearl's guards, standing as stiff and mute as mile-posts along the hall. They did not question the drudge with the hunched shoulders and lowered head going to clean up a spill. She went down the first stairway she could into the unguarded lower quarters, where she would have passed Ducon without lifting her head if he had been a step ahead of himself.

As it was, he rounded a corner just as she hurried past

it and they met precipitously, with a clang of bucket. Ducon, gripping Mag's arm to keep her upright, bent speechlessly to rub his shin. She stared in amazement at the fish-bone hair while the bucket rattled across the floor and rocked gently to a halt.

Ducon let go of Mag finally. He seemed to take her silence for a drudge's timidity, or fear of being punished for having been tripped over. He barely glanced at her, just reached for the bucket absently, his thoughts already proceeding down the corridor. The dry floor caught his attention. Water did not make its own way to those parts of the palace; an empty bucket made no sense. He looked at her for the first time.

He didn't speak immediately either. He took her arm again, moved her a step or two closer to the nearest spray of tapers along the wall, and studied her. "Hair," he murmured finally. "A pile of straw and full of pins. Eyes the color of walnut shells . . ." His voice trailed away; he looked suddenly puzzled, as though he had remembered her from some dream, perhaps, or within a different light. She felt it too. It was what had drawn her there, that sense of recognition. "Mag," he said finally, and she nodded.

"Why do I feel I know you," he wondered, "when I have never met you before?"

"I don't know." She stood rigid under his scrutiny, still startled by being seen before she chose. The hall was shadowy beyond the taper lights, and, but for their hushed voices, very quiet. "I was hoping you could tell me."

"You came looking for me?"

"Yes."

"Does Faey know you're here?"

"No."

He shifted slightly, as though to hide her from invisible eyes. "This is the last place you should be."

"I know." Her hand closed tightly on the locket hidden beneath the drab wool. "But there is no one else to ask about the charcoal."

He slid his own hand into a pocket as though to touch something familiar, reassure himself. "Faey made it," he reminded her. "You could have asked her."

"Faey doesn't know everything. She says that you see with more than human eyes, but she doesn't understand why. Maybe she doesn't remember why; she must be as old as Ombria."

He was silent, studying her again with his inhuman eyes. "Perhaps it's because you've lived underground and with her magic all your life," he commented obscurely.

"What?"

"There's something unhuman about you, too." He pulled the charcoal out of his pocket impulsively, then considered it ruefully. Faint, glittering colors washed over it in the candlelight. "I wish I had the time to draw you. Maybe that would answer some questions."

"You have drawn me," she said. "But not with that."

His silvery gaze flicked to her again, surprised. "Have I? Surely not. I would have remembered you."

"You drew me in a tavern, the day Royce Greve was buried. I wore a long black veil; it hid my face."

"That was you?"He regarded the drudge with amazement. "That mysterious, elegant woman in black?"

"That was me. You were surrounded by young nobles who were trying to persuade you that it might be a good idea to kill both Domina Pearl and Kyel and put you on the throne instead."

His face grew taut. "You heard that."

"I followed you to the pier." She looked away from him, suddenly inarticulate. "I had a decision to make. About you. About myself."

"I remember," he said, his gaze indrawn now, expressionless. "Lydea told me that you were spying on me. Trying to make some decision about whether I should live or die."

"About whether or not I should help Faey dispose of you," she amended. "As it was, I had no choice. I meant to meddle with her spell during the making, but she gave me no chance; I tried to steal it, but she hid it; I searched everywhere for you to warn you, but I couldn't find you —"

"Why?" he asked abruptly. "After what you heard in the tavern and on the pier, why would you try to help me?"

"That night after the funeral when you were summoned to stay with Kyel because he was having nightmares, I was trapped under his bed." Ducon, astounded, tried to speak; nothing came out. "I couldn't leave because of the guards. Kyel trusted you. You lay awake all night watching while he slept. You go everywhere in Ombria; you're not afraid of anything." She looked down at the bucket he had picked up for the drudge. "Not even kindness."

He was staring at her. "You see my life far more clearly than I do."

"It made no difference in the end," she said. "I couldn't rescue you from Faey."

"She rescued me herself. After she tried to kill me."

"That was business."

"But why reverse her own spell and let me live?"

"That," Mag sighed, "was Faey. Even I don't always understand her."

"Ambiguities," he said nebulously. "Like the charcoal. It drew such magic that I couldn't put it down. It would have been the death of me, but I would have fought before I parted with it. And you. Spying on me and trying to save me from sorcery when I didn't even know you existed. Lydea told me that she would have died on the streets but for you. Who are you? Where did you come from?"

"That is what I hoped you could tell me" She slid a finger beneath the neckline of her dress, snagged the fine gold chain. She opened the locket, turned the thin, gold-framed leaves of glass until she came to the charcoal. "Someone left me like the morning bread in a basket on Faey's doorstep. I was wearing this, she said, when she found me. I've seen the drawings you've made with the magic piece of charcoal. I hoped this might be magic, too. I thought — I thought maybe it might hold my mother's face."

He made a soft sound, took the locket from her to look more closely. He brushed the charcoal recklessly with a finger. "Perhaps it does . . . How strange. Blood, a rose petal, and charcoal. There's a story."

"I know. But what? Please," she begged. "Draw with it. Now, if you have the time."

"Time is what I don't have this morning." He paused as a door near them opened abruptly and a portly woman in black hurried down the hall away from them, keys chiming at every step. He closed the locket carefully, put it back into her palm. "The Black Pearl ordered me to bring

Camas Erl back from the undercity. How did he find his way down there? Does Faey know he is there?"

"Yes. I brought him to her."

"You—"

"I was searching for you in the secret palace after Faey sent you the charcoal—"

"How did you find your way there?"

"I saw you come out of the door in the wall beside that great, fat urn."

"You're everywhere," he said, astonished again.

"Well, I went too far that day. I got trapped by Domina Pearl in her library. She locked me in without knowing that I was there. Camas Erl found me. He freed me, but he asked me questions, and he made me promise to take him to see Faey."

"So that's how," Ducon breathed. "But why?"

"He has some idea—He thinks—" She shook her head bewilderedly. Another door opened and closed; he drew her away from the taper light. "He's treacherous and rash and he doesn't make much sense. Can't you leave him down there? You're safer with him wandering among the ghosts."

Ducon shook his head. "For now," he said evenly, "I must do as I'm told." He took her arm again, and caught an amazed stare from a young woman tying her apron as she passed them. "But wait for me—"

"Where?"

He led her around the corner, down the hall. "I'll be back as soon as I can. We'll see then what comes out of your charcoal."

He pushed open one of the endless, identical doors. A

woman still in her nightgown and bent over a basin raised her dripping face, startled.

"This is Mistress Thorn," he said to Mag. "Rose, to you. Don't leave this room before I come back."

He closed the door. The woman cupped water in her hands and splashed away the mask of soap to reveal her true smile.

"Mag!"

She told Mag, in a harried fashion as she dressed, why she was disguised and under the same roof again as the Black Pearl. Mag peered closely, but could find little trace of the helpless, grieving beauty who had flung her sapphire heels into the sunflowers. Faey had done her work too well. Breakfast tapped at the door; Lydea shared it with Mag. They passed the teacup back and forth while Mag showed her the locket, and explained why she had come searching for Ducon.

Too soon, Lydea rose. "I must go. I'll be alone with Kyel until Ducon returns. Do you know other languages?"

Surprised, Mag nodded. "A smuggler taught me."

"Mathematics?"

"The baker's wife."

"History?"

Mag's mouth crooked. "I live with it. Why?"

Lydea studied her, a thumbnail caught between her teeth. "I wonder—" Her hand dropped. "No. I'd never be able to explain you to Domina Pearl. But I wish you could help me tutor Kyel; I know so little."

"You know more than he does," Mag guessed. She watched Mistress Thorn straighten a cuff, touch a hair pin. "You look—you look—"

"I know. So Ducon says. If only I could feel the way I look." She turned to Mag, held both her shoulders lightly, and her eyes. "I know you like to wander, but don't. It's far too risky. Ducon may be back before I am. Until then, there's a stack of history beside the bed."

She left. Mag sat down on the bed and stared blankly back at the blank walls.

The halls grew silent again. Domina Pearl, Lydea had said, would be busy in her council chambers all morning. Ducon might be gone half the morning or all day, depending. Mag had passed the enormous urn with the secret door behind it before she ran into Ducon. She could slip into the hidden palace for an hour and no one would be the wiser. She had seen the drawings Ducon had left in Faey's house; they hinted at some mystery in the empty rooms and shadowy doorways. The mystery had flowed through the charcoal and onto Ducon's paper. It seemed a living thing, that stick of ash and spit, a blind eye that saw invisible wonders and reflected them onto paper. Ducon himself had sensed the marvels; only that could explain all the shadows he drew. As though he expected that, by rendering shadow onto paper, he might peel away the visible darkness and illumine the mystery behind it.

But—"Once warned," she whispered, "no fool. Twice warned: once a fool." And she had been thrice warned, by Faey and Ducon and Lydea. So against her inclinations, she stayed put. Inspired by the thought of charcoal, she riffled through the books beside Lydea's bed, not in pursuit of history, but for a likely page. She found one finally, a blank flyleaf in the back of a book. Coaxing the charcoal out of the locket proved a simple matter; it fairly leaped into her hand when she turned the open locket upside down and tapped it. She handled the charcoal carefully; it was scarcely bigger than her thumbnail and no thicker than three leaves of the heavy, deckle-edged paper. Unlike Ducon's charcoal, it did not glitter. But it did surprise: the first few lines it drew seemed to come out of itself rather than anything on Mag's mind.

She stopped, studied the lines. An indifferent artist, she could still have drawn a face that a child could recognize: an oval, two dots and a smile. But what came out of the charcoal was not, by any stretch of the imagination, a human face. It looked mostly like a small whirlwind. She hesitated, not wanting to whittle away the magic on nonessentials before Ducon returned. But the corner she drew with seemed as sharp as ever. Curious, she let the charcoal roam at will again across the paper.

She paid no attention to the distant, rhythmic crashes at first; they were, for all she knew, part of the daily life of the palace. What the charcoal drew seemed chaotic, unrecognizable, but it fascinated her, for occasionally she could put a name to something in that chaos: a ringed finger, an ear. As though someone were forming or falling apart in the whirling dark. It was only when the din grew near enough to separate into coherent sounds—a door banging open, a sharp voice, heavy, booted footsteps—that she realized she was in trouble.

She stood up as the door of the room across from Lydea's was flung open. Paper and charcoal slid to the floor. She glanced desperately around the room, found the only possibility: the untidy bedclothes on the unmade bed. She had barely pulled them, sheets and all, into her arms when Lydea's door slammed open.

The Black Pearl stared at her. She dipped a hasty curtsey, and emitted the faint squeak of the terrified drudge. But the ancient eyes were not deceived. They recognized, after all those years, the secret-eyed waif who had swallowed a heart.

"You," she said acridly. She stepped into the room. Her guards crowded the doorway; there was no place to run. The locket hung open against Mag's dress; the strange drawing had landed at her feet; the charcoal, whole and seemingly unused, lay on the floor beside it. Mag's thumb and forefinger were black with it. Her eyes lowered, she felt Domina Pearl's face close to hers, smelled the odd, musty scent of her. The Black Pearl ran a claw into Mag's hair, jerked her head up. "I warned you about spying. You should have listened."

She caught a finger on a barbed pin then, and hissed. Mag stared, overcome by curiosity. What came out of the bony, wrinkled skin looked more yellow than red. She had lost a thumb, Mag saw then. Her face, stiff with rage, looked odd, as Faey's did sometimes when she first awoke: unfinished, missing a bone or a nostril. The Black Pearl had misplaced an eyebrow. And an ear, Mag realized with astonishment. Then she felt the blood slide completely out of her face.

She stared at the drawing. So did the Black Pearl, searching for her missing ear. She made a strange noise with her teeth, like a door hinge groaning, and ground the flake of charcoal beneath her boot heel until there was nothing left but a smear of black powder across the floorboard. Then she picked up the drawing carefully, as though her missing pieces might fall out of it. Mag felt her eyes sting suddenly, and closed them. A few more moments, and something vital might have been sucked out of Domina Pearl into the drawing. If only she had begun it sooner, or if she had listened sooner and hid . . .

The locket chain bit into her neck and snapped. The Black Pearl pushed her roughly toward the door. "Take those pins out of her hair," she said to the guards. They held her, following orders ruthlessly and efficiently, until Mag's hair fell down and she was blind with unshed tears. She refused to blink; tears fell anyway, revealing a floor littered with barbed, jeweled pins to greet Ducon when he returned for her.

"So the waxling learned to cry human tears," the Black Pearl said. She seized Mag's hair again, found her eyes. "Did the sorceress send you here with that charcoal? Did she make it? Is she plotting against me?"

"No—" Mag gasped; the talons in her hair shook her silent.

"She is beginning to get in my way. She traps Camas Erl in the ruins of history; she sends you to pick at me like a vulture. Let's find out, shall we, exactly how much you are worth to Faey. If she truly cares for you, she will come and get you. Then I'll have you both, trapped in a place beyond the reach of time, where there is no history and the only ghosts are mine. You and you," she added to two guards, "wait here and bring me whoever comes through that door. The rest of you: take her and follow me."

The guards surrounded Mag, seized her arms, her hair. The Black Pearl led them through an unfamiliar door into the secret palace.

TWENTY-FOUR

Lost and Found

Ducon, having fallen blindly into the underworld, remembered only the door through which he had left
it. On the sign hanging above the door a pair of elegantly
gloved hands parted as though to reveal some marvel; bubbles of blistered paint floated between them. The tiny glove
shop was surrounded by hulking warehouses, pools of water and blood from a slaughterhouse, and stained wagons
bringing fresh hides to a tanner and taking tanned hides
away. Whether or not the shop had ever sold a pair of
gloves was as dubious a matter as whether anyone in pursuit of them would have ventured down such a bleak and
stinking street.

Inside the shop, there was nothing but a hollow of
walls and a stone stairway attached to the threshold and
leading directly down to the river. Ducon saw the lamps

along it still lit in the early morning hour. A sound below made him pause until he recognized it from his feverish stay in the sorceress's house: the rhythmic heave and sigh of gigantic bellows that was Faey snoring.

He was midway down the steps when the snoring stopped.

The sorceress was waiting for him at the bottom. She looked dishevelled, still half-dreaming, her face vague in the gentle lamplight, perhaps not all there. She yawned, voluminously and noisily, patting absently at the billows and snarls of her hair. It was completely white. One of her lovely eyes was turquoise, the other emerald, as though she had groped for them and put them on in the dark. Just beyond light, and just within his eyesight, Ducon glimpsed the glowing, restless currents of her powers that never aged, never slept.

She murmured something, pulled a mirror out of no-where and delicately straightened the line of one rumpled brow. The mirror vanished; she said, "Ducon, what are you doing here at this hour of the morning?"

"I've come for Camas Erl."

She sniffed. "He's not worth the rescue. I'd leave him, if I were you."

"Domina Pearl sent me to bring him back," he answered, and saw a glint in one lowered eye as if it had turned as darkly glittering as the wild magic around her. She sat down on the stairs, gestured for him to join her.

"Did she now?" she asked lightly. "He'd betray her, too, with no more thought about it than he'd spare to clean his teeth. He's demented."

"Maybe, but she wants him. Do you? Will you stop me?"

"No. Take him. I find him annoying. But you'll have to get his attention away from those ghosts. He's lost in history and babbling about transformations. I doubt that he'd recognize you unless you're dead."

"Will you help me? I was told to ask you. Domina Pearl said that you have never refused her anything."

Her face turned away from him; she leaned back against the steps, idly watching something, perhaps the play of her own magic through the underworld. "No," she said softly. "I haven't. And no, I won't help you. I find I thoroughly dislike them both, and I do not care a cat's breath if Camas Erl and the Black Pearl are ever reunited in the world above." She looked at Ducon again, lifted a finger and turned his face to examine the bruise on it. Her eyes grew suddenly black, pupilless, like the empty eyes of ancient statues. "Even you," she said. "Even you deceive."

"I have to, in that palace." The dark, rich currents of her magic flowed through her eyes then; he could not look away.

"You say one thing to the Black Pearl, another to Kyel, another to the man who nearly killed you. He tried again?"

He nodded, remembering the cold metal against his throat, the manticore's mad eyes. "But I never lied to him. He expected me to and panicked. I haven't seen him lately."

"There are others . . ."

"Yes," he heard himself say very softly. "They want me to kill her and rule Ombria."

"Will you?"

He hesitated, thinking of the Black Pearl and her mirrors watching him. The sorceress smiled. "She cannot hear you now. You are in my mirrors, within my illusions. So," she added, reading his mind. "These others, you never tell them yes, you never tell them no."

"For Kyel's sake," he whispered. His hands had clenched, holding all the possibilities, all that he tossed into the air and kept from falling in the world above. "They see no need for him; they would as soon be rid of him. They are young, ambitious, desperate—"

"So you are holding up the sky over the young prince's head."

"Trying."

"Which is why you are down here to rescue the unscrupulous tutor for the wicked regent."

"For now," he answered, "I do her bidding."

"For Kyel's sake. And for whose sake are you deceiving me?" He stared at her, his face slackening with surprise, and her eyes turned the pale matte brown of walnuts. "Why," she asked, "do I find my waxling on your mind?"

"I had no intention of deceiving you," he protested, startled by her perception. Intent on Camas Erl, he had forgotten Mag. The sorceress queried him with a sparse brow; he admitted, "I would have let Mag tell you that we met. I found her in the servants' halls; she was looking for me." Both brows went up at that. But she let him finish. "She wanted me to draw with the piece of charcoal in her locket. She thought I might coax her mother's face out of it."

"Did you?"

"I had no time. I left her waiting for me in Lydea's room."

The sorceress exhaled harshly; Ducon half-expected her breath to flame. "I told her to stay out of that palace."

"I warned her not to wander." He watched Faey, asked cautiously, "Do you know who her mother is?"

"I have not the slightest idea," Faey said. "Nor have I ever been much interested in the question." But she was now, Ducon guessed. Her brows had creased; she studied something invisible in the air between them. Then she studied him. The flare and welter of her powers transfixed him with their intensity and secret beauty; again he could not look away. "You see me," he heard her say, "in ways no other human can. Except Mag. I have hidden such things from her since she was small, so that she would do my bidding without being distracted by them. But when I first found her, I saw the reflection of my powers in her eyes. She would try to catch the glittering in her hands. Someone left her charcoal. She saw it and connected it to you."

"What are you saying?" His own voice sounded far away, very calm. "That we are somehow kin?"

"What do you think?"

"I had never seen her before this morning. But when I looked at her, I thought we must have met, in some other time and place."

"Perhaps you did."

She loosed him too abruptly; he felt stranded, bewildered, a fish out of water and all her haunting currents out of reach. Her eyes held human color again. She contemplated him dispassionately, as though she were examining a crooked stitch in a vast and complex tapestry. "I will be extremely interested to see what comes out of that flake of charcoal. But she could have asked me to summon you, rather than running off to the palace and putting herself under the Black Pearl's nose. I do wish at times that I had encouraged her to think."

She stood up. "But wait," he pleaded. "Tell me. What time? What place?"

"How should I know? Maybe the charcoal will tell you. Domina Pearl is right," she added, "about one thing. I will help you if you ask me. But don't ask me for help with Camas Erl. Deal with him yourself." She wandered away from him, yawning again. "I'm going back to bed."

He followed the path the lamps lit along the river; here and there the great houses illumined a window to watch him pass and then grew dark again. The river narrowed, quickened, its surface trembling like the eyes of dreamers. The sun rose. Gold, dusty crossbeams of light fell from forgotten windows, drains, the broken husks of buildings whose floors had long since fallen. The river ran deeper, sloping down toward earlier times. Houses on its banks grew smaller, clustered closely together; old streets looped and coiled like mazes. Once he smelled the sweet, astonishing scent of grass newly cut in a field, another time the scent of lavender.

He walked until he saw how far he would have to go to reach the beginning of time in the undercity. The fragmented, ephemeral memories of shadowy walls, towers, the river fanning into a vast black sea, seemed too far to reach except in dreams. Perhaps, he thought, kneeling on the riverbank for a handful of water, Camas had gone that far beyond history.

But the tutor had not yet reached the end of time. Ducon saw him finally, walking across a bridge of rough-hewn stone arching over the river. His head cocked in concentration, arms folded, he was listening to a huge, burly man in silk and fur, white fox heads dangling over one shoulder, his boots trimmed with fringes of ermine tails. Camas's tangled hair slid over his haggard face, caught in the ragged stubble on his jaws. His clothes looked dank, muddy, as though he had walked through water; he was missing a shoe. But he spoke earnestly, eagerly, to the ghost as if it had stepped for a moment into the palace library to help the tutor with his research.

Ducon appearing out of nowhere at the end of the bridge made no impression on the tutor. He continued his thought without a flicker of recognition, as he stepped down to the bank, "And all of this happened during the reign of Sisal Greve, whom you say, contrary to all our written histories, would never have — " What Sisal Greve would never have done about what was lost forever as Ducon's fist slammed against the tutor's jaw. Camas tripped backward against the end of the bridge and sat down on it heavily, all his attention suddenly riveted on the living.

The ghost, ignored, vanished. The tutor, his wide, stunned gaze on Ducon, permitted no distractions; no one else appeared. Ducon flexed the bruised bones of his hand, then reached down for Camas's bedraggled collar and hauled him to his feet.

"Ducon," the tutor said bewilderedly. "What are you doing here?"

"Domina Pearl sent me to bring you back."

"But I'm in the midst of my research. Ducon, you would not believe what I have learned—" He stopped suddenly, looking confused, caught, Ducon guessed, between lies. He shifted his hold to the back of Camas's collar, twisted it, and pushed him upriver toward the sorceress's house. The tutor, turning his head fretfully, complained, "I can hardly breathe."

"You didn't hear me."

"I heard you. Domina Pearl sent you."

"She showed me her secret room, where she makes her spells and her poisons, and puts her crumbling body to bed to regrow itself at night. She had me help her shift enormous mirrors to search for you. She said that you usually do such things, but you were missing, so—" His fingers tightened abruptly on the cloth at Camas's throat; the tutor, his breath rasping, flailed at his collar, tore a button off. He bent, hands at his knees, groping for breath. "All those years," Ducon said between clenched teeth, "you lied—"

"I never lied—You never asked—"

"Did you help her kill my uncle?" He heard Camas's breath stop for an instant. "Did you?"

"You must," the tutor said raggedly, "consider the consequences. The rewards are incalculable."

Gaunt as he looked, he still had more strength than Ducon realized. He felt it as the tutor straightened suddenly, and propelled a shoulder into Ducon's chest, trying to push him into the river. A ghost appeared, waited calmly for the outcome. Ducon shifted, rolling from under the tutor's weight, and caught Camas again as he lost his balance and reeled toward the water himself.

Camas fell to his knees on the bank. Ducon, standing behind him with one hand around his throat, the other clamped to his shoulder, said succinctly, "Don't fight me. Just explain. What is so important to you that you would kill one Prince of Ombria and put the next in such danger? Ombria is your passion, and Greve is its ruling house. Why?"

The ghost disappeared. Camas, shifting fitfully under Ducon's hand, said breathlessly, "I am so close — so close to understanding it myself —"

"Understanding what?"

"You must let me stay here. I've spoken to ghosts who have survived the last transformation of Ombria —"

"You've spoken to the sorceress's illusions," Ducon said flatly.

"No — They have been appearing to me freely. Listen to me. Perilous times, a desperate city, the ruling house in chaos, in danger — all of this signals the change, and causes it. The deeper Domina Pearl plunges the city into misery and hopelessness, the stronger its visions of hope and longing for change become. Do you understand? When the desire becomes overwhelming, the transformation becomes inevitable. It has happened before, it will happen again, and we are reaching that point —" He stopped, choking on his own words as Ducon's hand tightened.

"Because of you." Ducon felt cold fury bore through him like a blade of ice. "You and the Black Pearl are destroying Ombria for a fantasy — a child's tale —"

"No—" His fingers prying, Camas gained another word's worth of air. "Listen—"

"You listen. I'm not giving you back to Domina Pearl. Tale or true, you'll never know; you won't be here to see, and this change, if it comes, will more likely come from your absence than from any dream you spin out of history."

"What—"

"You are going on a very long sea journey to the outermost islands where Domina Pearl's ships stop to collect her strange plants and poisonous reptiles. You will never return to this city."

"Domina," Camas gasped, striving with Ducon's hands. "She'll stop you—"

"Not when I explain to her that you were conspiring with this sorceress against her. She'll put you on the ship herself."

"No—" The force of the tutor's desire overwhelmed him. One hand, groping upward, caught Ducon's shirt. "I must see it—I must be here—" He wrenched at Ducon; his other hand, scrabbling along the earth, found a stone. Ducon, jerking back, avoided the flailing weapon, but his grip loosened. Camas turned, his eyes desperate with visions. "No one," he said and swung the stone again as he pulled free. His weighted fist cracked across Ducon's face. The distant lamps turned suddenly to tiny pinpoints of light; Ducon fell endlessly into them, still hearing the tutor's voice. "No one will stop me."

"No one," the sorceress snapped, "is going anywhere."

Ducon raised his head. Blurred colors and textures took shape slowly into damp earth and the tip of the sorceress's blue silk shoe. He rolled unsteadily, spat blood.

The tutor, seeing yet another ghost in the willowy, red-haired beauty, stared transfixed across Ducon's prone body. Then he blinked as she said irritably to an elegant lord in black velvet and silver chains,

"Go away. All of you: back into the cauldron."

Blood streaked through Camas's face. He shifted, his mouth opening and closing soundlessly. "You didn't —" he managed finally. "You couldn't have made them all —"

"You," she said pithily, "are a fool of the first water." She held a slender, jewelled hand to Ducon and flicked him to his feet as though he were made of down. Then she skewered the tutor again with eyes the color of metal. "I didn't make them. I summoned them out of memory."

"You knew them all?" the tutor demanded hoarsely.

"Oh, stop," she said in exasperation. "I've been hearing you babble for days." She thrust a folded piece of paper at Ducon. The seal was broken, but he recognized it. He opened the paper. Faey, her words as staccato as the heels in the streets high above their heads, told him what it said before he read it. "That woman has Mag."

Ducon felt a sudden flare of pain where Camas had struck him. "I left her safe," he whispered, sickened. "I thought I did."

"She was never good at sitting still. The Black Pearl wants to know if my making of wax is worth anything to me before she unmakes it. And what I might consider offering her for its safe return."

"What will you do?"

"Whatever I must," she said succinctly. "For now, I'll consider an offer. You'll take it to her along with Camas Erl."

"No," he protested incredulously. "You must not give Camas back to her."

"I think that, under the circumstances, I should not like to offend the regent." She turned abruptly to Camas Erl, donning manners like a ball gown. "Forgive my brusqueness. I am distressed. I hope that before you go you will accept a pair of shoes?"

He spoke cautiously. "I would be grateful. I can't think what might have happened to my other shoe. As a matter of fact, I don't think I entirely understand what I have seen and done the past few — " He stopped, felt his chin. "Days?"

"And, perhaps, a cup of tea?'

"Yes. And if I could just speak to you for a few more moments, about your earliest memories? I know the regent will show herself grateful for anything that you can tell me."

"Then I will tell you anything," the sorceress said.

"I will not," Ducon said, his voice rising precariously, "put Camas Erl back under the same roof with Kyel." He took a step toward her, his fists clenched. "He helped Domina Pearl kill Kyel's father. You told me to deal with him. I will. I will kill him before I return him to the — "

She turned a face to him that seemed half bone, half nacre, and stripped of all human expression. Her eyes grew colorless, shrivelled; that white stare burned all language out of him, all thought. "I will do anything I must for my waxling," she said. He felt her voice like hoarfrost in his heart. "You will do as you are told."

Shedding centuries again, she slipped an arm through

Camas's, and accommodated herself, like one of her own ghosts, to his blistered hobble along the river, while Ducon, betrayed by his own spellbound bones, trailed helplessly in her wake.

TWENTY-FIVE

The Wild Hunt

Lydea, exposed to her own ignorance for the better part of a morning in the library and surrounded by guards who looked as though they might lop off her head for a misspelled word, was deeply grateful for Mistress Thorn's unruffled voice. She sat as close to Kyel as she dared, but did not touch him; she had no idea how much the Black Pearl saw out of the hard, unblinking eyes around them. Kyel seemed to sense her tension. He did not question her about Ducon, or why she only read him history and did not try to teach him words in other languages. She braved the silent guards stationed along the bookshelves to come up with *Simple Mathematical Principles*. She was struggling, in Mistress Thorn's sedate manner, to make sense of that for Kyel when Domina Pearl spun through the door like a bony, furious whirlwind.

She disconcerted Mistress Thorn, who sucked in a dust mote and gave a genteel cough as she rose. The Black Pearl, early by an hour or two, looked oddly dishevelled, peculiar, though she was scarcely there long enough for Lydea to examine. She carried a crumpled drawing in one hand; the other she held out peremptorily to Kyel.

"Come, my lord. Enough, Mistress Thorn. You may retire."

The thumb on that hand seemed withered and strangely dark. Mistress Thorn blinked at it, then curtseyed hastily. Kyel, taking the hand without expression, glanced back at Lydea as he left, his eyes wide, uncertain. Domina Pearl hissed something at him; he looked down at the floor instead. The guards followed her out.

Lydea, wondering, returned books neatly to the shelves, except for the book on basic mathematics, which she took with her to her room. The halls were silent at that hour before noon, but for the occasional passing bundle of rich and colorful laundry that had been removed quickly from sight in the upper world to be transported to the lower through the servants' halls. She remembered Mag, then, waiting in her room or not waiting, as the mood had seized her. Lydea quickened her step, expecting either Mag or a lack of Mag to greet her beyond her door.

Even Mistress Thorn's composure cracked at the sight of two granite-faced men looming up in her tiny chamber, drawing their swords as she opened the door. The mathematical principles crashed to the floor. Mistress Thorn, abandoning propriety, slammed the door in their faces and fled.

She heard the door crash open again as she rounded a

corner. She passed a stairway, but dared not run up. By
now, the image of her in those spellbound eyes must have
passed from mind to mind throughout the palace. She
heard a shriek behind her, partly muffled as laundry
dodged the swords. The guards' feet pounded hard on Lydea's heels as she ran a scared rat's path through the maze
of hallways, taking every turn. She could not lose them,
she realized with growing terror; it was as though she left
a glowing trail of footprints behind her.

Someone moved ahead of her. She saw a pale head
behind a huge urn standing grotesquely along the narrow
passage. "Ducon," she gasped on a rag-end of breath. He
looked back at her, then disappeared. She gave a half sob
of horror and despair, hearing the boots hammering the
floorboards behind her. Casting a hopeless glance back for
Ducon as she sped past the urn, she saw the narrow opening in the wall behind it.

She threw herself into it, closed wall and wainscotting
behind her. The inner passageway was empty; Ducon was
nowhere to be seen. Perhaps, she thought incredulously, it
had not been Ducon at all but his ghostly-seeming other.
Pausing only to kick off her shoes, she fled noiselessly
down the nearest turning, then up a stairway, angling her
way without thinking, without stopping, deep into the secret palace.

She paused finally to catch her breath, feeling her heart
rattle against her ribs. She heard voices beyond the wall,
a distant shout or two. Surely they knew those hidden hallways; they would search for her there. She moved as soon
as she could, parched and aching, and certain that this time
Mag would not appear out of nowhere and save her during

her wild run. The Black Pearl must have sniffed Mag out in some sorcerer's way, and left the guards in the chamber to trap her accomplice.

Lydea fled up another stairway, this one lined with ornately framed paintings that had grown so dark with age they might have been of faces or of cities, she could not tell. The balusters were trimmed with peeling gold leaf, and supported a railing of black wood. At the top of the stairs, the sconces along the walls were of finely painted porcelain. She realized something then that made her stumble a step. All along her way, there had been candles lit, random and unobtrusive. Had she, she wondered in that instant, simply chosen the path that she could best see? Or was someone ahead anticipating her, lighting candles to guide her way?

Down the shadowy hallway, something shifted. Lydea froze. Then Mistress Thorn, reasserting herself for a moment, reached up coolly and pinched the nearest flame out. A dim, perplexing shape moved into the frail light. Lydea, expecting guards to pour through the wall, didn't immediately recognize what she saw. A door had opened, she guessed, but what came through near the level of the threshold looked confusingly like an arm, several sheets of paper, and a small, dark head.

Her heart, which had been stopped for hours, it seemed, or days or weeks, gave a sudden, painful twist. She made an incoherent sound; the face turned toward her. She began to run again. Without hesitation, the small figure pulled itself into her path and carefully closed the door against the world.

She caught him up as she ran. He clung to her, his

arms around her neck, not speaking; she could hear his unsteady breathing. She held him tightly, fiercely. She felt his wet cheek against hers; she could barely see through her own tears. Beyond the hidden walls the palace murmured vaguely, undisturbed yet by the vanished prince, who had been left, Lydea guessed, to take a nap. She climbed another staircase, moving as far from his chamber as she could get until she could barely take another step. She pushed into the nearest room, an old ballroom by the look of it, empty but for half a dozen antique chairs spilling stuffing out of their tapestry seats where the mice had nested.

She put Kyel down and sank to the floor, heaving for breath. He crouched close to her, put his hands on the sides of her face.

"Lydea," he whispered. "Lydea."

She kissed him, wiped both their faces with her sleeve. Then she held him again, glimpsing her own fate if she were caught running away with the Prince of Ombria, but knowing that she could not leave him an instant longer in that deadly place.

"Where will we go?" he asked, echoing her thoughts.

"Well," she whispered back, "what goes up must come down. We'll go down as far as we can under the palace, and from there we'll escape to the undercity."

"Ducon went up."

"What?"

"When he took me here after my father died. He kept going up."

"He does come here, then," she breathed in sudden hope. "Maybe he'll look for us here and help us."

"He would look up," Kyel guessed, gazing at the ceiling on which people in stiff and elaborate costumes appeared to be dancing on clouds.

"Then we'll go up first," Lydea said, her lips against his hair, close to his ear. "And if he doesn't find us there we'll go down."

He drew back a little to see her face. "Where is Mistress Thorn?"

"She's still here. She hides me from everyone but you."

His face dropped against hers again; she stroked his hair, trying to think. Ducon had gone to find Camas Erl; he would come back eventually and report to the Black Pearl. Who would tell him then that she had trapped the sorceress's spying waxling in Mistress Thorn's room, and that Mistress Thorn had eluded capture and disappeared somewhere within the palace. And so, subsequently, had the Prince of Ombria. The inescapable conclusion being that she had stolen the prince for ransom, or other evil purposes. Camas Erl, who would hardly be thanked for introducing Mistress Thorn into Kyel's life, would tell the Black Pearl that he had been hoodwinked by Ducon into accepting her: that Mistress Thorn was actually the ensorcelled Lydea, obviously deranged by grief and a grave threat to the prince; she might hide him anywhere, in any hovel in the city. Ducon might be sent to look for them, since they both trusted him. In which case "up" was indicated. Or he might be tossed into a pit in the cellar somewhere for bringing Lydea and the prince back together. In which case, "down" seemed safer . . . down and out and onto the sorceress's mercy.

She heard footsteps.

She clung to Kyel again, her throat burning. So soon, she thought in despair. So soon.

He held her as tightly, and whispered, "Don't leave me."

"No," she promised blindly, "I won't."

Light footsteps pattered like rain, many of them on one side or the other of the ballroom, she couldn't tell which. On one side the double doors were open as she had left them. Across the room, matching doors were closed. The steps seemed quiet, disorganized after the guards' rigorous, mindless pounding, but who else would be gathered up there?

"In here," someone hissed, and the closed doors opened.

Lydea's arms locked around Kyel. She rose while the group of young men at the door pushing against one another to get in were brought up, transfixed, against the sight of the Prince of Ombria in a musty ballroom high within the secret palace, unguarded and alone except for the stranger who held him. Lydea recognized a few of them: the young sons of nobles and once-powerful ministers. They looked harried, she thought, desperate and reckless; most of them were armed.

For a moment they were simply stunned at the incongruous sight; their faces refused to believe their eyes. Then someone said it, his voice flat, expressionless, "Kyel Greve."

Kyel twisted in Lydea's hold, gazed back at them silently. Someone drew a sword; she backed a step.

"Who are you?" one of the young nobles asked bewilderedly. "What are you doing up here with the prince? Have you kidnapped him? Are you mad?"

"She must have," someone breathed. "She must be."

Half of them, she realized with wonder, had inherited the soft black hair and dark blue eyes of the House of Greve. Kyel's wayward kin, they were, each with a labyrinthine link to the throne of Ombria. She flung the question back at them.

"What are you doing here? Armed and gathered up here in secret, with your faces out of Ombria's history?"

They looked at one another, startled again and silently questioning. Lydea took another step backward toward the open doors. A sharp word sent two of the young men, both armed, circling her to stand guard at the doors.

"What shall we do with this?" one murmured. She recognized Lord Hilil Gamelyn's impetuous son, with whom she had once danced. He did not recognize Mistress Thorn, whose formidable self-possession masked a growing and terrifying perception of the dangers that had chanced into the ballroom.

"Kill him?"

Mistress Thorn's imperturbable face turned as brittle as glass. Someone else shook his head violently, scowling. "You heard Ducon Greve. I'm as afraid of him as I am of the Black Pearl. He does her bidding now; he's lost to us."

"But, we could blame it on this woman. He has no direct heir; I could make a claim as strong as anyone's." The young man moved out from the group to study the glacial Mistress Thorn more closely. "Who are you?" he asked softly. "How did you dare snatch the Prince of Ombria out of the Black Pearl's grip? And how long did you think you were going to live afterwards?"

Lydea, feeling the prince trembling in her arms, opened her mouth to plead, to make suggestions, to bargain like the tavern-wench she had been. Thunder rolled down the worn hallways, drowning her voice. The young men, blood startling out of their faces, moved abruptly, scattering through the ballroom toward the open doors. Caught up in their mute urgency, Lydea ran with them a moment or two before she realized what she heard. Domina Pearl's guards, boots echoing everywhere, burst through the doors on one side while the young nobles and the prince's kidnapper fled through the opposite doors. The last of them turned courageously to fight; Lydea heard the explosive argument of blades.

She tried to outrun the running nobles, lose them in sudden turns down the chipped, twisting halls, but they stayed grimly at her heels like hounds after the deer, while the guards, rumbling over the worn floors like a pack of horsemen, clamored after them. Breath like fire in her throat, her arms shaking under Kyel's weight, Lydea moved hopelessly, feeling his damp cheek against hers. Up and up the hunted ran, dodging, circling, dashing toward any shadow, down any empty corridor or stairway. The guards, relentless as flood water, flowed everywhere after them.

She glimpsed an impossibility ahead of her, as a window in a room she reeled into gave her a sight of Ombria far below, the crooked, winding streets she had fled down in the night spread out like a maze between the palace and the sea. A tall man with hair the color of ivory moved away from the window to slip through a shadowed doorway in the wall. "Ducon," she whispered, with barely strength enough to shape the name. Shadow lay as deep and stark as midnight sea across the door.

But there was no place else to go. Someone caught at her, tried to stop her, shouting at her that there was nowhere left to go. But Ducon had just walked through the doorway. And so she followed him, carrying the Prince of Ombria with her into nowhere.

TWENTY-SIX

Time Out of Mind

Mag, shackled to a wall in a room without a door, watched what looked like a huge moth with glowing golden wings beat incessantly at the glass sides of a jar on a shelf. The jar was sealed with cork and wax; the moth should have died long before Mag ever laid eyes on it. But it kept fluttering around and around in the jar, never resting, ceaselessly battering itself against an illusion of freedom until Mag could not bear looking at it. But she couldn't bear looking away, either. Then things half in shadow and glowing in the dark crossed her sight, like the pile of bones in a corner and the deformed creatures floating in other jars that seemed to study her curiously. The room itself, windowless, doorless, and steeped in smells, she recognized easily. It was Domina Pearl's most closely guarded secret, the center of the she-spider's web. That she had permitted Mag to see it, Mag found profoundly disquieting.

Earlier, Mag had watched her pull parts of herself back out of the charcoal whirlpool that had stolen them and reattach them, muttering a trenchant mix of spell and imprecation. The best she could do was a withered black carrot for a thumb, a crumpled leaf for an ear, and a dead-white eyebrow. Looking into a mirror, she had spat at her reflection. The glass melted where her spittle ran down. Then she had turned to Mag, who was slumped on the floor, one arm dangling from a metal cuff on a chain and growing numb.

"As for you," the Black Pearl said harshly, staring into Mag's expressionless eyes. "You will stay here as bait. I will refuse every offer she makes for you until she is forced to come for you. Then she will reckon with me. If she does not care enough to come, then you will be my waxling, in name, in thought, in heart. I will use you against her as she used you against me. That will teach the sorceress not to meddle in a world where she does not belong."

She left then. Mag watched closely, but it was as though the Black Pearl had seeped through the stained floorboards, or compressed herself into a speck and blew between slats in the wall. Mag stood up to work the blood back into her arm. Faey would rescue her somehow, sooner or later; she clung to that, trying not to demand *how soon*? or *how?* from thin air.

What seemed to be the Black Pearl's bed distracted her for a few moments. It stood open against the far wall, a chest as long as a coffin with a high, rounded lid. The outside looked as if it had been made of amber and the gleaming wings of thousands of beetles. Inside the box and along the lid, some strange substance had formed a mold of the Black Pearl, complete to the end of her nose and the tips of her outstretched fingers, as she lay enclosed within the box. The substance looked vaguely porous, spongy, like bread dough, and was the color of dried blood. It was that yeasty muck, Mag guessed, which nightly rejuvenated the Black Pearl, and gave her, judging from its smell, the peculiar odor of musty, unaired linen.

She sat on the floor again and watched with mindless intensity as the luminous, beautiful moth fought the prison around it. If it freed itself, she felt, then so could she; if it could just find the way beyond the invisible door, then so could she . . . The Black Pearl emerged out of the air. Her face seemed patchy, streaked with passion; her lips had all but vanished. She looked, Mag thought uneasily, as if she had inhaled a thunderbolt.

She went to what resembled a cast-iron tree that grew mirrors like fruit on every branch. She angled different mirrors rapidly. Mag caught fleeting images of the palace: a rich, shadowed chamber in which naked figures dimly moved on rumpled satin sheets; the kitchens where a cook carried a steaming pot high over the bowed heads of a row of girls peeling vegetables; the secret library where once Mag had been trapped. Domina Pearl whispered something, and every mirror showed her the harsh, expressionless face of a guard.

"Watch all entrances, even to the kitchens, and all the stairways to the cellar. Do not let them leave the palace. When you find them, kill her and bring the prince to me."

Lydea, Mag thought, feeling her skin grow icy. The

Black Pearl whirled suddenly, tore off her stiffly piled hair and flung it on the floor. A small knife bounced out of it, and a little glass vial of something green. Domina Pearl stared at the hair, breathing heavily. Mag stared at the bald, seamed head of the regent. She bent finally, grunting, and put her hair back on her head. The small black hillock seemed so rigid that Mag expected it to have cracked. But not a hair was out of place.

She vanished again. Mag, frightened thoughtless, threw whatever she could reach at the golden moth to break the jar, including her shoes. Everything bounced off the recalcitrant glass except for one shoe, which narrowly missed the reappearing regent and fell into her bed instead. The Black Pearl left a weal across Mag's cheek with her signet ring, and tossed the shoe into the bone pile. Mag swallowed, motionless again. Half the shoe had melted.

She could not see exactly how Ducon and Camas Erl found their way into the Black Pearl's secret, but there they were suddenly, standing in front of her. Ducon's face, even worse for wear, had a hard, hopeless cast to it, as though he had been forced to absorb something bitter. The bitterness, Mag guessed, was Camas Erl, safely returned from the backwaters of history to Domina Pearl. She was only partly right, she learned soon enough. Ducon gave her a harried look that took in her throbbing cheek and shackled arm. He said nothing, but she glimpsed the deepening despair in his eyes.

He handed Domina Pearl a sheet of dove-grey paper sealed with Faey's customary splash of black wax. She read it and sniffed contemptuously. "As I expected. She has begun to bargain for her waxling."

"What will you do?"

"Accept nothing until she has no choice but to come here. She has grown too free and unpredictable in her underground city. I want her here, under my control, doing my bidding. While I wait, I will make a few necessary adjustments to the girl."

"What kinds of adjustments?"

"She is too curious," the Black Pearl answered succinctly. "Like you."

"Let me take the girl back," the tutor pleaded. He had tidied his hair, but his chin still bristled like one of the Black Pearl's peculiar fleshy plants, and he wore a waterline across his shirt. "I still have many questions for the sorceress. Her past is extraordinary; it stretches back to the beginning of Ombria's history. She promised me — "

"You," Domina Pearl snapped, "have been gone far too long. You have neglected your duty, and because of you the history of Ombria is liable to take a deadly turn. Your Mistress Thorn has stolen the prince."

"What?" Ducon whispered. Camas Erl, wordless and blinking rapidly, seemed caught between lies and considering the more expedient of them.

"She is trapped in the old palace, along with another covey of conspirators flushed out by the guards. Nestlings, all of them, thinking they will succeed where their fathers failed and died. Of course, Mistress Thorn cannot elude the guards, but who knows what she may do to the prince when she is cornered — "

"She won't harm him," Ducon interrupted rashly. "She loves him."

Domina Pearl eyed him bleakly. "You know this Mistress Thorn well enough to assume that she would snatch the prince away from his guardian and his family out of love rather than malevolence and greed? I think she is yet another conspirator, trying to force my hand."

"I know her. So do you. She was Royce Greve's mistress. The sorceress disguised her beneath a spell so that there would be someone in this decaying, dangerous, bloody-minded palace who would give the child love instead of a daily dose of poison—"

Mag didn't see Domina Pearl move, but Ducon was on his knees suddenly in front of her, struggling to speak, his face as white as bone. "She," the regent said very softly, "will not be as fortunate this time. She will die where she is found, in front of the child. You will be even less fortunate. You will live. Here. Obeying me in all things, without question. You will never leave this room again." She turned away from him to the cauldron standing on its grate above the floor. "You can begin now by helping me return this waxling to her proper state of wax." Ducon loosed a harsh sound between a curse and a sob. She ignored him, her eyes going to the unusually silent tutor. "And you. How well did you know this Mistress Thorn?" He hesitated, torn between answers; she gestured, exasperated. "Never mind. I'll have the truth out of you later. Go and find the prince. Make sure that my orders are carried out, and return here with the boy. You want to witness history: witness that. Cut off her hair when she is dead; I can use it in my—"

She stopped abruptly, caught by a face within one of the mirrors. It spoke, silently except to her. Ducon, freed for no apparent reason, got to his feet unsteadily. He watched her, his face haggard and slick with sweat. She seemed to be listening to something of enormous portent. Mag held her breath, but heard nothing. The Black Pearl's face smoothed like eggshell; all expression startled out of it. She eased down slowly on the edge of her bed. For an instant, as she sat staring at the unforeseen, she looked almost human.

Her wide eyes went first to Ducon. "The child is dead."

Again he could not speak; her words had struck like a spell. He shook his head a little, holding her eyes, beginning to tremble as he waited.

"Lydea," the Black Pearl began; she had to stop and clear some acid out of her throat. "The guards cornered her at the top of the hidden palace. With no place left to go in the world she leaped out of it with the prince in her arms. The guards are searching for the bodies." Ducon made a sound finally, soft, meaningless. Domina Pearl stilled a sudden twitch beside her mouth and rose. She said wearily to Camas Erl, "You will have to plan another funeral, suitable for a child-ruler. And untangle the genealogy charts to find out exactly who rules after him. I want no ambiguities left in this house."

Ducon, swaying forward to grip the rim of the huge cauldron in front of him as though to catch his balance, rocked it off the grate and heaved it into the air. He staggered under its ponderous bulk, but kept his balance as he swung it like a bell and hurled it. It seemed such an impossible task that even the Black Pearl was transfixed by the flying cauldron until the instant before it passed over the place where she had been standing. It crashed onto her bed. The bed splintered into a thousand pieces; beetle wings flew everywhere. Domina Pearl, reappearing to stare at the wreckage, gave a long, high-pitched wail. Mag, the bones of her face singing before she heard the sound, clamped her ears between her arms. Ducon reeled, but stayed on his feet, and followed the cauldron doggedly with the cast-iron tree of mirrors, in which, briefly, his harrowed face appeared in every mirror before they shattered.

He hauled at the iron grate, his hands coming up black with ash. Mag held her breath, for the golden fluttering moth in its prison was just above the Black Pearl's head. But, screeching like a hinge, she gave Ducon no chance. He froze before he could throw the massive grate, stood spellbound in her murderous gaze, trembling again at the weight dragging at him.

She drew breath to speak, or perhaps just to spit and let her acid eat into him. The jar shattered abruptly above her head. They all looked up, except for Ducon, who seemed, even ensorcelled, still intent on throwing what he could at Domina Pearl. The moth flew free, spiralled an erratic flight across the room and came to rest in Mag's hair.

She felt a flame spark behind her eyes, in her throat, for no reason except that the moth was free and it had come to her. The room shuddered suddenly, oddly, under them. Shards of amber glittered and clicked; bones shifted. Domina Pearl stumbled, caught herself, her eyes searching wildly through the broken fragments of her mirrors. The walls shook again, as though in the heart of the hidden palace, or at its foundations, something massive and un-imaginable was taking its first ponderous steps.

The grate tore out of Ducon's hold, gashed the floor

as it hit. Jars rattled together on the shelves; things within them shivered. A shelf groaned as nails bent within the wood. It broke abruptly in half, showering glass and liquid and various stenches over the Black Pearl. She hissed a word, watching a crack growing across the ceiling.

Camas Erl whispered, "She said she would do anything."

Domina Pearl looked at him, her face seamed like dry mud and as brittle; she might have broken at a touch. The room lurched around them, twisting, Mag realized, like one cog against another. The wall she was chained to had shifted behind the Black Pearl, giving Mag a clear view of Ducon's stark, motionless face, and the tutor behind him, trying to see through the ceiling.

"What is it?" Camas pleaded of whatever was shattering the boundaries of history as it moved to meet them. "Is it her? Or is it the beginning?"

Domina Pearl, suddenly shedding illusions like old leaves, lost an eyebrow as she shrieked at him, "Why don't you know? You've been studying this for years!"

"The ending?" the tutor guessed, his face bloodless, rapt. Walls turned again as though the enormous being beyond the room were trying to open it like a jar. A voice, more wind than human, or the angry hiss of an enormous reptile, swept through it; the words it spoke seemed of some ancient language, only half-human and completely incomprehensible.

Domina Pearl waded through splinters of glass and amber, picked up a broken piece of mirror. As she turned it futilely this way and that to see the speaker, her withered ear fell off. She cried out, searching for it in the rubble.

Camas Erl, his yellow eyes flickering nervously, moved a step away from her.

The voice flooded the room again with the furious energy of a roiling storm, its threat unmistakable, its words unfathomable.

The Black Pearl spat a rotten tooth or two, tried to catch them. "Who is that woman?" she asked Camas hoarsely. "Where in Ombria did she come from?"

"You must know her," Camas answered frantically. "She has always been here."

Ducon came to life again unexpectedly; his arms, still straining around the fallen grate, finally dropped. He looked around bewilderedly at the wreckage, found Mag again within the shifted walls. Then a floorboard or a door tore itself apart just beyond the walls and he froze again, trying, as they all were, to see beyond the visible world.

The voice boomed against them and shattered like tide hitting rock. "Give me my waxling!"

The Black Pearl's withered thumb fell off. She screamed suddenly, furiously back, "Take her!"

She vanished. Camas Erl, shouting incoherently, wavered between history and magic, then followed the fleeing path of what he understood best.

The moth fluttered out of Mag's hair, touched the floor, and turned into Faey.

She had cobbled a face of some sort together; her skin was iridescent and one eye smaller than the other. She straightened a strand of unnaturally glowing hair the color of the moth wings, and touched the iron cuff at Mag's wrist. The cuff sprang open; her numb arm dropped. Mag, melting like wax, could not move even then. The moth in the jar in her mind kept turning into Faey, who had come out from under the world to rescue her. Fire spilled out of her eyes, burned down her face; she was blind with it, words changing to fire in her throat, until she hardly knew any longer if she were the wax or the wick and the flame.

She heard Ducon's voice, raw with rage and grief. "Where did they go? I want her dead. Will you help me?"

Faey settled down on the floor beside Mag, put an arm around her shoulders. "Domina Pearl is dead even as she runs," the sorceress told Ducon. "You killed her. She can't regrow without her bed, and she will have no time to make another before she needs it. A form of mold, I think she must be. Or fungus. Something grown in the shadow of the world."

"Her guards ran Lydea and Kyel to death like animals." Ducon's face glistened, furrowed with sorrow. "Please. Can you tell me where they are?"

"From what I saw, they went out that door. The one you drew so often, with the iris beside it. Or did they go into it? You'd know better than I. Look for them through there."

He stared at her uncertainly, tormented by her riddling. A short, harsh sob shook him; he vanished, without answering, out the Black Pearl's invisible door.

Or had he, Mag wondered, vanished *into*? "We should go after him," she said uneasily. "Help him. She's not dead yet, and her guards are everywhere."

"I can keep an eye on him from here," Faey answered. "Unlike some, I don't need all those mirrors for spare eyes."

Mag wiped at tears with her sleeve, said huskily, "I came here trying to find my true mother in a piece of charcoal. I don't think that seeing her face could ever move me as much as seeing you now. Whichever face you happen to put on."

Faey, adjusting her mismatched eyes, said pensively, "I have been wrong in my life almost as often as I changed my face. We learned something together, you and I. Just when I thought I knew everything I would ever need to know, you taught me how to see beyond my sorcery into my heart."

"Can you show me how to see without eyes?"

"You've seen Ducon that way already," Faey said simply. But she reached for a piece of broken mirror. "Here, use this; they still work. Think of his face."

Mag summoned Ducon to memory and looked in the mirror. The thing outside took another immense step that seemed to shake the palace from weathercock to wine cellar. Mag started. The mirror shivered in her hand; the image forming in it rippled like water. The walls made their clockwork turn.

"I thought," she said uneasily to Faey, "that it was you making all the noise out there. What is it?"

"It happens," Faey answered obscurely. "This is a good place to wait it out. It's outside of time, and you'll remember better afterward."

"Wait what out? Remember what? What exactly is going on out there?"

The sorceress shrugged slightly; an eyebrow tilted. "I'm never sure. But it seems to happen whenever I come up from the underworld."

Mag stared at her, speechless. The secret room revolved like a star in an orrery, following its immutable pattern across the night.

TWENTY-SEVEN

Ombria in Shadow

Ducon had to fight his way through the slit in the air that was the Black Pearl's invisible door. Even air and time seemed to be warping within the palace along with floorboards and joists. He pushed back illusions of falling beams, shoved through bare walls closing together, all in a narrow corridor of time which led in and out of the Black Pearl's inmost chamber. In abandoning her secrets, she had all but trapped him. The misshapen door at the end of her corridor was growing smaller, odd angles closing in on one another in a blind iris of moldings and boards. He reached it just before it grew too small to pass through.

Emerging from within that brief pocket of time, he was startled to feel the floor shake under him. Something other than the sorceress was happening in the ancient palace. It stirred like a living thing, murmured and groaned like a dreamer. He stepped out of the little antechamber in the hidden palace within which the Black Pearl had built her door, and stopped, swallowing drily. Death had stalked those empty, forgotten passages. He recognized the hot-eyed young cousin who lay in his own blood in the hallway. He still wore the shallow scratch on his neck from Ducon's blade. Ducon coaxed the sword out of the stiff fingers and listened. But for the faint trembling of the crystal prisms in an enormous chandelier, the place was soundless. He began to run, inward and upward toward the secret heart of the palace.

He was unprepared for the virulence of the Black Pearl's guard. The first one he met nearly impaled him before he remembered that he would be their quarry now; Domina Pearl, who had nothing left to lose, would not let him live a moment longer than she wanted. He fought desperately. The sight of him in one barren, mindless pair of eyes attracted other guards. Ducon heard shouting down the distant corridors, the crack of boot heels along the bare, aged floors. The palace shook again. Fire sprang briefly alive in the dusty tapers along the wall. Ducon, ducking a slash that might have blinded him, smelled an astonishing scent of violets.

But it was a dream, a child's tale. The threshold Lydea had crossed had led her to her death; the silent man who wore Ducon's face and drifted unexpectedly across his past was already a ghost. He had seen enough of them in the sorceress's house to recognize one more. The ceiling above him groaned; a beam had twisted or straightened itself. Ducon, distracted again by possibilities, was forcibly reminded of the most likely when the guard's blade burrowed past his attention to shear a bloody ribbon down his sleeve. He jerked back. The blade, arcing toward his throat, flew abruptly upward as the floor shook again. The guard stumbled and fell. Ducon turned on his heel and ran.

He went up the nearest stairs, and up again and farther up, until he could hear the doves rustling in the rafters beneath the rotted openings in the roof. He could no longer hear the guards thundering down the hallways, throwing open doors that had been closed for centuries. They would also keep going up, he knew; in the end, like Lydea, he might be forced to run out of time. The doorway he came to at last seemed unchanged: one post painted with irises, the other worn bare long ago. The blackness across the threshold looked absolute.

"I told you," the Black Pearl said behind him, "that he would come here."

He whirled, his back to the open dark, the sword raised futilely. She spoke to Camas Erl, who watched Ducon with burning curiosity, as though he were not quite human, something unnameable whose movements would be entirely unpredictable. The Black Pearl, missing various parts as though she had pulled herself together too hastily in a grave, glowered at him malevolently.

"He has drawn this doorway many times," she continued. "Something pulls him here to this place. Draw something for us now, Ducon. Draw a door for us. You have that charcoal. You always carry it."

The great palace shuddered; the city beyond the warped glass in the windows blurred briefly, became distinct again. Standing in the ancient, decaying room overlooking the twisting streets below, overgrown piers crumbling into the blinding afternoon sea, Ducon felt his heart break apart like something battered too long by rain.

"It's nothing," he told her wearily. "No place. It's where Lydea and Kyel died. You think you can walk into that and come to life again?"

"Draw a door."

"The door is open."

"Is it?" Camas asked, still studying him. "You've seen such places all your life. You recognize them. What draws you to them?" Ducon was silent, the blade still raised between them, guarding the place where his ghosts lived in some other, tranquil world. "Shadow," Camas told him. "You draw shadow. The shadow city."

"So," Ducon said tersely, "it is full of shadows."

"Is it?" Camas took a step toward Ducon in his fervor. The sword followed him. Domina Pearl spat something, and the blade flew out of Ducon's hand, pierced a broken piece of molding across the room.

"I may be dying," she told him, "but I am not powerless. You are dead. You will die either on this side of the threshold or the other, as you choose."

"But either way I will not draw you a door."

"Yes, you will," Camas said softly. "Because you have been drawing doors to find this door all your life. You could not die without knowing if we are right: that you are the door and the key and the threshold between worlds. Are they alive or dead? Kyel and Lydea? They could be either, within that dark. Draw the door and find out."

Ducon felt a door open somewhere in his thoughts; he glimpsed himself across the threshold. The palace lurched again, jarring them. He felt it from a distance, though it had flung him off balance onto his knees. He caught himself, leaving a bloody handprint on the floor. He did not answer, only took the charcoal from his pocket and began to draw the outline of a door on the floor where it might have fallen if dark could cast a shadow.

As he drew, he remembered all the strange corners he had turned, the unexpected alleys, the crooked streets that had led him to that moment, where he crouched at the Black Pearl's feet, giving her the last thing he would ever draw. She and Camas had conceived the idea of the shadow door; it had never occurred to him. But he, with his strange compulsions, his eye for whatever was obscure, ambiguous, paradoxical within their lives, and his restless charcoal had led them to that conclusion. Lydea might have leaped to her death across that dark threshold. The Black Pearl saw a different door: its shadow, opening to light.

His fingers grew black, swirling charcoal into shadow. He left the bright splayed handprint showing through it as both door latch, and the hand reaching out to the latch. He outlined it heavily in black, for it was his hand and his heart's blood, and as close as the Black Pearl might allow him to get to opening that door. He was right about that. When the black rectangle on the floor could not possibly hold another stroke of darkness and the charcoal hesitated, Ducon felt the blade at his throat forcing him back. Guards she had summoned surrounded him, their mad, passionless eyes watching his every breath.

"Choose," the Black Pearl said, "my lord Ducon. The quick predictable death here, or the long fall into the unknown or the palace cellar, whichever rises to meet you first."

He started to stand, to turn and face the dark rather than carry the final memory of her face with him into oblivion. The floor shrugged and rippled as though the entire palace were trying to uproot itself, walk away from the doomed city. It scattered the guards and threw Ducon down again on the charcoal. His hand, outflung for balance, slid in longing and despair across the dark to meet the shadow hand on the door.

It opened.

Light poured out around him, blinded him. He heard Camas give a sudden shout. The Black Pearl snapped something. An unbearable streak of silver light swung down at Ducon. Another seared below it, bore it up and out of the luminous, dazzling flood he knelt in, that was nothing he could name or understand except that it was the opposite of shadow.

Then a hand gripped him, pulled him out of the light. Blinking stars out of his eyes, he saw himself.

And not himself.

For the first time, he could see the shimmering flow of power that trailed endlessly away from the man whom Ducon's charcoal had set free in the taverns of Ombria. It melted through his silvery eyes, turning them a shade darker than Ducon's, now a shade lighter. Ducon tried to speak, could not. The man studied him as silently. Time and sorrow had etched the thin lines along his mouth, left their memory in his eyes. He still held Ducon's arm; his fingers tightened slightly, before he spoke.

"You don't look at all like your mother."

Ducon whispered, "I look like you."

"You see what I am."

"Yes." He stopped to swallow. "Now I do. I couldn't see it before."

"You drew me into Ombria. I was a shadow of myself. Being charcoal, I could never speak. I could only watch you."

"Watch over me," Ducon amended. All around them, he realized, other faces from other drawings were crowding into the room, igniting battles with the ensorcelled guards. The shadow doorway, pouring light like a sun, had illumined the impenetrable black opposite it. An army seemed to be spilling out of it along with gusts of rain-streaked wind, the smell of grass, the harsh cries of ravens. His father still kept watch over Ducon's shoulder at the tumult behind him, his sword raised to guard Ducon's back. Ducon heard the fighting from a distance; he could not look away from the sorcerer's face.

"Did my mother find you?" he asked huskily. "Or did you find her?"

"Your mother leaped to meet me. Like you, she was drawn to this door."

Ducon's fingers, closing suddenly on his father's wrist, melted slightly into a glinting aura. "She lived?"

"She lived and bore you. More than that, I never knew. She returned to the doorway to show you to me. I never saw her again, though for a time I haunted that doorway, and I searched through fire and water for glimpses of her. I knew the moment she died. I knew that you existed in her world, but until you drew me, I never saw your face again."

"I followed you that day I first saw you. You led me —"
A shadow across Ducon's thoughts faded; the familiar
glimmering currents of power illumined him. "You led me
to Faey."

"Is that her name? The sorceress who lives underground? We never knew."

"What are you, in your world?"

"I rule, in the reflected world. I do not live underground, and though I am very powerful, I am not immor-
tal." He loosed Ducon's arm, touched his face lightly with
long, hard fingers. "You seem to have inherited that power
in odd ways. You can recognize it and it comes out of your
drawings. But you are not a sorcerer?"

"Neither sorcerer nor ruler. Just a man with a piece
of charcoal." He started at a fierce brawl of swords close
behind him. The elusive, gleaming swaths of power seemed
to draw closer around them, blurring the battling figures,
the noise. "Is the door open forever now?" he asked without hope. "Can you stay?"

"We came because in your utter despair you found a
way to open the door between our worlds. The shadow
world is your hope. When you no longer despair, you no
longer need us; we fade and you forget. When the sorceress
who lives underground is disturbed enough by events to
make her way up into the troubled, desperate world above,
then she shifts the balance between despair and hope, between light and shadow. She draws us to your world, to
restore the ancient balance between us. But it was you who
searched for us in your drawings, you who saw into
shadow, you who opened the door."

"Camas guessed that much," Ducon said, balanced between bitterness and wonder. "Will I forget you? Did my mother? She never spoke of you."

"Perhaps," his father said gently. "Perhaps not. I never forgot her. There have been other children born belonging to both worlds. They stay where they were born. Like you, they seem haunted by the world they lost."

"My mother was able to return to this world through that door?"

"She belonged here."

"My small cousin —" His throat burned; he began again. "My cousin who is — was — Prince of Ombria, and the woman who loved him ran for their lives through that doorway. They belong here. Is there a way back for them?"

His father shifted a little. The luminous air around them faded enough for Ducon to see the few scattered battles around them, the stray guards still obdurately obeying the Black Pearl's commands. She herself was nowhere to be found. Camas had vanished with her, into her erratic, secret passageways, perhaps, or into the streets of Ombria, where she would find no opening door that would save her, and no bed except her last.

"Draw them," Ducon's father suggested, and Ducon turned, raised his charcoal to the wall beside the door.

The first few lines that came out revealed a face that was neither Kyel's nor Lydea's. He lifted his arm to brush it away. The eyes seemed to watch him as they had done in life, and he paused, puzzled, then began to draw again. When the charcoal shaped the jet head of a pin floating above a tangled cloud of hair, he stopped again, disturbed by what he recognized, wondering if she, too, had somehow vanished beyond the door. The darkly glittering hues of color that streamed briefly through the charcoal eyes illumined him.

"Who is that?" his father asked. Behind them, the room was finally silent. "She sees like you do."

"Mag," Ducon said. "She is watching us." He moved to the other side of the door, where the iris still bloomed, and told his father a story of charcoal and wax while he drew out of the dark the faces of his heart and around him the world he knew drew its own conclusions.

TWENTY-EIGHT

Ever After

The Prince of Ombria and his governess sat together on his bed, gazing at the array of puppets spread across the vast expanse of silk. The prince, who had just finished his midday meal, looked heavy-eyed and drowsy. But he still stifled his yawns, and his hands moved busily among the puppets, choosing, discarding, until they pounced finally on the moon with her crystal eyes and her hands shaped like stars.

"I will be the moon," Kyel said. "You must make a wish to me."

Lydea slid her fingers into the fox's head, with its sly smile and fiery velvet pelt. "I wish," she said, "that you would take your nap."

"No," the prince said patiently, "you must make a true wish. And I will grant it because I am the moon."

"Then I must make a fox's wish. I wish for an open door to every hen house, and the ability to jump into trees."

The moon sank onto the blue hillock of Kyel's knee. "Why?"

"So that I can escape the farmer's dogs when they run after me."

"Then you should wish," the prince said promptly, "that you could jump as high as the moon."

"A good wish. But there are no hens on the moon, and how would I get back to Ombria?"

The moon rose again, lifted a golden hand. "On a star."

The governess smiled. The fox stroked the prince's hair while he shook away the moon and replaced it with the sorceress, who had one amethyst eye and one emerald, and who wore a black cloak that shimmered with ribbons of faint, changing colors.

"I am the sorceress who lives underground," the prince said. "Is there really a sorceress who lives underground?"

"So they—" Lydea checked herself, let the fox speak. "So they say, my lord."

"How does she live? Does she have a house?"

She paused again, glimpsing a barely remembered tale. "I think she does. Maybe even her own city beneath Ombria. Some say that she has an ancient enemy, who appears during harsh and perilous times in Ombria's history. Then and only then does the sorceress make her way out of her underground world to fight the evil and restore hope to Ombria."

"My tutor goes everywhere in Ombria. Maybe she knows where the sorceress lives."

"I wouldn't be surprised at anything your tutor knows."

The sorceress descended, long nose down on the silk. Kyel picked another puppet up, looked at it silently a moment. The queen of pirates, whose black nails curved like scimitars, whose hair was a rigid knoll in which she kept her weapons, stared back at him out of glittering onyx eyes. Kyel put her down as silently, frowning slightly. He lay back on his pillows. Lydea pushed the puppets away from him and began to rise.

"No," the prince said sleepily. "Stay. Tell me a story."

"And then you must sleep." She settled herself beside him, absently picked up the black sheep, whose eyes were silvery, whose long mouth curled into the faintest smile.

"Tell me the story of the locket."

"Once upon a time, my lord, in the best and the worst of all possible worlds, a princess fell in love with a young man who loved to draw pictures."

"Like Ducon."

"Very like your cousin. Every day for a year, she gave him a rose. She would pick it at dawn from her father's gardens and then take it to the highest place in the castle, a place so high that everyone had forgotten about it except for the doves that nested beneath the broken roof. There, she had found a secret door between the best and the worst of the worlds. Every day, they would meet on the threshold of that door. She would give him a rose, and he would give her a drawing of the city he lived in. They loved each other very much, but of course they could never marry, because they were from different worlds: she was a princess and he an artist who had to paint tavern signs to keep himself fed.

"One day, after a year had passed, the princess brought him a child along with a rose. It was the happiest day of her life because she had given him their child, and also the saddest day of her life, because he came to her with his heart's blood on his paper instead of a drawing. Someone had seen him with the princess and had punished him. So, in her love and sorrow, she crossed the threshold to his world, to stay with him while he breathed his last."

"His last what?"

"Breath. In her grief, she pulled the locket from her throat and placed into it a rose petal, three drops of his blood, and a sliver of his charcoal. But after he died, she found that she could not get back into her world with the child, because it was half of the best and half of the worst, and neither world would accept the baby. But the princess, after many days and nights of ceaseless weeping and searching, finally left the child with a wise and powerful woman who would know, with her vast knowledge and experience, how to raise a child of both worlds. At last the princess could return to her own world. The only thing she had to leave with her child was the locket, which held all the memories of her love . . ."

Lydea heard Kyel's even breathing and stopped. She pulled the coverlet over him and slid gently off the bed, seeing only then that the regent stood in the doorway.

How long he had been listening, she did not know. She dropped a curtsey, which erased the hairline furrow in his brow. He gave a last glance to the child in the bed and followed her out; the prince's attendants slipped in after her to wait for him to wake.

Ducon had regained something of his sense of humor after having lost it for weeks to the precarious position he had attained. The footloose artist had been forced to learn to rule a city after his uncle's death. He looked older, harried, and much tidier. It was as though at his uncle's death he had suddenly seen Ombria for the first time. All the broken piers he had wandered over must be fixed; the troubled, dangerous streets he had roamed at all hours must be made safe; the street urchins must be caught like stray dogs, fed and schooled. He had declared war on the black-sailed ships that had commandeered the ports. Every day brought him an endless list of complaints, injustices, charges, petitions. Lydea expected him to vanish out of the palace, as had been his habit once, leaving it anyone's guess where he had gone.

So far he hadn't. She found him with her at odd times, as though he used her in some way as an escape. Perhaps, she thought, it was the tavern-wench he saw beneath the governess's sober garb that drew him. She was as close as he could get to the life he had lost.

"Lavender," he commented, looking at the ribbons in her sleeve.

"The prince was tired, he said, of looking at so much black."

"So am I," he breathed. "It seems we have been in mourning forever."

Sorrow caught her, as it did sometimes unexpectedly: a thumbprint of fire in the hollow of her throat. She swallowed it, said only, "Because you have been working so hard, my lord."

"I'm not used to it yet." He measured a trailing end of the ribbon at her wrist between his fingers, oblivious of the guards and hovering officials who had followed him. It was the color, she understood, that caught him: her hair, the ribbons, the little brush strokes of satin and jewel that the puppets made, scattered across the deep blue silk. He added impulsively, "Perhaps I'll come with you this afternoon."

The thought made her smile. "To my father's tavern? It's hardly for the likes of you."

"I've been to—"

"I know, my lord: every tavern in Ombria but the Rose and Thorn. I wonder how you missed it." Then, out of nowhere, a chill of fear blew through her; she heard herself say, "We can't both leave the prince. Not both of us at once."

He gave her a strange look, not of surprise, but a reflection of her fear, which she found odder still. He loosed the ribbon, nodded, his eyes returning briefly to the prince's door. "Perhaps you're right. He knows where you're going?"

"He knows, my lord. But I'll be back before he remembers that I'm gone."

"Be careful," he said. "Tell your father that I will come and draw in his tavern some day."

But that was idle wishing, she knew. Already he was a legend in certain parts of the city, and legends, having made themselves so, rarely returned to repeat their feats.

He seemed to read her mind. His eyes, clear, faintly smiling, held hers a moment.

"Not," he said, "an idle wish."

A promise, his eyes told her. She blinked, then dismissed the half-glimpsed idea that had rolled like a sea creature on the surface of her mind, then dove back down, so deeply that she had forgotten it before she returned to her chamber.

High, she found herself thinking, and low, and now in the middle. She had a view of the trellises in the gardens, but not of the sea. But she had never been that low in the palace, except once, with the regent, who had taken her there for some obscure reason . . . Perhaps he had simply wanted her to see how they lived, those who never raised their eyes in passageways, who never spoke.

"This palace," he had said, "is a small city, past lying close to present like one shoe next to another. If you look at them in a mirror, left becomes right, present becomes past . . ."

Shoes . . . Her mind turned oddly on them, as she tidied herself and drew on a hooded cloak. The days had grown shorter; the direction of the wind had changed. She was walking down a hallway, well lit and guarded, when a small door hidden in the wall clicked open and she froze, both hands over her mouth to stifle a scream of terror.

Mag came out of the wall. She looked stricken herself at the sight of Lydea, who dropped her hands quickly and wondered at her own pounding heart.

"I'm so sorry," the tutor said guiltily. "I was exploring."

"I don't know why I was so frightened."

"I know. It's all right. Here." She stooped to pick up the elegant rosewood box that Lydea had dropped.

"It's for my father," Lydea said dazedly. "He keeps his money in an old boot."

"Have you seen him since Royce Greve died?"

"Only once. He'll be wondering. I was — somewhat distraught, then."

Mag nodded gravely. She was young to be tutoring a prince, but the regent had chosen her. She replaced Camas Erl, who had taken a long journey to study flora and fauna in the outermost islands of the southern seas. He had left shortly after Royce's death, and would be gone, he had said, indefinitely. Lydea found Mag's knowledge astonishing, and had gotten into the habit of taking lessons with the prince. They helped each other study, sometimes with the aid of puppets.

Lydea, past her strange terror, was piqued. "What's in there?"

"Another palace. Rooms no one uses, dusty passageways, secret doors everywhere." She was watching Lydea, her calm eyes taking note of every change in Lydea's expression. Mag saw everything, it seemed, and she remembered everything . . . She added, unpredictably, "I saw your father two days ago."

"You were in that part of the city? Alone?"

"You go alone."

"But it's where I grew up."

Mag nodded. She had a confused past herself, involving brothels and alchemists and the grimier face of Ombria. Which was why, Lydea assumed, Ducon had chosen her.

"So did I," Mag said. "I looked in on your father. The Rose and Thorn was quite full; I imagine his boot is filling up."

"What were you doing there?" Lydea asked curiously, wondering if the grave and willowy Mag, with her hair like straw spun into gold, had a lover. She was used to the vague, wide-eyed expression Mag assumed when she was questioned. But sometimes she let slip details when she answered, that Lydea pieced together later.

"I was visiting a friend," Mag said. "She's teaching me something of her trade. I'm an apprentice, you might say."

"What does she do?"

"Oh, this and that. She's a sort of historian. And something of a healer. You might say. People go to her for help."

"A physician."

"After a fashion."

"Where does she live?"

But Mag grew very vague at that, nearly inarticulate. "Along the water," she intimated, which Lydea took to mean overlooking the sea. Mag added earnestly, by way of changing the subject, "I think the best way to teach well is to be always learning something. Don't you agree?"

Who could not? Lydea thought, descending to the west door of the palace to her waiting carriage. Mag was as riddled with secrets as the palace. She found herself remembering, as the carriage drove past the crop of blind, withered sunflowers beside the gate, some old tale that she might have told Kyel once or twice when Royce was alive and she had been in love or in fear, it seemed, at every waking moment. What was it? A city in shadow . . . Something about a fan . . .

   She forgot about that, too, as she watched the familiar

streets flow past and the tavern signs above her change like playing cards, until time dealt her the Rose and Thorn and she saw, through the open door, her father's smiling face.